James Calbraith is a Poland-born writer, foodie and traveller, currently residing in South London. His debut historical fantasy novel, "The Shadow of Black Wings", has reached ABNA semi-finals in 2012. It was published in July 2012 and hit the Historical Fantasy and Alternate History bestsellers lists on Amazon US and UK.

Praise for *The Shadow of Black Wings*

"Fast paced and full of energy."
— Adrian Tchaikovsky,
author of the *Shadows of the Apt*

"This manuscript is full of highly crafted detail that will make readers shiver at times with fear and delight...a familiar yet highly original fantasy that is a worthwhile read."
— Publishers Weekly

"The real-world cultures are incredibly well-researched and truthful, and yet well-balanced with the fantasy elements. An intriguing and impressive series."
— Ben Galley,
author of the *Emaneska Series*

By James Calbraith

THE YEAR OF THE DRAGON

Book One: The Shadow of Black Wings

Book Two: The Warrior's Soul

Book Three: The Islands in the Mist

Book Four: The Rising Tide

The Year of the Dragon Books 1-4 Delux Edition

Transmission

Dragonbone Chest

Visit James Calbraith's official website at
jamescalbraith.com
for the latest news, book details, and other information
Or sign up for the newsletter at:
tinyletter.com/jcalbraith

The Shadow of Black Wings

Book One of

The Year of the Dragon

James Calbraith

FLYING
SQUID

Published July 2012 by Flying Squid

Second Edition May 2013

ISBN-13: 978-83-935529-1-7

Cover Illustration: Yue Wang

Map Illustration: Jared Blando

Cover Design: Flying Squid

Thank you once again for buying this book. A reader's trust is the only thing that makes a self-published author, like myself, thrive.

This book is a love letter to a country and its people. It is a work of fantasy — hence the dragons and the wizards. It is an alternative history — hence the unvanquished Roman Empire. But it is, foremost, a historical fantasy — based on the events that have really happened and on characters that have really lived at a certain point in time and space: in and around Japan, in the turbulent middle decades of the 19th century.

I have decided to leave many of the names of the historical characters as they were, to make it easier for the curious among the readers to follow their real life stories. The geographies of Gwynedd and Chinzei — otherwise known as Wales and Kyūshū — have been rendered as faithfully as possible for a work of fantasy. The Fukusaya bakery still serves the best Castella cake in the city.

Throughout the books I use a modified Hepburn transliteration of Japanese, in which long vowels are indicated by a macron: ō and ū should be read as long o and long u.

I hope you will enjoy reading this book as much as I enjoyed writing.

James Calbraith

TABLE OF CONTENTS

THE KINGDOMS and PRINCIPALITIES
OF THE MODERN WORLD

EURASIA

Unchanging the river flows, and yet the water is never the same.
In the still pools the foam now gathers, now vanishes, never staying for long.
So in the world are men and their dwellings.

Hōjōki

PROLOGUE

A single gear whirred and clicked into place. A valve opened, letting out a thin plume of grey steam with a quiet hiss. A gold-plated dial moved by a notch. A tiny mallet sprang from its compartment, striking the brass gong - one, two, three, four, five, six times.

Master Tanaka looked up in surprise - an hour of the Hare already? He turned towards the window and the pink light of dawn illuminated his face. The temple bell only now started to ring out the time. He sighed then yawned, rubbing tired eyes. Another night had passed without him noticing.

The elementals inside the clock awoke with a soft purr and the automatic brush began to move swiftly inside the glass cloche. A slot opened in the mahogany pedestal and spat out a piece of paper upon which was written the day's divination. Hisashige reached for it absentmindedly, his attention focused on the piece of complex clockwork on which he had been working. He glanced briefly at the calligraphy - *Oku*, "a gift". He smiled to himself and nodded knowingly.

A higher-pitched chime rang eight times – counting out the hours of the Western reckoning. The door slid open noiselessly and a small boy entered the workshop. With his long and angular face, puffed lips and wide straight nose, he bore no resemblance to Master Tanaka.

"It came from Kiyō this morning, Father," the boy said, presenting Hisashige with a large, ornately packed wooden box.

"Excellent!" the old master exclaimed.

He put the box on the workbench beside the clockwork and began to unwrap it eagerly.

"Shūhan-*sama* was supposed to send me some Walcheren glass."

He stopped abruptly and his shoulders sank when he saw the crest on the box, in golden leaf – three lines in a circle. He lifted the lid without enthusiasm. Inside was what seemed like a small human head, completely bald.

"Some *gift*." Hisashige looked at the clock with reproach. "It's just another of Zōzan's broken dolls."

He took out a small paper envelope containing his fee, and gave it to the boy.

"Put it in the treasure box later."

The old master opened a hatch in the top of the doll's head and studied the complex web of gears, cranks and pulleys for a moment. With one swift twist of his fingers, he snapped a rubber band back onto the hooked lever.

"Hardly worth the effort," he murmured, closing the head and the box. "I really need those divinations to be more precise in the new clock."

"Is that the new year-plate?"

The boy craned his neck to see over Hisashige's shoulder to view the mechanism sprawled all over the workbench.

"Yes. You have a good eye, Daikichi," the old master said with a gentle smile.

"Still can't get it to work?"

4

Hisashige shook his white head.

"Come, I will show you."

He put the loose screws and gears back into place and lifted the plate gingerly. He moved across the workshop to a tall sculpted cabinet of Western make, and opened the oaken door.

There was another clock inside, similar to the one standing in the corner of the room, but larger and with even more dials, switches and levers.

Hisashige inserted the clockwork plate precisely into its slot and turned the key. The gentle warm hum of the elemental engine filled the cabinet. Steam hissed from the valves.

"I don't understand. Everything seems perfect," the old master commented as the dials turned to their desired positions, showing exactly the same time and date as was visible on the old clock. "I can't find any fault within the mechanism. The minute hand is even more precise than before. All the Major Trigrams match. But look at that zodiac dial..."

A round ivory plate turned slowly. Pictures of animals, encrusted in black lacquer, appeared in the glass lens one by one – monkey, rooster, dog, boar, mouse, ox...

"It should stop now," said Hisashige, and the boy nodded.

It had been the Year of the Ox for a few months now – water ox, to be precise. But the plate continued to turn inexplicably past the tiger and hare until, at last, it halted.

The black lacquer silhouette of a coiled sleeping dragon glinted mockingly from the lens.

THE SHADOW OF BLACK WINGS

CHAPTER I

Gwynedd, May, 2606 ab urbe condita

The distance from Llambed to Dinas Bran is computed at seventy miles, as the crow flies. The prevailing wind is north-westerly, steady at fifteen knots along the entire distance. Given an average velocity of an unladen Purple Swift equal to forty knots, and allowing for the pressure pocket of Berwyn Hills – oof!

Bran bumped into someone and dropped the exercise book to the ground, his notes scattering all over the freshly cut grass. He knew who it was just from looking at the thick leather boots. Only the Seaxe wore shoes on the sacred meadow of the Scholars' Grove.

"Honestly, Toadboy, it's as if you wanted to be beaten up," a familiar vile voice mocked.

Bran looked up and sighed. Wulfhere of Warwick towered above him in his impeccable blue uniform. His sky-blue eyes stared at Bran from under a neat flaxen-yellow fringe with disgust.

"Sorry, Wulf." Bran stooped to pick up his papers. "I'm in a hurry for the Octagonometry exam..."

"Pah!" snorted the Seaxe. "What's the point? You and your Toad will never pass the Aerobatics."

"Its name is Emrys," Bran said coldly, "and it can outfly any dragon in this school, including your fat thoroughbred."

Wulfhere narrowed his eyes and tightened his fists. Tiny sparks crackled around his knuckles and Bran prepared himself for a blow. The Seaxe glanced towards the red brick arches of the Southern cloister where the house prefect stood, watchful.

"Out of my way, serf, you're lucky I'm not in the mood today," he scoffed and pushed Bran aside.

The papers scattered again. Gathering his notes, Bran mumbled a Prydain slur, loud enough only for Wulfhere to hear. The Seaxe stopped and turned back slowly.

"What did you just say?"

Bran looked around helplessly. Nobody was coming to his aid, of course; this wasn't a fight worth joining in. Somebody was paying attention though. The red-haired Pictish lass, Eithne, stood under a large oak tree with several giggling friends. Their eyes met. He saw pity and embarrassment in hers, and something inside him sank.

She wore the robes of the Geomancers, although Bran knew her dream was to one day become one of the *Derwydd* – Druids, guarding Gwynedd from their fortress at Mon Island since ancient times. The brown-green, plaid cloak suited her auburn hair and green eyes, framed in a delicate spiral tattoo. They liked each other but never went any further than a few walks under the oak trees and an occasional awkward teenage kiss. In the end their relationship had simply fizzled out, to Bran's sporadic regret.

He repeated the slur, suddenly feeling brave. Now everyone heard him. Several people stopped curiously, waiting to see what would happen. But with only a few days left until the final tests, Bran no longer cared. After the exams none of it would matter, anyway.

"You've done it now, Taffy. You'll have to take your tests in the infirmary!"

The Seaxe grabbed Bran's neck and the boy tensed. With an electric crackle and sizzle, a cloud of painful sparks appeared around Wulfhere's hand. Paralysed, Bran made no sound, though his eyes welled up when he felt his nerve endings scorched. His neck was on fire, but he knew too well the electricity would leave no marks on the skin. The ability to tap into the lightning power of his mount, Eohlsand – a Highland Azure – made Wulfhere's punishments both immensely painful and perfectly undetectable.

Just as Bran felt he could no longer take the pain and would have to cry out for mercy, the provost finally appeared, heading towards them. Wulfhere let go of his victim. Bran fell to the ground, gasping.

"I'll get you next time, Taffy," the Seaxe hissed and shuffled off, unhurriedly.

"Are you alright?" the provost asked, reaching his hand out to Bran. "Did he hurt you?"

"I'm fine," Bran murmured with embarrassment and raised himself slowly, wincing as he massaged his aching neck. He glanced towards the large oak tree. The girl was nowhere to be seen. Sighing, he retrieved his papers from the grass for the third time and headed towards the dormitory cloister.

He tugged both sets of reins sharply and leaned back. The dragon pulled up and rolled on its back in a tight half-loop. Ground whizzed past the top of Bran's head. He jerked the top leeward rein. A leather strap fastened to the base of one of the dragon's horns tightened, and the mount turned upright. With one beat of its leathery wings it caught a strong waft of the Ninth Wind and its flight stabilised. The boy breathed out.

The series of manoeuvres finished, Bran brushed an unruly fringe of black hair out of his flying goggles and bade his mount swoop fast down towards the target range. The dragon needed no guidance here. They had been practising on the range for two years and both knew exactly what to do. The beast turned confidently towards the first objective: a large bale of straw. The dragon's neck stretched in a straight line. Its jaws opened but it coughed to no effect as the target dashed past. Shaking its head, the beast turned around to try again. Again it merely coughed and spluttered with great effort and a thin plume of smoke puffed from the dragon's nostrils.

"What's wrong, Emrys?" Bran asked, distraught.

The dragon whimpered. It could not breathe fire. The boy recognised the acrid smell in the dragon's breath: Iceberry water!

Only one person was capable of such a cruel prank on the day of the exam; but there was no time to think of vengeance and Bran was starting to panic. Seconds were running out, the teachers below were no doubt already frowning at his lack of performance. Not one of the targets had, as yet, been set on fire.

Fire. He didn't need Emrys' breath. He could channel the power of flame himself. It would have a far shorter range and energy, but it could still work. He focused on the Farlink, the mental connection giving him far greater control over the dragon than just reins and knees. The beast, following his unspoken orders, dived once more towards the bale of straw. He only had a split second as the mount sped past the target, whooshing a few feet above the grass at a dazzling speed. He reached out with his fingers.

"*Rhew!*" he cried in Old Prydain spell-tongue.

A blazing bluish spark of dragon fire shot from his fingers. Its tip reached the straw and the bale burst into flames. Elated, he repeated the exercise with the next target, a wooden horse, then with yet another and another, five more times in total. With each objective destroyed his exhaustion grew. Channelling the dragon flame drained his energy immensely, and reduced his control over the magic. His hands began to shake and his fingers grew covered with swollen blisters from the heat. With bleary eyes he searched for the next target, but couldn't find it.

At last, he realized there was none. The exercise was over. He managed to land before the teachers' observation tower, panting, sweating, too tired to even dismount. Struggling to keep his eyes open, he listened to the Master of Aerobatics assessing his trial.

"That was certainly… unorthodox," the teacher said, coughing nervously, "but I appreciate the initiative. You *did* hit all your targets in time, so I have no choice but to pass you."

Initiative? This was not the kind of school that encouraged initiative… Bran sighed deeply and closed his eyes. All thought of revenge disappeared from his mind. It didn't matter anymore. He had passed his final exam and was out of the wretched place at last.

Bran's fingers played with a fiery-coloured tassel on the grip of his heavy cavalry backsword, a proud, solid three feet long single-edged blade, a pattern tested in the Mad King George's wars. The quillon was curved in the shape of a rampant dragon, the brass mountings and circular guard ornamented in the form of claws, flames and leathery wings. The wyvern-hide grip culminated in a pommel sculpted into a dragon's head. Anyone looking at the sword would have little doubt as to its owner's profession.

He sat among thirty other similarly armed boys and girls, all excited and relieved at the same time, all wearing the uniforms of the dragon cadet corps, steel blue with golden stripes. They hailed from all over the Dracaland Empire. Most of them were Prydain, like Bran, with black hair, Roman noses and olive complexion, or the golden-haired, blue-eyed Seaxe from beyond the Dyke. A few dark-eyed Cruthin from Ériu across the sea and tattooed Picts from the northern realm of Alba were keeping to themselves at the back.

The headmaster was nearing the end of his speech. Short and impish, he had to use an ornate mahogany step to reach over the pulpit. His long red beard was forked neatly and tucked under a gem-studded belt. Wind tore on the bushy tufts of his hair – there was no roof above the ruined keep inside which they had all gathered. The headmaster was a Corrie, a member of an ageless race of wrinkly-faced, pointy-eared and red-haired dwarves living among the dales and lakes of Rheged in the North.

The headmaster finished the main part of his speech, waited until the din of whispers quietened and then held up a sword in a trembling hand. The straight, broad blade was rusted and notched in a few places, although the hilt was new, gleaming gold and encrusted with gems.

"It was seven hundred and ten years ago that Owain the Wyrmslayer established this illustrious Academy for the purpose of studying the ways and lore of the mighty Beast, after defeating the Norse dragons at Crug Mawr with this very sword," the headmaster shook the old blade.

He gestured around and Bran's eyes inadvertently followed towards the familiar thick walls of the Great

Auditorium, rising towards the sky like the crooked teeth of a long dead giant. Tapestries of red and white dragons had been brought to adorn the cold stones of this vast ancient ruin for the duration of the ceremony. The heavy oaken chairs upon which the teachers were sitting recalled the time of the War of Three Thorns and the realm of Harri Two Crowns. Leaves rustled and sparrows chirped on the branches of ancient oak and elm trees growing in a dense circle around the keep. Far in the distance a booming sound of a siren announced lunch break at the local elemental mine.

"The graduates of the Sixteenth Year of Victoria Alexandrina, the Queen on Dragon Throne! Today you finish your first four years at the Academy. The bards will now take my place on this stage to tell tales of past glory much better than I can. Let me just put a final touch on all of you before I release you into this dangerous ever-changing world."

This was the moment Bran had waited for the whole day. The headmaster straightened himself, full of youthful vigour. He raised Owain's Sword towards the blue sky and whirled it around in a complex pattern. The air sparkled and buzzed with powerful magic, and the fresh scent of ozone spread throughout the auditorium. A flash of dazzling light flared above the heads of the gathered, taking the form of a great white eagle hovering in the blue sky. The raptor shrieked and a shower of stars rained down from under its spread wings, each dazzling star landing upon a shoulder of an astonished student.

"You have all been marked with the Seal of Llambed," explained the headmaster after the spell dissipated. "Those who know how to look will always see it upon you. Bear it proudly. It is not only a sign of education - it is your talisman, a precious gift. Three times in your life you will be

13

able to call upon its power - and it will deliver you from any danger."

A murmur spread throughout the keep. For some of the students this was the first time they had heard of the magic mark and its power, but not so for Bran.

"You will use up your Seal before you know it," his father, Dylan, had told him. "It's only there to help you through the first years of life as a dragon rider outside the school walls."

"When did you use yours for the first time?" the boy had asked. "Was it in a battle?"

He had been only eleven then, just about to enter the Academy, as was expected of the son of a Prydain officer.

"No, nothing as glamorous as that," Dylan replied, chuckling. "I was still in the Academy, getting my baccalaureate. I was racing another boy, one of the Warwicks, along the Dyfrdwy Valley and I broke my dragon's wing under the Pontcysyllte Aqueduct. A hundred feet drop, that is. I had no choice but to call on the White Eagle."

"And what happened?"

"It brought me straight into the Dean's office!" Dylan laughed. "I got a right telling off for wasting a charge so recklessly. But that's how the Seal works – unexpectedly. You never know where it will take you. Other schools have similar charms, but none are that fidgety – or that powerful. It will save your life, always, one way or another."

"*Mages of Llambed! Arise!*" the headmaster's voice boomed.

The school bard entered the podium to lead the choir, and the crowd erupted into the Academy's anthem enthusiastically, startling a flock of sparrows hiding in the branches of an oak tree.

> *Men of Llambed, on to glory*
> *Victory is hovering o'er ye,*
> *Pride of Prydain stands before ye,*
> *Hear ye not her call?*
> *Rend the skies asunder,*
> *Let the wyrm roar thunder!*
> *Owain's knights fill world with wonder,*
> *Courage conquers all!*

Dean Magnusdottir, head of Dracology, a gentle-faced, mousey-haired woman, browsed the piece of paper unhappily.

"Bran ap Dylan gan Gwaelod. I can't say I'm not disappointed," she said, tutting and shaking her head, "your father was – "

"The best student this Academy ever had," muttered Bran, rolling his eyes. "I know, ma'am, but aren't you being a bit unfair? I did quite well where it matters."

"Where it matters, boy? Where it *matters*? Every single subject in this school matters. You have barely passed the athletics, your history knowledge is non-existent and your alchemy score was the worst in your class."

Bran looked down, feigning embarrassment, but he couldn't bring himself to care. He had graduated, and nothing else was important right now. He did not wish to spend anymore unnecessary minutes within the college walls.

"You are a good rider, certainly," continued Madam Magnusdottir, calming down. "One of our best. Your Farlink quotient is frankly astonishing. That much of Dylan's blood shows, and you have his magic talent, of course. You could easily take up wizardry as the second faculty – we could help you develop the necessary skills. But it takes much more to achieve real success in a dragon rider's career. In truth, I would rather you stayed in school for four more years. Catch up a bit on the old *scientia vulgaris*."

Bran looked up, startled.

What?

Stay in school for four more years? That seemed like such a nightmare right now. Besides, usually remaining for a baccalaureate was considered a reward, not punishment for bad grades.

"Think about it, my boy," the dean insisted when Bran did not reply, "you have time until October, hmm? Will you consider?"

"Er... I will, ma'am." Bran hesitated. "Will there be anything else, ma'am?" he asked, reaching for his diploma.

The teacher stalled, still holding the paper.

"Son," she said, looking earnest, "I don't mean it in a bad way, but - we could get you a better dragon if you remained with us."

Bran stood up, barely concealing his anger.

"There is nothing wrong with Emrys!" he exclaimed. "How many more times do I have to prove it to you all?" He grabbed the diploma from the teacher's grasp, tearing off a bit in the corner. "This is all my father's doing, isn't it?"

"I assure you, your father had nothing – "

"I've heard quite enough, ma'am." Bran raised his hand. "I bid you farewell."

He turned around and stormed outside, heading straight toward the stables.

CHAPTER II

Yamato, Spring, 6ᵗʰ year of Kaei era

Hendrik Curzius sweated profusely.

A servant brought him another silk handkerchief and took away the previous one, damp and smelly. The wizard put the cold wet cloth to his bald forehead. *And it's only May*, he thought. *What an accursed place.*

The Nansei Islands lay far to the south of Yamato. Even in the deepest winter it never got really cold around there. In spring the weather became fickle, alternating between gusts of cold northerly winds, bringing showers of freezing rain, penetrating to the bone, and waves of heat coming from beyond the southern horizon, foreshadowing the unbearable tropical summer - like today.

"I wish there was somewhere else we could meet," said Curzius, quaffing cold spring water from a clay cup.

"You know very well it's impossible, Overwizard-*dono*. We can never be seen together. Only this island is truly free of the *Taikun*'s spies."

The man speaking these words was broad-shouldered, balding, had a long oval face and close-set eyes. He wore the flowing silk robe of a Yamato aristocrat. His name was Nariakira Shimazu.

The small cosy villa they were in belonged to this man, as did the garden around it, filled with the fresh scent of azaleas exploding everywhere in bursts of maddening pink. In fact, the entire island and the surrounding archipelago was Nariakira's property. This was one of the most powerful men in the country, a daimyo – lord of a province. Curzius recalled what little he had learned about the complex feudal power structure of the Yamato from a small booklet given to him before he had left Bataave to take over the post of the Overwizard of the trading factory at Dejima. Below the daimyo were their many retainers, forming the samurai warrior class. Above them – the Tokugawa *Taikuns*, a dynasty of generals ruling from the eastern capital of Edo. And watching over all of this, at least nominally, was the half-divine *Mikado,* an emperor-like figure whose true name could never be spoken without first ritually purifying one's lips.

But the *Mikado* had no real power over Yamato, and even the *Taikun* had no power over the Nansei Islands. This was the Shimazu clan's sole domain, by right of conquest and cunning. Never officially recognised as part of the greater Yamato archipelago, the islands were suspended in a kind of diplomatic limbo. They had their own laws, own customs, even own language. The government's edicts did not reach the islands and the foreigners could come and go as they pleased – as long as they knew how to reach them, of course, and for the last two hundred years this had limited the number of visitors to just the Bataavians.

He waved a paper fan, desperately trying to cool himself enough to think clearly. What he had come to discuss with Lord Nariakira required his utmost concentration. Curzius may have been a newcomer to Yamato, but he was an experienced diplomat and had been thoroughly briefed by his predecessor. He could only hope it was enough to deal with the deceptively gentle-faced man before him.

"Three hundred years ago, when the Westerners first arrived in Yamato, we were all awestruck and terrified of your power and wealth," he started. They were conversing in his own language which the daimyo knew fluently. "It was the same with Qin and Bharata, and Sri Vajaya, and everywhere else in the Orient. There were just so many people in the world, so many riches, so many warriors! We could only hope to gain some profit by subterfuge and cunning, never by force. Yamato itself had more men than Rome's entire Imperium, Qin, ten times of that, and in those days of sword and musket, sheer numbers mattered most. Now the Bharata jungles are overrun with mercenary armies led by Dracalish generals. The Qin is thrown to its knees by the West, and everyone is looking for the next conquest. There are not many left here in the East."

Lord Nariakira nodded. Curzius guessed the daimyo must have been well aware of the recent events in Qin - the Cursed Weed trade, the Emperor's futile edicts, the countless rebellions and the war so badly lost by the imperial army.

If mighty Qin fell so quickly, what hope was there for Yamato?

"When you first arrived, you were but children and we were like your ancient ancestors," the daimyo said, pausing often. "Your priests like beggar monks at the *Mikado*'s court, your merchants like village peddlers trying to hawk their wares on the festival market. Now the children have far outgrown the parents. The teachers have fallen asleep, their *dōjō* overgrown with moss, while the world outside turns faster and faster. How many people live in your greatest cities now?"

"More than a million in Ker Ys, twice as many in Lundenburgh," answered Curzius.

THE SHADOW OF BLACK WINGS

And only two hundred thousand in Noviomagus, he thought, *but you don't need to know that.*

"*Pah!*" The daimyo clapped his knee in an expression of helplessness. "That's already more than Edo, and I bet it won't stop at that. How is it that you can spawn so fast?"

"It is not that we bear more children than you; our medicine and science help us keep more people alive. You may have your shrine healers, but we have conquered the pox and cholera, and those kill thousands more than battle injuries. Our crops are more plentiful, our storage and transportation systems more efficient, so we keep famine at bay. There are also many other improvements that allow us to combat death and disease. You know it as well as I do - we finally caught up with the East."

Nariakira nodded again.

"Yes, the world outside seems to spin much faster than in Yamato. It's as if every year passing on the Sacred Islands is merely a day in the lands of the West. The Divine *Mikado* in his everlasting palace and the illustrious *Taikun* behind the impregnable walls of his castle are barely aware of what's happening just outside their shores."

"The winds of history blow fast and strong, Shimazu-*dono*."

"I know what you're after, Curzius-*sama*. Don't think that your reports to the *Taikun* are the only source of my knowledge of the West."

The Overwizards of Dejima were responsible for providing news of events overseas to the court in Edo. They had abused this monopoly to produce reports that were increasingly further from the truth, as Bataave was losing its significance as a major Western power. The *Taikun* had no knowledge of the revolutions rolling through the continent,

20

or of how close the Kyrnosian Imperator and his invincible legions had come to vanquishing the tiny merchant republic sixty years before. How the small nation had been split even further by wars and rebellions and economic crises, how they were slowly losing their hold on all colonies, until only the precious trade monopoly of Dejima remained as the main source of income. All this was omitted from the annual report on "Western matters".

"You are as frightened of other Westerners as the *Taikun* himself, aren't you?" Nariakira continued. "That is why you came to me so eagerly, because, unlike the old Tokugawa, I understand your plight and can assist you - *if* you assist me. What is that funny saying in your country? You scratch my back…"

"…I'll scratch yours," Curzius said, nodding.

"I hope there can be a mutual understanding between the two of us. I have great respect for the men of your talent."

Curzius sensed a hanging "but". Respect did not mean leniency.

"I know of the little network of friends and allies to your cause that your predecessor has been building around the Southern provinces," Nariakira pressed.

"It is well known that your web of spies is second only to that of the *Taikun* himself," Curzius said, having no choice but to admit the truth.

"There was barely need for spying; you Westerners are too clumsy. I also know why you asked to see me today, but be warned - a daimyo's price is far greater than that of some grey-haired scholar or masterless samurai."

"Of course, I am prepared to make many concessions."

"Ah, concessions. Is a warship an acceptable concession?"

The Overwizard's eyes narrowed.

"What kind of a warship?"

"A mistfire engine," said the daimyo, and started counting on his fingers. "Hull clad in iron plate, armed with repeating cannons, lightning throwers and rockets, and with a small dirigible for long-range observation."

"I'm surprised you know of these things," Curzius said, raising his eyebrows.

The mistfire ironclads had been around for some time, but the armaments the daimyo mentioned belonged to the latest trends in the fashion of war. He himself had only seen a few such ships so far.

"You shouldn't be. Has not the previous Overwizard told you what kind of a man I am? What kind of people live in Satsuma province?"

"He has, but I did not believe it. I now see he has even underestimated you."

The daimyo dismissed the pleasantries with a wave.

"Never mind the flattery. Can you give me such a ship?"

"Would you be able to keep it a secret from the eyes of Edo?"

"The eyes of Edo cannot see over the mountains. It would be safe and hidden until the time would come to use it."

"And when would that be?"

"Perhaps never…" Nariakira shrugged. "*Butsu-sama* knows war is the last thing on my mind. But it's always shrewd to be prepared."

"If we were certain the *Taikun* would never learn about the ship and where it came from, and if you could afford it, then yes, I believe we could provide you with one."

"Don't worry about the gold. I cannot spend it fast enough. How long would it take?"

"It would leave our shipyards in less than a year. Before next summer it could reach Kagoshima, or wherever you would wish it to sail."

"Excellent."

"Then you would join us?"

"No," Nariakira said unexpectedly.

Curzius was taken aback.

"No, but I would let you join me."

"I'm not sure I understand."

"Do you think you're the only one conspiring and conniving?" The daimyo laughed heartily. "The Shimazu have been plotting for centuries. It's in our blood. Our influence is vast, our allies powerful. Your little network of scholars and *rōnin* would make a fine and valuable addition to it, but that is all it would ever be – a single cell in the sprawling network."

"I… I see."

The little man wiped more sweat from his forehead. The tropical sun did not suit his pale skin.

"Good. I had hoped you would. Yes, if you promised me a warship, I would consider letting *you* join *my* conspiracy. My resources would be yours, and vice versa. Of course, the ship would only be the beginning, you understand - a token of friendship."

"There must be no war in Yamato," Curzius warned, wondering what exactly he was getting himself into. He was only beginning to perceive the undercurrents of ancient vendettas and grudges these people must have been holding for centuries. *Of course, the Shimazu hated the Tokugawas with a burning passion,* he remembered. *Perhaps it had been a mistake to come here after all.*

23

"We can provide you with defensive weapons only."

"I have no need for anything more," the daimyo replied, smiling sweetly and falsely. "It is just a precaution, you understand. Also I need to satisfy my urge to study your magical sciences and technologies, and a modern ironclad is the finest example of both, wouldn't you agree?"

"That is true," the wizard replied with a nod.

"A year is a long time. I will need another token of friendship before that."

What else would this old fox ask for now? Curzius thought with a shudder. *A squadron of dragons?*

Those he could not grant him. Bataave had no more dragon riders.

"Send me the plans for a smaller vessel. A mistfire ship good enough for me, and a few men. Just a little something to pass the time before the real prize arrives."

The Overwizard sighed with relief. Just that? That was easily arranged.

"I will have the plans sent as soon as I get back to Dejima."

"We can do better than that. Sign this document and they will be delivered to my men on the morrow."

The daimyo pushed a sheet of paper towards the Overwizard. Curzius picked it up and neared it to his face. It was a letter to the quartermaster of Dejima – written in his own handwriting, sealed with his own seal. He looked up. Lord Nariakira smiled gently, but his eyes mocked the Bataavian. Curzius swallowed.

"Why not forge my signature as well?"

"That would be dishonest of me. I'm not trying to cheat you, I only wish to hurry things up. We are still allies."

"I hope we can become more than that, Shimazu-*dono*. I hope we can become friends."

24

"Signing this letter would greatly improve the chances of that happening," the daimyo said with a grin.

The Overwizard reached for the pen. Despite the heat his hand was shivering as he wrote his name on the paper.

The rain poured incessantly with the noise of gravel beating on a tin plate, with the force of a great waterfall, with the coldness of a mountain stream. A million cascades gushed from the blue clay roof tiles and gutters of the narrow wooden townhouses. The packed dirt roads turned to treacherous swamp paths. All the late blooming trees had lost their flowers, their petals washed off by the rain like make-up that had gone out of fashion.

A shallow brook, which in good weather trickled quietly along the town's southern limits, now swelled to a roaring river. An old heron stood on the edge of the thundering waters, unmoved, enjoying a feast of eels and sweetfish, battered dumb on the cobbles by the swift current. The rolling billows licked the brink of the causeway dangerously, the last of the late farmers hurrying across it with their belongings.

Nagomi stared at the raging waters, trembling. A straw cloak and a wind-tattered umbrella did a poor job of protecting her sodden clothes from the elements. Water dripped from the strands of her long, luscious amber hair sneaking out from under the indigo-striped hood of the raincoat.

She was rarely so far from the comforts of her home city of Kiyō, so exposed to the raw elements. The swollen river carried tonnes of yellow mud, debris and flotsam, gathered along its way from the hills, but there was something else in the water, something Nagomi knew only she could see. Streaks of blackness, threads of un-light

flashed among the waves. She knew at once what it was –
somewhere upstream the river had disturbed a cemetery
shrine, and released the troubled Spirits into the world. She
shivered, only partly from the cold.

"I thought as much," her mother, Lady Itō, said,
observing the chaos before them. She straightened her silk
yukata robe, once dazzlingly colourful and light as a feather,
now grey and heavy with water and dirt. "We cannot cross
today."

"It's still safe!" said Satō, a ponytail of black hair
bobbing up and down with her every agitated move.
Nagomi's best friend cut her hair and wore her clothes like a
samurai, down to the long katana sword in a red lacquer
scabbard dangling from her silk sash.

"Look, if we hurry…"

"It's too risky," Lady Itō said, shaking her head.

"Can't we just go back to the inn, Mother?" Nagomi
asked quietly. "Drink some hot *cha*..."

"I don't like their *cha*," muttered Satō, "it's bland and
dead. They boil it too hot, and serve it too cold. If we go
back now, we'll have to wait for days until this calms down."

Lady Itō looked at the river doubtfully.

"All right, but be very careful. Let the porter through
first."

She waved at the servant, who entered the causeway
with trembling legs, the heavy bundle of their belongings
bending his back. They followed him across. A small group
of men and women in simple linen clothes, tattered and
mud-stained, waited on the other side – the causeway was
already only wide enough for single file.

"Almost there," said Satō.

They now waded through shallow mud as the swollen
waters started breaching the crest of the causeway. The other

side was now closer than the one from which they had started.

Nagomi said nothing. She clutched her cloak tight. It was neither the water she feared nor the cold, but the dark Spirits in the water, now floating around her legs. It was like wading through sewage. The souls of the dead whispered and buzzed with an incessant droning hum and, worst of all, they seemed to be gathering around her, sensing a holy presence. She was almost certain she could hear her name repeated in their humming.

"*Nagomi*," they whispered. "*Nagominagominagomi…*"

A horseman appeared on the road ahead, a governmental courier speeding on a white stallion, crying for them to make way. The peasants on the shore dispersed before the horse, and the three travellers managed to wade to the side, but their porter lost his balance and stumbled into the water. The courier did not stop, bound by duty to deliver his urgent message, splashing the yellow muck all around. The commoners rushed to the servant's aid. With Satō's help, they managed to pull him out of the raging current, but the man was already unconscious, his head cracked, bleeding.

Without thinking, Nagomi dropped to her knees beside the porter, straight into the brown-yellow sludge. The black Spirits still swirled about her, repeating their monotonous mantra:

"*Minagominagominagomi…*"

"Nagomi, dear," Lady Itō tried to admonish her in exasperation, "it's just a hired servant, not worth your attention…"

The girl didn't listen. She examined the porter's wound. It was not as severe as she had feared. She threw back the hood of her cloak and the people around gasped at the sight of her copper-coloured hair. Some pulled back, crooking their fingers against bad luck.

The girl ignored them. She was used to this reaction whenever she showed herself outside her hometown, and understood the cause. Nobody in all of Yamato had hair of the same colour. Some – a few close friends and family – regarded it as a blessing from the Gods. Most, however, treated it as a curse, an abomination. Luckily it did not affect her healing powers.

She drew a tasselled paper wand from her sash and started waving it vigorously, chanting a prayer. She could feel the holy energy filling her body with warmth. It was the warmth of a fireplace in winter, of the summer sun, of a mother's arms. She forgot all about the other-worldly coldness of the dark Spirits in the water below. At last, when she was almost at the point of bursting, she released it into the unconscious man's body. It blazed with a blue light for a moment and the wound started sealing up almost immediately. The man stirred and moaned. She staggered as blood rushed from her head. It was an exhausting exercise.

The villagers eyed her suspiciously, as if she was a demon in disguise.

"Take him somewhere warm. He should be back up in a few days," she said, trying not to let their hostility get to her. The response was silence and accusing glares, as if the villagers were telling her "you healed him, you take care of him."

"Are you deaf?" Satō glowered at them, putting her hand on the hilt of her sword. This made them move. A couple of men carried the injured porter across the sinking causeway, and the remaining peasants followed, throwing fearful glances over their shoulders.

"You did well," Satō said, helping Nagomi up with a smile, "and see, we've crossed to the other side."

She turned to Lady Itō with a beaming grin.

"Yes, but *all* our luggage is lost in the river," her mother replied, shaking her head with disappointment.

"So we'll travel faster." Satō said with a shrug. "We'll be back at Kiyō in no time."

The girl hurried onwards. Nagomi stuck her wand back into her sash, sighed, recited a quick prayer of gratitude and followed her friend into the rain.

It was a busy day, a happy day, the Day of the Ship. A new Bataavian merchantman had arrived at Dejima with news and visitors from the mysterious exotic world beyond Yamato's shores. The streets of Nishihama-machi, the old merchant district of Kiyō, bustled with handcarts and porters carrying wares from all over Chinzei – the southernmost island of the Yamato archipelago, of which Kiyō was by far the largest and richest port – to storehouses and shops. Pottery from Arima in the east, knives and blades from Matsubara in the north, silver from the mines of Ginya, malted rice from nearby Kojiya, dyed cloth from Bungo on the north-eastern coast; anything the Bataavian representatives could be persuaded to spend their gold and silver bullion on. To serve the crowds, food and drink stands sprouted along the main streets. Summer fruit and pickles were brought in from the countryside. Fishmongers hawked their morning wares; marinated eel from inland waters, and freshest mackerel and skipjack from the sea. There were boiled sweets and rice crackers for the children. There was saké and strong shōchū for adults.

Any other time, Satō would have been the first to venture among the stalls, looking for bargains on Western accessories and magical ingredients; lenses and copper tubes from Bataave, dried herbs and powdered bones from Qin, elemental essences and black iron from Chosen. All these things were always much cheaper and more abundant on the Day of the Ship, but this time she was simply too tired to care. All she wanted was a bath and a hot meal.

"Do come with me," she said to the others, "I'm sure Father will love it if you stay for dinner."

"That is most kind," replied Lady Itō politely. "Nagomi, you go with Satō. I will come later."

Nagomi agreed eagerly. The Itō house was farther up the hill, beyond the Sōfukuji Temple, and Satō's family residence was much more luxurious, commanding a beautiful view over the city.

The Takashima household was a massive compound, built on the very top of Maruyama Hill, dominating the neighbourhood with its thick stone walls. Two spearmen stood by the main gate, vigilant. The younger of the guards lowered his weapon threateningly as the girls approached, but his older companion shook his head.

"It's all right - that's the young *tono*."

Satō stopped by the younger guard. To him she was a samurai boy, son and prospective heir to her father's school of *Rangaku* – the study Western magic.

"You're new here, aren't you?"

The man nodded. He couldn't have been more than five years older her.

"What do they call you?"

"Kaiten, Takashima-*dono*."

"You're supposed to be keeping people *in* that house, Kaiten, not out of it."

"Yes, Takashima-*dono*," he replied pursing his lips, uncomfortable and irritated.

30

Satō didn't worry about his discomfort. She enjoyed mocking the guards, playing pranks on them and being generally obnoxious towards the frequently changing spearmen. The soldiers did not belong to her household – they were employed by the city magistrate, who, in turn, took their orders straight from the *Taikun*'s court in far-away Edo. Her father was under house arrest ever since he had tried to convince the magistrate to put the masters of Western magic, like himself, to work on the city's defences. The idea proved too radical and deemed a treason: even in Kiyō, a city more open and diverse than any other place in Yamato, nobody trusted the wizards enough to give them access to military secrets.

"It feels more empty than usual," remarked Nagomi, entering the residence.

"Everyone's either helping their families in the stores or has just wandered off to see the Ship," explained Satō, "besides, we don't get that many students these days. It's been six years since my father lost favour with the *Taikun*, people are starting to lose faith he will ever regain it."

A white-haired figure lurked in the hallway. The old servant cried out in joy and disappeared to summon the master of the household. Shūhan hurried down from the library wing. He was a short man, long-faced and small-eyed, clad in a short, black pleated skirt, a kimono of the same vermillion silk as Satō's garment – the colour signifying he was a scholar of *Rangaku* – and a black vest bearing the Takashima clan crest, four diamonds in a triangle, embroidered on the shoulders. His head was shaven in front, with a small bun of tied greying hair at the back. He hugged Satō, who flushed with embarrassment, and greeted Nagomi warmly.

"Do you have it?" he asked. "Show me the blade!"

THE SHADOW OF BLACK WINGS

Satō drew the sword and presented it proudly. The blade was magnificent; long, slender, perfectly balanced, with distinct temper lines forming a small circle at the tip, the signature of the Matsubara swordsmiths. The hilt and hand guard were decorated with the cherry blossom seal of the Ōmura clan and the *tsuba* handguard carved with the butterfly insignia of the Heike clan.

Satō smirked every time she saw the butterfly crest. The Heike clan had been vanquished eight hundred years earlier, and still the Matsubaras, their once-sworn vassals, clung to the ancient allegiance. This unwillingness to change was exactly what her father had always warned her about. "The elements are always mutating, always transforming, and so must a wizard", he had taught her. "That's why the *Rangakusha* are so feared and hated in Yamato. We are the harbingers of revolution".

"Splendid, *splendid!*" exclaimed Shūhan, admiring the weapon in the sunlight. "Shigehide-*sama* has truly outdone himself this time. I dare say it's even finer than my own. It was worth the trip, eh? You know, the old fools say a sword is the warrior's soul – but I can see how this one truly fits you. You must tell me all about your journey… but you are dying for a bath and change of clothes, right? We'll talk at dinner. I've ordered eel from Yorozuya today!"

The girls bowed and hurried to the bathroom. Nagomi threw her travel uniform into the washing basket, while Satō removed the *Rangakusha* garments and began to unwind a bandage that flattened her breasts.

"Phew! Finally," she groaned, "you've no idea how uncomfortable this is."

"Believe me, I do," replied the younger girl, "you've been complaining about it every night since this trip started. I thought you'd got used to wearing boys' clothes. Weren't

32

you always trying to sneak into kendo trainings in this disguise?"

"I was an urchin then, and didn't need those." Satō threw the bandages into the laundry basket. "Still, it's a small price to pay for being able to walk around the city with a sword."

When they came out of the bath, relaxed and refreshed, clean summer *yukatas* waited for them folded neatly on the straw mat. Nagomi changed into a pink floral robe, while Satō dried herself with a fragrant towel. "I like this blue dye," said Nagomi, picking up the other *yukata*, "I haven't seen it before."

"Father must have bought it as a surprise. I don't think it's local."

"Looks like Arimatsu cloth. It must have cost a fortune!"

"Sometimes I think he doesn't really know how much things are worth... Since Mother died, he's been useless with money. Like this sword he got me – it's marvellous, but was it really necessary to buy a *Matsubara* blade? He always says the blade is only a tool..."

Satō shook her head and stood up to put on the *yukata*.

"What about your father and sister? Will they be coming tonight?"

"I believe so," answered Nagomi. "I just hope Father doesn't have any patients booked for the evening."

The girls tied their sashes and Nagomi finished braiding her long auburn hair. The sound of the kitchen gong and the smell of broiling eel coming from downstairs announced it was time for dinner. Satō felt her stomach rumble with the thought of a good meal. She had forgotten how hungry she was.

THE SHADOW OF BLACK WINGS

CHAPTER III

Gwynedd, June, 2606 ab urbe condita

The buxom barmaid glanced at Bran sipping his half pint of Llanfairfechan Black and passed the table without stopping. The Red Dragon *tafarn* was overflowing with guests. Tonight, the graduates of Llambed came in great numbers to celebrate.

Bran was alone at a small table in the corner, trying to listen to the old harper over the din of the lively crowd. The bearded bard was just finishing the last of the Royal Triad, three epic poems recalling the deeds of the most famous kings of Gwynedd: Owain the Wyrmslayer, vanquisher of the Norsemen; Llywellyn ap Gruffud, the Hammer of Rheged and Harri Two Crowns, the first to sit on two thrones.

The triad finished, Bran saw the bard look hesitantly around. Failing to spot anyone still paying any attention to his poetry, he bowed to nobody in particular and removed himself and his bulky instrument from the open space by the fireplace. Three other musicians moved to replace the lofty tones of the harp with a coarser tune of fiddle, drum and pipes, more suited to the playful mood of the patrons.

"What about you, Bran?"

The dragon rider looked up, surprised. Two boys slammed their pint tankards, filled to the brim with dark foaming *cwrw*, onto his table. Hywel and Madoc came from Llyn, north of Cantre'r Gwaelod. Like Bran, their families lived by and from the sea and, like Bran, they were commoners. They were the closest Bran had to friends at the Academy.

"Sorry…?"

"What are your plans for after the summer?"

"Oh, I haven't decided yet…"

"I'm off to join the dragoons in September," said Hywel loudly, taking a great gulp from his mug. His face was flushed red, his brown eyes bloodshot. "Father's already arranged everything."

"The Third or the Fifth?" asked Madoc, wiping froth from his proud Prydain moustache, dyed with lime for the Graddio in the ancient fashion. It was the envy of all other boys in the Academy.

"The Twelfth," Hywel said ruefully, "they don't take the likes of us into the Guards."

"My folks want me to stay for the baccalaureate," said Madoc. "I've got no real prospects in the army."

Hywel nodded. "Yeah, I figured you would stay. You always had the best grades of the three of us."

"Surely your *tad* prepared a spot for you in the navy?" questioned Madoc, turning to Bran, "with his connections…"

"I haven't talked to him about it yet," Bran replied, "in fact, I haven't even seen him yet since last summer."

"Ah, well, that's the navy for yous," Hywel said, his speech starting to slur. "You'll have to tell him about your areo… aero… flying exam! That was something!"

Bran shrugged. He was certain all his father would get from the tale was that Emrys had failed as a mount – just as he had always predicted.

"I see you have your trinket out," Hywel continued, pointing to a ring upon Bran's left hand, a simple twisted band of gold with a single blue gem, an irregular, jagged shard, semi-translucent like a pearl. "Trying to get the girls' attention with jewellery?" he guffawed.

He was wearing two golden bracelets upon his left wrist and a bronze torc around his sinewy neck.

"It's a family heirloom," explained Bran. "I figured it's time I started wearing it."

"I see, I see," said the other boy nodding absentmindedly, his attention already turned to the musicians.

The band was playing "The Trouble at the Tavern", an old bawdy jig, and Madoc and Hywel joined in with the loud singing, leaving Bran again to himself.

As he brooded over the half-empty glass, the boy noticed another student sitting alone at a table across the room: Wulfhere of Warwick. The other sons of Seaxe noblemen, his usual entourage, were for some reason sitting together at another table, in another part of the room.

What's going on?

Wulfhere of Warwick noticed Bran's curious stare, stood up and, slightly swaying, crossed the hall in quick steps.

"What are you looking at, *Taffy*?"

Bran blinked, surprised.

"What's it to you, *Sais*?" he replied. Now that they were on equal footing he was no longer frightened. Blue sparks appeared around Wulfhere's tightened knuckles, but dissipated when a heavy hand fell on his shoulder.

"Go back to your ale, Wulf." Hywel said threateningly. The Seaxe's uniform under his fingers started smouldering faintly – Hywel's mount was an Eryni Ruby, a firedrake. "You shouldn't even be here."

He was one of the few Gwynedd-born boys who could stand up to the tall burly Seaxe. The Warwick stared at him for a moment then grunted something and staggered away towards the *tafarn* door.

"What's up with him?" asked Bran. "What did you mean, he shouldn't be here?"

"Didn't you know? Look at his Seal."

Bran looked after the Seaxe. Among the many enchantments woven into Wulfhere's aura his True Sight could not spot the mark of the white eagle.

"It's not there... He failed to pass!" he whispered, astonished.

"Aye," nodded Madoc, taking another gulp of ale, "for all his *Sais* boasting and bullying, he turned out to be one big failure. I wouldn't like to be in his skin now!"

"Serves him right," Bran replied, remembering the Iceberry water and all beatings he had to endure over the years.

The song was finished, and so was Bran's glass. The musicians started another dance tune, and the other two boys moved into the crowd to find themselves partners for the jig. Bran rose and headed for the door to get some fresh air.

Once outside, looking at the starry sky above the empty cobbled street leading towards the faer iron gates of the Academy, he decided it was time to go home. Having sat at the table for an hour and drank a glass of ale, he felt his social duty fulfilled. His head was beginning to hurt from the noise of the crowd, banging of the drum and screeching of the fiddle.

I will not be missed.

38

He headed for the dragon stables, a wide, high-roofed building of sandstone, with long, slate-tiled eaves. Somebody emerged out of the shadows and walked towards him.

"Hullo, Wulf."

Bran tried to walk around the Seaxe, but the flaxen-haired boy moved to the side, blocking his passage again.

"So you've passed, Toadboy," the Seaxe snarled.

"And you haven't," Bran said, unable to stop himself gloating.

Wulfhere pointed his finger at him accusingly.

"You've had your *faeder* pull the strings, haven't you? You'd never pass otherwise. Not with that flying frog of yours."

"No, Wulfhere. I simply practiced for the exams instead of wasting my time beating up others and playing with poisons. Besides, your father knows plenty more 'strings' to pull."

"*Pah*-!" the blond-haired boy scoffed. "I should have known not to go to a *waelisc* school. You guys always stick together."

"If you choose to believe this, so be it. Now, please let me through," Bran said and made a step forward.

"No." Wulfhere stood firm. "Not before I see whether you really deserved to pass."

"What?"

The Seaxe crooked the fingers of his left hand, summoning a *bwcler,* semi-translucent shield protecting his forearm, and tightened his right hand into a sparking fist.

"Don't be absurd, Wulfhere." Bran raised his hands. "It's over. I'm tired and just want to go home."

"Oh, but that won't do at all! I need to see what it is that a peasant's boy can do better than one with royal blood."

Three hundred years earlier, at the end of a long civil war, the first of the Warwicks, Richard the Kingmaker, had reached for the Dragon Throne. His triumph was brief; Harri Two Crowns had crossed over from Gwynedd and destroyed him at Bosworth a mere two years later. The Kingmaker's blood ran thinly in Wulfhere's veins, but all the Warwicks still harboured deep resentment towards the people west of the Dyke.

"I'm not a peasant," protested Bran, raising a weak single-layer *tarian* shield just in case Wulfhere was seriously intending to hurt him. "I'm townsfolk, and I don't need to prove anything to you. You can see I have the Seal."

"Then I will have to make sure you're dead three times to make it disappear!"

Bran reeled back. Dead? Had the Seaxe gone mad? *Is he drunk?*

There was desperation in his voice that worried Bran more than the smell of liquor in the boy's breath.

A blue electric spark struck from Wulfhere's outstretched fingers, piercing Bran's shield with ease and hitting his chest painfully. Bran waved his hand defensively, summoning a plume of bluish flame. Wulfhere covered his nose.

"You're trying to scare me away with your swamp stink?"

He punched Bran again, this time simply with a fist. Bran gasped, grabbed Wulfhere's hand instinctively and cast a Strike of Repel.

"*Gwrthyrru!*"

He was still determined not to let himself be dragged into a senseless fight. The Seaxe slid away a few feet across the slippery cobbles. He regained his balance and shook his head.

"Oh, *come on*, you're not even trying!"

His blue eyes glinted. He raised his hand again and this time Bran ducked, barely dodging a shot of lightning. Another bolt deflected off Bran's *tarian* and hit an iron lamp post, showering the street with sparks.

"You can't win a *gornestau* like that!" Wulfhere laughed. "Show me what you're really made of, swabbie. *Draca Hiw!*"

He roared and leapt towards Bran, shape-shifting midflight into a blue were-drake. He was now six feet tall, covered in scales and hovering above the Prydain boy, his great azure wings spreading, his bright eyes blazing.

In a reflex, Bran jumped backwards and crouched, compressing his *tarian* into a stronger thrice-layered shield. He clapped his hands then spread them apart. A Soul Lance shimmered between his palms and solidified. He hoped the sight of it would bring the Seaxe to his senses. The Soul Lance was a deadly weapon when used against dragons and Dragonforms, the only blade certain to pierce through any dragon scale. Wulfhere pressed on though, with claws and lightning, pounding relentlessly against Bran's *tarian*. The lightning strikes bounced off the shield in all directions, throwing tiles off the stable roof and scorching the wooden beams. The dragons inside the building woke up and started snorting and screeching in agitation.

The magic duels, *gornestau*, never lasted long. No man could keep casting spells or sustain shields for long. The victory was usually a matter of who ran out of energy faster, or first made a mistake…

Bran's shield fizzled and vanished. He raised his lance in both hands. Wulfhere grabbed it with his talons and they wrestled for a while, lightning crackling around them, scorching the hair on Bran's head.

"*Rhew!*" cried the Prydain boy, summoning a little dragon flame.

The lance burst with bright blue fire, blasting the opponent's clawed hands and the Seaxe pulled away briefly. A scream of pain turned into a roar of rage.

Bran darted inside the stables and tried to slam the gate shut, but the thick fireproof door burst open, and the impact of the explosion threw him back. Wulfhere leapt inside. It was difficult for him to move in the confined space, but he still pressed on towards the hapless Gwynedd boy, who stood up on shaky legs and continued his retreat.

The dragons around them went mad with excitement, filling Bran's head with a buzz of Farlink messages and emotions. He swayed and almost fell down again. His skull throbbed with pain. He hit something with his back: a ladder leading to the stable roof. He grabbed a rung and hoisted himself upwards in a flip. Wulfhere's claws smashed the ladder underneath him, but Bran managed to grab onto a ledge and climb outside.

A slight breeze cooled his aching head. The slate covering was damp and slick. He only managed to tread a few steps away from the ladder chute before the roof exploded. The dragon-formed Seaxe flapped his vestigial wings and landed clumsily on the tiles.

"Wulf…" Bran pleaded. "Stop this, *please*. I don't want to fight you…"

But the Seaxe was too far gone to be reasoned with. He opened his mouth and let out a mindless bellow. His clawed hand scratched at Bran and the boy leaned backwards in a reflex. His feet slipped on the edge of the roof. He had been learning how to take falls for four years and the training kicked in instantly. He imagined his legs and torso following the perfect curve of spiral rotation. He had a split second to

42

calculate the optimal trajectory for the manoeuvre. The air around him heated up as the dragon magic enveloped his body…

A memory flashed in his mind: a student in the second year who, failing to perform a proper rolling leap, had lost focus and fallen to the ground from a dragon's back, a hundred feet down. The medics had carried him off the training field and nobody had ever seen him again. The enchanted acrobatics had always made Bran uneasy since. He wasn't built for physical prowess and found it difficult to grasp the complicated calculations necessary for merging his own body with a stream of mystic force…

Landing, his feet slipped and he fell face first into the mud. He hissed with pain and cursed aloud. He tried to scramble to his feet clumsily, but slid on the wet cobbles whenthe Seaxe landed before him with a massive thud, instantly reached out a clawed hand and lifted Bran by the collar of his blue uniform. The Gwynedd boy grasped powerful talons, trying to wrestle himself free, in vain; the Dragonform was unstable and a risk to the caster but for a moment provided him with almost unlimited strength.

There was a whoosh of wings and the sound of claws scratching against the cobbles and Bran was thrown aside by an impact of a large warm body. He looked up and saw a large grey dragon standing before him, pinning transformed Wulfhere to the ground with its fore talons like a hawk holding a mouse. Bran turned his gaze away; it hurt to look straight at the beast for too long. The glamour cast on its scales caused them to shimmer and shift, making the dragon seem transparent, half-invisible. It was easy to forget it was there at all.

The Highland Greys were bred exclusively on the Isle of Scathach in the north-western Alba, to be used by spies and scouts. Only one person in the Academy rode one. Madam Magnusdottir, the Dean of Dracology, sat calmly in the saddle. She nodded at Bran to stand up.

"Thank you ma'am," he said, half-relieved and half-embarrassed.

"You're lucky. I was flying close enough to see everything! This is very serious."

"It was just a *gornestau*, ma'am."

She eyed him suspiciously. The Dragonform had to be fed on a very strong emotion and was too powerful and intense enchantment to be used on a whim. Even soldiers on the battlefields were reluctant to transform unless their life depended on it.

"Transformation is forbidden in magical duels."

"We're not at the Academy anymore, ma'am."

She laughed briefly, clicked her tongue and the shimmering dragon raised its talons. Wulfhere, back in his human form, cast Bran a furious look, scrambled to his feet and ran away into the night without saying a word. Madam Magnusdottir looked after him pursing her lips in thought, then turned back to Bran.

"Is your leg all right? You're limping."

"Yes, it's just a bruise."

"That was a particularly shoddy performance, young man. Enchanted acrobatics is an essential skill to the dragon rider!"

"I'm sorry."

He scratched his head, not knowing what else to say.

"That's all right," she smiled, her features softening. "You've passed the exam, after all – barely, if I recall. I suppose all that ale does hamper one's abilities a little. Give my regards to your father when you see him," she added before launching into the air. A moment later the dragon shimmered and disappeared in the darkness.

Just then several boys and girls had run out of the *tafarn*, intrigued by the noises of combat and their dragons' distress calls.

"What's going on?" asked Madoc.

"Wulfhere Warwick transformed. I think he had too much to drink tonight," replied Bran, rubbing the bruises on his face.

A red-haired girl tugged Madoc back towards the *tafarn*.

"They're playing 'Farmer's Fancy'! I want tae dance!" she said, rolling her "r's". She noticed Bran and lowered her head, bashful. It was Eithne.

"You coming back, Bran?" Madoc smiled, wrapping a muscular arm around the girl. "The night is young."

"Thanks, but I think I'll fly home." Bran sighed heavily. He knew, no matter what his own decision after the summer, he would not see her ever again – she was moving to the Mon Island in October. This was his last chance to say goodbye – the *Derwydd* lived in monastic fortresses where none but them could enter.

"I don't feel so good. I think I've bruised my ankle," he said instead.

"As you wish."

The other boy shrugged and returned to the Red Dragon with Eithne in tow. She looked back once, briefly.

Bran limped towards the stables. The dragons were slowly calming down. He patted his mount on the neck soothingly.

"Let's get out of here, Emrys," he said quietly.

The beast grunted in response.

THE SHADOW OF BLACK WINGS

The unmistakable whoosh of a landing dragon came from the front yard. Dylan ab Ifor put away *The Cambrian* and stood up from the black wood armchair to welcome his son. The boy entered the living room straight from the door, staining the carpet with dirt. The white mice Bran's mother employed as household imps scurried to clean away the mud. Dylan cast him a quick glance.

He's really grown.

"I see you didn't even bother to come to my Graddio."

Dylan scratched the scar running across his cheek with discomfort.

"I only just got here from Brigstow, son. We had to pick up survivors from the *Birkenhead* and then our Weatherman came down with jungle fever," he explained. "I really hoped we'd get here much sooner."

Bran shrugged dismissively. Dylan moved to an awkward embrace when his wife entered the room, wiping muddy hands on a linen cloth. The sweet smell of vervain and betony followed her from the garden. Certain herbs had to be picked at night.

"Oh, back you are!" she exclaimed with a smile. Dylan always wondered why Rhian still spoke with the gentle southern valley lilt, even after all the years of living on the coast. "How was it? Did you get the Seal? Dylan, did he get the Seal?"

"Do you not see it?" Dylan raised his eyebrows. "Ah, right, I forgot." Rhian had some magical talent, but she had never pursued the scholarly path, preferring the ways of the Cunning Folk – making potions and casting small mending charms. She had never developed the True Sight necessary to perceive the Academy's secrets.

"It's just above his right shoulder, as bright and beautiful as any I've seen."

"What did the dean say?" Rhian asked.

"She... asked me if I wanted to stay for baccalaureate," said Bran.

"See, I told you they'd want him back!" She beamed to Dylan. He smiled knowingly.

So the old Magnusdottir had received my letter.

"You seem tired... Your face is dirty and your hair is singed. Did something happen?" Rhian continued her investigation.

"Nothing, I was just playing with Emrys," Bran replied.

Dylan knew this was not the case – he could still detect the faint lingering traces of battle magic. He chose not to say anything; there was no point in worrying Rhian. Boys would always be boys, but something else in Bran's response made him frown.

"Do you still have that toy drake?" he asked, sharply. "You know I could get you any breed you wanted."

Bran scowled.

"I have Emrys. He's my friend."

"Bran," Dylan looked his son straight in the eyes, "you can't get attached to a dragon. They are the most egotistic of creatures. Sooner or later it will betray you, no matter how kind you are to it."

"Emrys is more loyal to me than any human."

"There's no such thing as a loyal dragon. I have scars to prove it."

"Well, maybe you just don't know how to handle them! What have you told Magnusdottir?"

Before Dylan could answer, Rhian intervened.

"Can't you stop quarrelling even for a moment? Let him have his pet *dab* for a while yet, Dylan. The lad's just graduated. Starting his holidays, he is. He won't need a new *draigg* for some time."

She went on to put the kettle on the stove and the two men sat down in front of each other, uneasy.

"You've been away for almost a year," said Bran, interrupting the silence.

Dylan looked vacantly around. The room, with its white-washed walls, heavy oaken furnishings and a roaring fireplace, seemed at once familiar and unreal. Had it really been just a few months since he had been sitting in the tent in the middle of the savannah, negotiating with the Bataavian commander?

"I was overseeing the Transvaal agreement," he said, more to himself than to Bran. "The negotiations were very difficult."

The herd of wildebeest the only witness to our quarrels.

"How did it go then?"

"Her Majesty finally granted sovereignty to the Bataavian settlers. Our borders in the South are secure and our friendship with the Bataave strengthened."

"You sound like a royal pronouncement."

Dylan chuckled. "I had to talk like this for a year."

"What about the *Birkenhead*? There was something in the papers, but I didn't have time to read before the exams."

"She was brought upon the reefs by Xhosa illusions, off the Cape. We had to run twelve sorties to bring everyone safe."

"Then the war with Xhosa is still on?"

"More than ever…"

"It must have kept you busy."

"Rest is a rare privilege in a war zone."

That was as much as he could say. Most of his work had to be kept secret even from his closest family. In the silence that followed Dylan decided to change the subject.

"So, have you been thinking of what you will choose for your baccalaureate?"

"I'm… I'm not sure. I don't really like that place," Bran replied with a shrug.

"I know, son, but believe me, things change later. As an alderman you're too highly ranked for – "

"It's not just that... I want to…" Bran paused. "I don't want to go back."

Dylan glowered.

"Look, boy, you can't just decide your future on a whim. What else would you do? Work down the pit, herding fire elementals?"

"I could join the navy…"

"You don't know what you're talking about."

"Most of my... friends will be enrolling in October."

"Most of your friends didn't get a choice. By Owain's Sword, you're not some farmer's son!"

Rhian entered the room with a tea tray. Dylan leaned back, putting a smile on his face. He relaxed the grip of his fingers on the leather armrest.

"Are you two still arguing?"

"No, dear. Oh, I just remembered. I brought some tinned fruit from the South. Why don't I go get them?"

CHAPTER IV

Yamato, Summer, 6ᵗʰ year of Kaei era

From the window of her room on the top floor, overlooking the quiet suburb sprawling along the hillside, Satō first saw the herald bearing the orange standard of the Merchant Republic of Bataave. A retinue of servants and guards followed and then, at the end, an ornate palanquin climbed up the steep hill road, carried by six porters. The guards halted the procession at the gates of the residence.

"His Excellency, *Oppertovenaar* of the Dejima domain, Hendrik Curzius, here to see the master of the household, Takashima Shūhan," the herald announced in a loud shrieking voice then presented a rolled up paper to the elder of the guards. The spearman checked the seals and nodded at his companion. The two bowed and stepped aside.

She leaned further; she had not seen the new Overwizard before. A short portly Westerner stepped down from the carriage, straightened his long vermillion tailcoat and put on a wide-brimmed green top hat.

"*Welkom, Oppertovenaar,*" a voice spoke in nigh impeccable Bataavian. Satō's father was proud of his ability to speak the language without a strong accent. He claimed it made his spells work that bit more precisely. "I'm grateful for your visit."

"I'm grateful for your welcome, Takashima-*sama*," the guest replied in the language of the Yamato, in a correct, but rather coarse, manner.

She ran down to the main hall just in time for the two men to enter the building.

"My heir, Satō," Shūhan introduced the girl and sat down beside her by the low table. The Westerner bowed and joined them, his legs crossed casually.

"Aah, my limbs are not what they used to be," he explained.

Shūhan laughed politely, poured saké into three shallow cups and raised a toast.

"To the eternal friendship of Bataave and Yamato! *Kanpai!*"

"*Proost!*"

Satō swallowed the warming liquid and felt immediately relaxed. She reached for another portion, but her father discreetly moved the cup away.

"I'm so happy I can finally meet you, Takashima-*sama*," said Curzius, sipping saké. "It's so difficult to be granted the permit. The Magistrate finally agreed when I threatened to delay my visit to the *Taikun*'s court."

"I'm honoured," bowed Takashima.

"No, no," protested the guest, "the honour is all mine. I've heard so much about you from previous Overwizards. The great Takashima Shūhan, one of the finest *Rangaku* scholars in all of Yamato! The airgun, by the way – marvellous, one of my marksmen shot a pheasant from two hundred yards last week! I'll be sending it to the *Stadtholder's* court in Bataave; he enjoys game hunting."

"That pleases me greatly."

"But let's get down to business!" The wizard looked around, watchful. "Are we in a safe place?"

"There are only the three of us here."

"I'm not sure if it's a conversation for a young... boy," Curzius said.

He knows, she realised. *Of course he does. He's the chief wizard of Dejima. He must have spotted through my disguise the moment he entered.*

"Satō is my heir," Shūhan replied, "whatever is said or done in this house, he is part of it."

"I'll get straight to the point, then. I come not of my own accord, but on a mission from my master, the *Stadtholder* - a very special mission."

"You intrigue me."

"There is something... *new* in the air. Our soothsayers are anxious. They say the threads of Fate are tangled, disordered, and they all seem to focus here, on Yamato."

"Surely, your soothsayers are mistaken," protested Shūhan. "We are an isolated and peaceful nation, far from the events of the outside world."

"And yet the world seems to be reaching out towards you. The Westerners are encroaching on the lands of the East. The realms of Bharata have fallen. The Qin barrier is breaking."

"I'm familiar with all this," said Shūhan, "but I would think the spoils of Bharata and Qin are quite enough to entertain the Westerners for generations to come."

"You underestimate our greed, Master Shūhan," Curzius said, "and the soothsayers of Dejima are rarely wrong – after all, they have learned their skill from your priests. The Empire of Yamato is on the brink of a major change – a change that may have repercussions far beyond your borders. The *Stadtholder* wants me to be more than just aware of it happening. I am required to take an active part in the events, however should they unfold, and for that, I need trusted men on my side."

"You want me to stand with you against the *Taikun*?"

The Overwizard puffed his cheeks and looked sharply at Shūhan – as did Satō.

"I… I did not say that."

"But that is what you meant."

"I only wish to know what you will do when the time comes to choose sides."

"There can only ever be two sides in Yamato: those with the *Taikun* and those against him. I've learnt it the hard way – this is why you found it so difficult to come here. Tell me, have you spoken to anyone else about it yet?"

"I have," the Overwizard replied, nodding. "I cannot give you the names, of course, but there is a… network of likeminded people, growing slowly."

"A *conspiracy*, you mean."

"I would not call it that."

"Call it what you will, you're still talking about sedition and treason."

"This is not just for our benefit, you must understand. We care about the good of your people. You make decent trade, and are an honourable and trustworthy race. We are happy with our agreements. The others, however... they will not care for deals, they will come to steal and conquer. We need to work together against this new threat."

Shūhan pondered this for a while, scratching his greying beard.

"Will you speak to the *Taikun* openly about these - signs?" he asked

"As much as I am allowed to divulge, yes, but from what I've heard of His Excellency, he is unlikely to be interested in what I have to say."

"Yes, the *Taikun* can be a stubborn man," said Shūhan, "and tough to deal with. There was a time when I desired nothing more than to serve His Excellency, but he chose to surround himself with advisers who cared for little but themselves. The 'reforms' they've introduced have only served to keep people like me away from the court."

There was bitterness in his voice Satō was familiar with; he sounded like this every time he spoke of the Edo government.

"What about the *Mikado*?" she blurted. "If the news are as grave as you say, shouldn't he be notified as well?"

The two older men looked at her in great surprise. She realised immediately how ridiculous she sounded. She might have as well proposed to discuss current affairs with the Gods.

"The *Mikado* has even less freedom than I do," said Shūhan, "you know that. Only the *Taikun* matters."

"Are we in agreement, then?" Curzius pushed, ignoring Satō's question.

"It is yet too early to decide, Overwizard-*dono*," Shūhan replied. "As your soothsayers say, the threads of Fate are tangled, but I can promise I will always do what I believe is best for my people and country, not just for *Taikun*'s courtiers."

"That is as much as I wanted to hear."

Curzius extended his hand and Shūhan shook it awkwardly. They both rose and headed for the exit. Shūhan held the Westerner back just before they were about to cross the doorway.

"This 'network' of yours…" he said in a low voice that Satō could barely hear from where she was sitting, "would they be in a position, should anything happen to me, to take care of my heir?"

"Is this your price?"

"It's my condition."

"Then I will see to it that they would. Farewell friend."

She watched her father return to the table, sit heavily on the straw mat with a sigh and pour himself yet another cup. The room was deadly quiet, even the cicadas in the garden fell silent.

"Well," he said at last. "What did you think of that? Not my noblest moment. To stand against my ruler and master, betray him in the hour of trouble... is that the way of a true samurai?"

"And is it the way of a true master to give ear to false accusations and imprison those who only wished to serve him? Kōshi the Philosopher said a faithful servant must – "

Shūhan smiled bitterly and raised a hand to stop her. "Quoting Kōshi is not as popular as it once was. Make sure not to repeat such words outside this house."

"Of course, Father. I'm not a child anymore."

"No. You're not."

He swallowed his saké in one gulp and stared grimly at the bottom of the empty cup. A lone raven cawed in the distance.

The great Suwa, chief of Kiyō's shrines, lay to the north-east of the city on the steep slopes of Tamazono Mountain. Beyond the long stairs and many gates, beyond the souvenir stalls and main worship halls of the shrine, beyond the cemetery, lay the forested inner grounds where only the priests could enter.

There were many sand and gravel paths climbing among the camphor trees, connecting the separate wooden buildings. Some led to lesser shrines dedicated to the worship of various local *kami*, others to warehouses or storage sheds, or, farther up the mountain, huts of hermit priests who chose a life of separation. A few disappeared into the underbrush, their original destinations long forgotten.

Nagomi scaled one of those white gravel paths, wearing her finest ceremonial gown of pale green silk embroidered with red thread, a wreath of flowers and ribbons of paper in her braided copper hair. On her wrists and ankles she wore bracelets of tiny brass bells. She was following Lady Kazuko, the wrinkle-faced, bright-eyed High Priestess of the entire Shrine. Despite the woman's drab plain garments, she displayed an aura of authority and wisdom.

The gravel path led past a persimmon orchard then along a grove of tall green bamboo swaying gently in the wind. Nagomi and the High Priestess reached a square building with walls of cedar logs, curved tiled roof and a narrow entrance without a door. Nagomi hesitated a moment before passing under the thick straw rope tied across the entrance to mark sacred ground.

The inside was dark and musty, a faint smell of sulphur and brimstone permeating the air. The High Priestess pulled out a small clay vessel and blew on it – a tiny Spirit of light living in the pot awoke and an orange flickering flame burst forth, casting disturbing shadows on the wooden walls. The building had no floor or foundations. Its walls were sunk deep into the forest soil around a flat rocky outcrop. A narrow jagged crack ran through the rock, venting dizzying fumes from the depths of the Earth. A large bronze bowl stood on a tripod above the crack, steeped in smoke, filled with dark motionless water.

The source of the foul-smelling exhausts and vapours was hidden somewhere deep inside the Tamazono Mountain. They leaked through cracks in the ground in many places throughout the shrine grounds. The savage deadly movements of the Earth that produced these cracks were both a curse and a blessing. They provided fertile soil and the relaxing hot springs, but once in a while the *kami* of the Earth would show their terrible wrath and bring fire and death upon common and noble folk alike. Such was the lot of Yamato: what the Gods gave with one hand, they took with the other.

Atop certain holy mountains, like Tamazono, the sulphuric vapours had yet another valuable property. They enabled a suitably attuned soothsayer to see into the future. It would take years of practice for a priest to read the Waters of Scrying properly, to not be overwhelmed by the Spirits of the mountain's heart and understand the secret signs. But Lady Kazuko, as if in anticipation of this day, had brought Nagomi to the Waters when the girl was only thirteen and had done so for a year now, getting her accustomed to the fumes surrounding the rock fissure.

The High Priestess nodded and Nagomi, as instructed so many times, approached the tripod and inhaled the pale yellow vapours until her head started spinning. She leaned over the bowl, stared into the cold surface and softly chanted the prayer. Lady Kazuko joined her encouragingly. In the stuffy darkness Nagomi recalled the dark dreams she kept having since returning from the excursion to get Satō's sword. The Spirits in the flood waters, calling her name... A house of red stone by the sea... a black ship that moved without sail... a winged shadow in the night sky. It were these dreams that caused the High Priestess to take her to the Waters today, to peer into the bowl on her own for the first time.

She sang a droning chant and clapped her hands in a slow deliberate rhythm, the tiny brass bells around her wrists ringing in unison. As she became entranced, the mists grew thicker, almost tangible, like wisps of pearly sea foam engulfing her, the tripod and the bowl. A rip in the air opened and a waft of the cold wind blew from the depths of the Otherworld. Nagomi sensed the presence of the Spirits before she saw them, little faces in the smoke, studying her curiously, attracted by the sound and movement. The surface of the water stirred and muddied. One of the faces spoke unexpectedly, startling the apprentice.

"What do you seek from the Waters of Scrying?" enquired the Spirit.

"That which lays ahead," she answered, as taught.

The Spirit giggled and disappeared, replaced by another.

"Look into the Water," demanded the new spectre, "if you can see, of course!"

It laughed and swept aside.

"Can she see? She's so young!" whispered another.

"We know her. Yes, we do," replied yet another, "we called her and she came."

Nagomi focused on the bowl and the dark water within, ignoring the giggling, prattling Spirits around her. A red spark suddenly appeared in the bowl then a blue one followed by a green one. Three round jewels in a triangle glistened in the water. They twirled for a moment, and one of the giggly voices whispered in her ear:

> *Turning, turning, jewels three,*
> *What through blood stone can you see?*

The ruby came to the fore of the vision. The other two jewels vanished.

Nagomi peered deeper into the dark mist and saw that the ruby orb was lying upon an altar in some ancient shrine, calm and timeless, shining with soft inner light. A hand appeared over it and grasped it firmly. The hand belonged to a long-haired man wearing a red flowing robe. The apprentice looked up from the jewel, but could only see a black oval where the man's face should be, a shadow darker than night itself. The man leaned closer as if sensing Nagomi's presence, and the shadow that was his face grew and grew until it engulfed the entire bowl in the darkness.

The other two gems appeared, and the whispering voice returned.

Turning, turning, jewels three,
What through tide stone can you see?

It was the turn of the blue jewel, the sapphire. This one started growing fast, encompassing the entire surface of the bowl within seconds. The water turned a stormy dark blue, dotted with tiny white streaks. Nagomi realised she was looking at the sea from high above, and the white streaks were billowing waves.

Something was stirring beneath the waves. The water bubbled as if a volcano was waking up at the bottom of the ocean. An enormous dark shadow appeared, rising fast, greater than any beast, a sea monster with broad, black wings. Just as the creature was about to break through the surface of the sea, the vision shattered into a myriad of tiny blue shards of sapphire glass.

The water was calm again, and dark. All three stones came into view one last time.

Turning, turning, jewels three,
One stone left, what can it be?

The third jewel, the jade, shone with a warm, hopeful life-giving glow. Nagomi sighed with relief and joy, her heart warmed by the gem's radiance, but her sigh broke the spell before the last jewel could fully unveil its vision. The mists scattered, the portal to the Otherworld closed and the water in the bowl turned to its usual, no longer ominous, murkiness. The apprentice swayed and staggered away from the bowl.

"What did you see?" the High Priestess asked.

The vision was only ever given to one soothsayer. Exhausted, with a weak voice, Nagomi described what had been revealed to her in the water. Lady Kazuko's eyes narrowed.

"Are you *sure* this is exactly what you have seen?"

"Yes, High Priestess. What did it mean?"

"Come with me, child."

They trudged down the gravel paths towards the living quarters, past the narrow corridors into Lady Kazuko's private chambers and library.

"Wait here," she said.

She walked up to an octagonal rotating bookcase, wherein sacred musty scrolls lay on many shelves and turned it until she found the right compartment and took out an incredibly ancient-looking document. The priestess blew off the thick layer of dust and unrolled the paper.

Nagomi gasped at the beautiful illumination, a detailed image of dragons drawn in black ink, flying over the brightly red rising sun, the colours still vivid after uncountable ages. Below and alongside the dragons were calligraphic letters in the script so old and elaborate that Nagomi barely recognised it as ancient Yamato writing. She squinted, trying to decipher it, but the High Priestess started reading the squiggly words aloud.

> *"Ruby, the blood of the Dead,*
> *Sapphire, the jewel of Awakening,*
> *Jade, the bringer of Life,*
> *Black, the wings of Despair.*
> *The monsters come from without,*
> *But the foe lurks within.*
> *The Eight-Headed Serpent rises,*
> *But the Storm God's sword is sheathed.*
> *At the breaking of the world*
> *The Mightiest will fall"*

Here the scroll ended abruptly, the edge torn off and scorched.

"What is it?"

"This is one of the oldest prophecies given to us by the Spirits of the Cave of Scrying," explained Lady Kazuko, "older than the shrine itself, passed through untold generations of first shamans and later, the priests. That it survived for so long is a miracle in itself – as you can see, part of it was lost in one of the fires. No living person remembers the rest. Most of the divinations in these scrolls have already come to fulfilment," she continued, carefully rolling up the paper and putting it away onto a shelf. "This is one of the few still remaining unrealised. It is said that when all prophecies of Suwa come to fruition, Yamato will no longer require the Gods and the priests to guide it. I wonder…"

"But what does it mean? Why has it been shown to me? Who else saw it?

"I know of nobody else witnessing the prophecy since it was first recorded, and very few even know of its existence," the High Priestess said. "The *Taikun*s were always very keen to keep it secret – as I'm sure you understand."

"I… I don't think I do."

"*The Mightiest falls*, child. There is only one man in Yamato who fits this description. This is most portentous. I must meditate on the meaning of what has occurred today, and you…" she neared the young apprentice with great seriousness in her eyes, "*you* must be very careful. Do not tell anyone what you have seen today. Not your family, not even your friends. Can you do that for me, child?"

"Y-yes, High Priestess," Nagomi stuttered, frightened. The priestess had never before asked of her anything of the sort. *A secret of the* Taikuns…?

"Good." Lady Kazuko's face wrinkled in a relieved smile. "Now you should rest. It must have been a tiring experience."

Satō wiped the sweat from her brow, grasped firmer the sharkskin-covered hilt of the Matsubara sword and raised the weapon to chest level, aiming straight at the unseen enemy.

"Once again! *Ei!*"

She made a sudden thrust. Half a dozen boys repeated her movements, their swords glistening in the late summer sun, feet slipping on the gravel.

"From the stomach!" She pointed at her abdomen. Her own muscles tightened as her concentration grew. "*Ei!*" – the blade went sideways in a perfectly straight motion.

"*Ei!*" cried the boys, more or less in unison.

"Good, Shōin," she praised the only boy who managed to repeat the cut precisely. "Now, gather the energy. *Ie!*" She raised the blade over her head. A chill went through her arms, her skin was covered with goosebumps. She could feel the sword grow icy cold. "And release - *tō*!"

Satō struck down powerfully, finishing drawing the rune. Even without pronouncing the spell word, a wave of cold air spread from the tip of the sword. The boys repeated after her, but their movements were imprecise and had no effect.

"Listen to the cicadas," she explained, "that's the rhythm we use in this exercise. One, two, three and *four*!" She accented the fourth prolonged cry. "No pause. Focus on that final strike, put your entire soul into it. Come on. *Ei*! *Ei*! *Ie - Toooh*!"

The boys tried again, and again they fell out of rhythm by the last strike. Satō sighed. She had never imagined teaching others would be so difficult. As a prospective heir to the Takashima *Dōjō* she had to take over some of the training duties. She was given the youngest pupils, six thirteen year olds, sons of samurai and wealthy merchants at a cusp of puberty, to teach them the very basics of the Takashima method and assess their innate abilities.

"Don't think of the sword as a weapon," she explained one more time, "it is just a tool. This," she said, pointing to her heart, "and this," to her head, "are your weapons."

The boys looked at her blankly. To them a sword was both a symbol of prestige and the power of their parents, and a toy they could play with pretending to be grown-up samurai. They had only recently been given real metal blades. Normally boys of their age would still train with wooden ones, but the Takashima method required affinity with steel from an early stage. Satō struggled to keep discipline among her unruly pupils, but as a girl she could hold no authority over them whatsoever.

As they tried the exercise again one of the boys, supposedly by accident, bumped into another and a quarrel quickly turned into a bout. The cheap blunt blades soon broke and Satō's pupils started punching each other with fists.

"*Stop it!* Oh, I can't stand it," the girl despaired. "*Bevries!*" she cried and drew an ice-shackle rune with her sword. A simple holding spell froze all six boys in a chain of ice, binding their wrists and ankles together.

"Calm down and think of what I have taught you today. I'll be back before dusk to release you – maybe…"

She grinned mischievously, enjoying the look of panic in their eyes. She knew the ice would quickly melt in the scorching summer sun. One of the boys cried in protest, but the rest accepted the painful punishment in silence as was proper. The cicadas laughed.

The wizardess walked up the hill near Sōfukuji Temple, and entered the small house of the Itō family, where Nagomi lived with her mother Otakusa, father Keisuke and elder sister Ine. It was empty and quiet, only the wind bells chimed in the breeze.

"Hello, anybody here? Nagomi? Itō-*sama?*"

She heard light steps on the wooden floor. Nagomi ran out to meet her, tying a red ribbon around her copper-coloured ponytail.

"Sacchan! Finished the class already?"

"I can't do it anymore today, it's too hot. Where is everybody?"

"Daddy was called off to Nagoya. There's an outburst of smallpox there. Mother went to see him off at the harbour. Ine is on a house visit, so I'm left to look after the home."

"Nagoya? But that's on Hondo!"

The main island of the Yamato archipelago lay days of journey away from Kiyō, and the city of Nagoya was right in the middle of it. One needed to have a really good reason to embark on such a journey.

"Daddy was born there, actually," Nagomi explained. "He only came here to study."

"I always forget your family is not originally from Kiyō."

"It was so long ago... He was just a herbalist's apprentice then. Now the lord of the domain himself requested his presence."

"You must be proud."

"I am," Nagomi answered, "but I wish he'd come back soon."

"Do you want to go to the bathhouse?"

"I was going to prepare some talismans for the shrine shop, but I guess I could do it later..."

Soon they lay naked on the stone bottom of a shallow steaming pool, only their heads bobbing above the surface. The spring water was steaming hot and crystal clear, with only a slight scent of sulphur. It was early in the day, so they had the bath all to themselves.

"Aah," sighed Satō, "that's just what I needed. These kids make my head ache. They can't even hold the sword straight!"

"They are only thirteen."

"I could cut down a straw pole at their age!" protested Satō, "and shoot an ice lance through a wooden plank one sun thick!" She spread two fingers to show the thickness of the imaginary piece of wood. "But, of course, boys are so useless." She sighed and lay back onto the stones. "All they care about is fighting. They just can't focus. No wonder none of them could ever beat me."

"My parents say Takashima-*sama* should officially name you his heir already. No one in Kiyō would be better suited to the position – and he's not getting any younger."

"That's very kind of them, but there is no law for a daughter to inherit a *dōjō*. It wouldn't be very wise for us to draw attention to ourselves."

"He's not planning to marry you off to some snotty-nosed son of a samurai, is he?"

"Gods, I hope not!" Satō laughed briefly. "I doubt if he even thinks about these things. He's not interested in anything apart from his experiments."

At least that's what I must believe, she thought, *that he's just forgetful, or waiting for the right moment.* Why else would he wait for so long? Nagomi's parents were right – she was the best pupil her father could ever dream of having.

"I hear there's a new resident wizard on Dejima." Nagomi reached for a face towel to wipe droplets of steam from her brow. "Have you met him yet?"

"I have," Satō replied with a nod, "he came to talk with my father before leaving for Edo. He's… different. Small and round, but very clever."

And frightening.

"Did he bring any gifts?"

"Just another sparkleball," she scoffed. "As if I was a child."

"I love sparkleballs! I need to come over and see it! What colour is it?"

"It's red, yellow and blue, a bit bigger and flashier than the last one. Father and I had really hoped for a new spell scroll or a blueprint, but I guess they're not allowed that anymore."

The apprentice lifted herself up and sat on a cypress board lining the edge of the spring, with only her legs still in the water. She ran her hand through her long hair, sparkling fiery red now that her locks were wet. Sometimes they seemed to change their hue according to Nagomi's mood.

"It's so hot today," she complained, "I can't sit still for more than ten minutes."

"It's better to come here in the winter," Satō agreed.

"I won't be able to do it as often when the summer ends."

"Why not?"

"After the Kunchi Festival I'm moving into the shrine permanently. I'm becoming a full-time apprentice."

"That's…" Satō hesitated. "That's great!" she said without conviction.

"Oh, you are always welcome to come up and see me." Nagomi smiled. "I'll just have to pay more attention to my duties, that's all. Besides, I'm sure you will be busy too, with all the training and teaching…"

"I guess so." Satō nodded solemnly. The lazy, relaxed mood perished. She became keenly aware of the passing of time.

Even in Yamato nothing ever remains unchanged, she thought.

She stood up abruptly. The hot water rippled before splashing onto the cold stone floor.

CHAPTER V

Gwynedd, July, 2606 ab urbe condita

Bran sipped on his ale and winced. It was too warm; everything was too warm this summer. The eldest of the yeomen gathered at the Red Dragon *tafarn* could barely remember a July as hot as that of Victoria Alexandrina's Sixteenth Year. The south-easterly wind bringing rain and fog from over the bay was gone. The air was stale and dry.

"I'm telling you, it's all the damned navy's fault," said a tall stout fellow wearing a blue felt cap crooked over one ear. "They've taken all our best Weathermen and left us only the shoddy ones, who messed everything up instead of fixing it."

"My well is running dry," another yeoman added to the complaints.

"What if there is famine, Huw?" a younger lad said. "I don't want to have to leave my land and sail to Gorllewin."

"Gorllewin? Those merchant folk across the sea?"

"That's what they did in Ériu. My cousin said the entire villages packed and left overnight. Swathes of land left abandoned…"

"They say nobody ever came back from Gorllewin," the man called Huw said grimly.

"And who would?" scoffed the third of the farmers, stroking his greying beard. "I've heard that anyone who sails there gets a piece of their own land the size of a village."

"A piece of wild forest you have to fell yourself, or a piece of stony grassland you have to till yourself," said Huw, shaking his head.

"And they're all Grey Hoods there. Sun worshippers," added the youngest, spitting, "as devoted as the Romans. You'd have to convert back to the Old Faith."

"It's better than seeing all your crops wither," the third man snorted, "and all your livestock perish with famine."

"Don't worry, Rhys, the Llambed boys won't let us starve. Right son?"

Huw raised a tankard towards Bran. He smiled weakly, knowing too well that if the crops *would* fail, the villagers would soon find somebody to blame, even though there never were any Weathermen at Llambed. Even his father showed some concern about the weather. There had already been recruiters from Gorllewin sneaking around the town – shifty, grey-hooded men, speaking an oddly twisted version of the Seaxe tongue, offering land and untold riches across the ocean.

"Why, I can feel the rain coming already."

The man in the felt cap winced and rubbed his elbow emphatically.

The weather was beginning to take its toll on Emrys. The dragon was of the race the scholars called Draco Palustris, a Swamp or Marsh Wyrm, said to be descended from the great Tarasques of the Rodanus delta. Its domain was the wet mud pits, peat moors and shallow brackish pools. Now the swamps along the Teifi river, which flowed through Gwaelod, were scorched dry and the beast's parched body demanded moisture. Bran did what he could to accommodate the beast's needs, but bathing in seawater brought only a little respite to the land-born creature. When

70

Bran had to help with something at home he would have Emrys sleep by the well and, from time to time, pour buckets of cold water over the dragon's jade scales.

Sometimes when he glanced at the windows of their house, with its old walls painted bright red, he saw his mother observing these efforts with concern. The dragon was a constant source of problems – and mockery from neighbours, family and other pupils at Llambed. It was a child's toy, the first dragon Bran had ever ridden. By the time of the Graddio most dragon riders would already have moved on to one of the large races, Belerion Crimsons, Forest Viridians or Highland Azures, but Bran grew attached to his mount and had never considered replacing it.

The jade green drake looked particularly wretched next to Afreolus, Bran's father's mighty mount. Reserved for the noblemen and soldiers of the Royal Dragoons, the Mountain Silvers or Wyrmkings, as they were more commonly known, were rare and expensive. Larger than any other race, bred exclusively on the royal pastures of the Pictish Highlands in the far north or imported from overseas, these were the dragons with the most strength and stamina of all the known Western races, and Afreolus was a prime specimen.

Dylan was spending most of the summer away from home, always finding something with which to busy himself. Between shopping excursions to Penfro, hunting trips with army colleagues and helping with research at the Llambed Academy, he was almost as rarely seen in the small, slate-roofed house as when he'd been sailing. They rarely talked. Most of their conversations turned to quarrels.

Bran was restless as well. The days of reckless adolescence may have been over, but he did not care much for the duties of a grown-up yet. He wasted away the days swimming in the cold sea, wandering the hills, and picking berries and nuts in the forest. In the afternoons, when it was cool enough, he and Emrys flew around, training acrobatics over the green tops of the five-peaked Pumlumon, or chasing red kites over the Elenydd uplands, enjoying the solitude of the blue sky.

On calm warm evenings they glided over the shaded hazel groves and slate-walled sheep pastures. Rising currents of the Ninth Wind carried the dragon effortlessly along the elm-lined brooks and across the green marshes, all the way towards the tall brick chimneys and iron towers of the Enchanted Mines along the southern coast, where the wizards cut deep into the Earth's crust to reach the realms of the fire elementals. Sometimes the air got so hot and stagnant Emrys refused to fly. Then Bran wandered alone about the wilderness of Eryri, far to the north, until he reached the summit of the mighty Yr Wyddfa and looked down over the misty crags, ridges and peaks towards the northern sea and the dreaded Ynys Mon, the foreboding island fortress of the Druids, Guardians of Prydain, in a foolish hope of catching a glimpse of Eithne's red hair among the oak trees.

These were the limits of his world. Here, unbound at last from the walls of the Academy, he could go wherever he wanted. From Mon in the north to Ynys Dewi in the south, from the sunset-facing beaches of Gwyddno to the peaks of Brycheinniog where the dawn rose and the silver-haired Tylwyth Teg, the Fair Folk, danced around the ruined gate to their long lost homeland.

He could just wander these wild lands forever, chasing deer and falcon, growing old, watching Emrys grow and mature. He could live the life of a small town mage, settle down somewhere near Penfro, meet a nice girl... but of course his father would *never* have that. He had to come up

72

with a better idea for his future and his time was running short.

Old Huw's rains neither came in July nor August. It was now September and while the evenings got somewhat cooler, the clouds were still scarce in the azure skies.

The earthy scent of fresh peat and dew on wet heather rose on the breeze. Bran stooped as he neared the pond in the middle of the dried-up moor, hiding in the brambles and thorn. He brushed the sun-scorched yellow fern aside and sniffed. There it was; the unmistakable smell of sulphur and methane. It was very faint - a less experienced tracker would have dismissed it as the natural aroma of the swamp. The beast was very careful not to let itself be detected.

The young stalker sneaked through the hazels and rowans around the pond, to stay downwind. He was now entering a shallow treacherous bog – the river flowed freely here in spring, but now it was all but dried out. It was harder to move quietly and smoothly. Soon Bran had to half-creep, half-swim in the brackish mire, his jacket now blackened with mud. He suppressed a sneeze.

He could see it now, almost submerged in the shallow water, larger than a fully grown bull, horned head covered under a leathery wing, long tail coiled neatly around the scaled body, sleeping - or feigning sleep. Bran unsheathed his sword, pointed it in the direction of the creature and murmured the Binding Words. The spell was not powerful enough to fully chain its target, but it should make its movements sluggish and restricted.

The dragon stirred as it detected magic. This was the moment to strike. Bran raised his sword and jumped ahead with a battle cry but his boot got trapped and he fell face-first into the water with a loud splash.

By the time he got up, cursing, the dragon was fully awake. It bared its teeth, hissing at short intervals.

"Oh sure, laugh", muttered Bran, trying to wipe the mud from his leather tunic and squinting his bright green eyes, full of brackish stinging water. "I almost had you this time, you know."

The dragon yawned and stretched to its full six feet, still sluggish from the effects of the spell. Bran licked the blood trickling from his knuckles, grazed against something hard in the water.

"What the *Duw* did I trip on? There shouldn't have been any roots here…"

He stooped to investigate by the light of a conjured flamespark and saw what looked like bones of some great ancient animal submerged in the mud. As the riverbed dried out in the heat, the falling water levels had revealed the ageless fossil. Bran touched the remains gingerly.

"I wonder what it was. Something big – an elk maybe, or a wyvern – "

The blue gem on his left hand suddenly burned up with a bright, warm azure light. Bran stared at the jewel in disbelief for a moment, before something else drew his attention.

"By Owain's Sword…"

The fossilised bones stirred and started moving, crackling, slithering in the mud like ivory snakes. Bran jumped backwards, frightened. Emrys whinnied anxiously as the shattered parts of the massive skeleton combined into one and the creature slowly started rising from the moor.

There was now no doubt as to what manner of a beast had died and left its remains in the peat. What had once been a great dragon – easily twice the size of Emrys – towered over the boy menacingly, swaying and staggering as it tried to find its balance after waking from aeons of sleep.

"W-we'd better go, Emrys," Bran stuttered, retreating onto the higher ground, searching for the wind goggles in his pocket.

The ring was now almost burning his finger. The jade-scaled dragon crouched towards its master, whimpering. Through their Farlink connection, Bran felt primeval fear growing in his mount's heart as the skeletal creature began stumbling out of the mud pool. The bone dragon spread its wings – or what remained of them. Names from the anatomy manual popped into Bran's head - *humerus, radius, phalanges…* It felt surreal to see the skeleton in reality, in full scale, dried-up joints grinding against each other.

Can it fly? Impossible, there is no membrane to give it lift…

The jaws, still full of teeth, opened as if the beast wanted to roar. There was no roar – there couldn't have been, the monster had no throat, but, disturbingly, there came a sound, a stifled, echoing humming rumble, as if from the depths of the Otherworld.

Bran managed to mount Emrys, his hands shaking with terror. He was trying to spur the terrified dragon to flight, when the bone monster flapped its wings and pounced onwards.

"*Duck!*" Bran cried out loud and in his head.

Emrys flattened itself in the marsh as the skeletal dragon, capturing the Ninth Wind in its phantom wings, soared above their heads. The monster circled in the sky once before swooping straight back at Bran, its jaws open, the unearthly noise rising again within the non-existent throat.

The boy tugged on the upper reins and pushed his heels into the dragon's sides. Emrys stood on its hind legs and spewed bluish methane fire. The skeletal monster reeled in its dive and ascended again, gaining altitude for another swoop. With a single beat of wings, Emrys leapt over the tops of the trees, and farther up. Alone, it would stand little chance against the dragon twice its size, but Bran had been trained to fight exactly this kind of aerial battle, and now it seemed his life depended on his skill.

A summoned Soul Lance hardened in his hands into an unbreakable crystal. The bone dragon plunged forwards in a mad head-on charge, like a raging stag. Bracing himself for attack, Bran adjusted his goggles and raised the lance in an outstretched arm as he had trained so many times, although his hand was shaking with dread and excitement. He could not guess whether the weapon would work against a living skeleton – there were no internal organs to penetrate after all, no scales to pierce. He could only hope.

He waited until he could feel the buffeting of the Ninth Wind coming from the skeletal wings. He tugged on the reins, banking Emrys to the left and pushed his right arm forwards. He missed – the lance hit the air. The bone dragon flew past, the stench of death around it so nauseating it almost caused Bran to fall off his mount.

The bone dragon turned back and roared again. The tops of the trees beneath turned black and withered; the monster was spewing *something* from its maw, not fire or lightning, but some invisible veil of death.

I won't get another chance, Bran realised, spurring Emrys to a charge. The two dragons sped towards each other, air whistling around them. Bran closed his eyes and focused on the Farlink connection he had with Emrys. Only this gave Bran the precise control he needed.

Down!

Emrys's wings folded and the beast dropped down, underneath the belly of the bone monster. Bran opened his eyes, breaking the Farlink, and struck upwards with all his strength. He felt the lance smash through the monster's ribs and penetrate further, piercing through something that was as unlike a real chest and heart, as the unworldly rumbling was different from a real dragon's dying roar.

He let go of the lance – the weapon disappeared in an instant – a fraction of a second before the impetus would've broken his arm. He watched as the monstrosity tumbled downwards and crashed into the marsh below, bones scattering into pieces again.

Emrys snorted and flew up higher and higher, until it deemed it was at a safe distance from the cursed pool. Bran was too exhausted and confused to command the beast, so he let his dragon do as it pleased for a moment.

The blue gem on his finger was as calm and dark as it had always been.

Bran welcomed the sight of the familiar, tall sandstone towers and oak tree groves of the Llambed Academy with relief. Usually he went go out of his way not to pass it, but this time he wanted to see something real, something certain, and he needed some answers.

A flag with the four lions of Aberffraw flew proudly over the pile of grey stones. A remnant of a Norse castle, at the confluence of the Rivers Teifi and Dulas, only a few months ago had served as the Great Auditorium for the Graddio ceremony. The ruin had been left standing as a reminder of Owain the Wyrmslayer's great campaigns against the Norsemen of Niflheimr and their Frost Armies. It was here, on the shores of Teifi, that the freedom of Gwynedd had been won once and for all, and the alliance with the oppressed Seaxe on the other side of Offa's Dyke forged for the first time of many.

The grapevine leaves clung to the cracked walls, lush green when the summer had begun then scorched yellow by August heat, growing scarlet now. The oak trees in the sacred groves turned golden-bronze. The college grounds, sprawling to the north and east of the castle ruins, were eerily quiet during the summer holidays, with only the gardeners and janitors remaining. Gone was the daily hubbub of hundreds of boys and girls, learning, training and playing around. Gone was the noise of dozens of dragons stationed in the Great Stables, the flapping of wings, roar of wyrm flame and crackle of lightning, but there were always lights and fires coming from the Research Tower, and there Bran landed his dragon.

"I don't see anything peculiar about the ring, I'm afraid," said Doctor Campion upon finishing a long examination of the jewel. "The band is a local work, of that I am sure. The gem seems valuable – a sapphire, I believe, although we would need to do an analysis to make certain. Interesting shape. Where did you say you got it?"

"My grandfather."

"And he...?"

"I... don't know."

I never really asked about it.

"Mm, mm."

The doctor nodded distractedly, playing with knobs on his telescope. They were sitting in the astrological observatory on top of the Research Tower. Doctor Campion was the only scholar who had time to meet with Bran at such short notice, as during the day he had little to do other than browsing through old horoscopes and solar tables in the library.

"What about the bone dragon, Sir?"

"This is an ancient land, boy, full of mysteries. You would not have heard of such things – it's deep in the archives... Old, forbidden magic."

"You mean - raising the dead? It's just a legend, isn't it...?"

"Nay, son." The doctor leaned forwards and lowered his voice. "It's more than that. The dead walked the land when the wars with the Sun Priests ravaged the world. It was almost the doom of us all…"

The clergy of the Bull-slayer God, the Old Faithers of Rome, had once been sworn enemies of all magic users, so much Bran knew. It had taken two centuries of war to settle their mutual differences at last. Many gruesome tales were told of the terrible Wizardry Wars, but this one Bran had not heard before.

"I'm not surprised," the doctor said. "We have kept it secret – us, magic users and the priests alike... I'm only telling you this because you've already met one of those creatures, and because I know your father."

He leaned closer to Bran, his eyes narrow and focused.

"It started with the Grey Hoods, the elite of the Sun Priests. They have discovered some ancient scrolls in the monasteries of Illyria, in the East. They were appalled at first, but when faced with defeat from the wizards they began to turn to anything that could give them advantage."

"Necromancy…" whispered Bran. The word had a dark taste on his tongue.

The doctor nodded.

"They were using it to raise fallen soldiers at first, but soon discovered that by using blood magic curses they could imbue the walking dead with great power, and keep them under control. They started raising *our* dead and send them against us. Then the wizards stole the secret and began doing the same. Not only with humans, but as you have also seen, dragons and other beasts. It was a travesty of a war; lifeless armies that could not be killed. Ere long the abominations learned to disguise themselves as if they were still alive. Bonds of trust have been broken – anyone could be killed at night and wake as an undead. Soldiers returning from the battles were no longer welcome home. And worst of all, some of the Abominations started to work together, turn against their masters…"

"But we've prevailed in the end."

"At a great cost. We signed a truce with the Sun Priests, a temporary alliance against what we had created. Both sides had to agree to abandon such pursuits, destroy the Abominations, unravel the magic, erase the very memory of the evil power. You must have stumbled upon some remnant from just before the Truce, some bone golem cast in the river when the war was over."

Bran scratched his forehead, trying to absorb all he had just heard.

"But what does my ring have to do with it?"

"Oh, I don't think it does, to be honest." The scholar leaned backwards. "It must have merely resonated to the magical energies abundant in the marsh. Some minerals do that, nothing mysterious about it. It's a neat trick, certainly, but that is all."

"I see…"

"Mars is in Sagittarius," the doctor added, raising a finger, "which means people and beasts awake, stir, become restless. The heat doesn't help – there hasn't been a summer this hot for decades. The water reveals what it had once

80

taken. I would advise you to stay away from dried up riverbeds, landslides, ancient ruins... All these places may be dangerous right now."

"Yes Sir."

"You did well." The doctor smiled and patted Bran on the shoulder. "To have faced such a creature and defeated it takes skill and courage, especially when riding such a weak dragon. I would expect no less from the son of Dylan ab Ifor."

Bran let the insult towards Emrys go.

"Thank you, Sir."

"By the by, would you like to see your father?"

"He's here?"

"I believe so, I've seen him heading for the Chambers of Precision."

Bran hesitated.

"I... I'm sure he wouldn't like to be disturbed at work."

"As you wish. Now, you must excuse me." The doctor sighed, reaching for a pile of densely scribbled documents. "I do have a few divinations to prepare for tonight..."

CHAPTER VI

Gwynedd, August, 2606 ab urbe condita

Bran raised his ring to the light, straining his True Sight to the limits. There wasn't even a trace of magic to it.

"Something wrong with it, is it?" Rhian asked.

"Nothing," he lied. "Where did *tadcu* get this ring?"

Dylan had given it to him on his eleventh birthday, just before Bran's entrance to the Academy; he had worn it on a cord around his neck then, his little hands much too small for the piece of jewellery.

"Oh, Ifor brought it from one of his travels," Rhian answered vaguely, "he kept bringing us trinkets like this all the time, he did."

"So why was I given *this* one?"

"Before he left, he insisted you be given this ring. I don't really like it myself – a Prydain boy should wear a torc."

"What was he like, grandfather?"

"Shouldn't you ask your *taid* about that?"

Bran shrugged.

"Father never tells me anything. You know what he's like."

Rhian smiled and pulled up a chair.

"You know, you're beginning to look a bit like young Ifor on the True Images, you are," she said, "soon you'll start growing a tidy moustache then you'll be the same *dap* exactly."

"Father's not wearing a moustache."

"Ah, well, he's in the Lloegr Navy now, he is. They like 'em clean-shaven." She laughed briefly, but then turned serious. "Ifor was… a funny old man, as we call them down south. He never was much of a family man. You could tell he was a sailor through and through. I don't know why he decided to settle here in Gwynedd after Dylan went to school – it was obvious he wasn't in his oils on land."

"Is that why he ran away?"

Rhian brushed a dark lock from her brow.

"Well, he did *not* run away – he promised us that he would return, one day, but he wasn't all there at the end."

"What did he think of Father going to Llambed?"

"Oh, tamping mad, he was! At least that's what Dylan told me. He hated wizards - superstitious, like all sailors. He wanted Dylan to be a Sun Priest."

Bran's eyes widened.

"*A Sun Priest?*"

There was still a *mithraeum* in Caer Wyddno, serving the small community of Old Faithers, but Bran had never seen his father as much as go near the cavernous building.

"Aye. *Only the Unconquered Sun will save us when the Abomination returns*, he used to say. I don't know what he meant. He had the house painted red, to ward off *evil*. I told you - funny old man."

Abomination?

"I had no idea about that."

"You'll find there are many reasons why Dylan is not eager to talk about his family. Now see, it's getting late - I'll run the bath, shall I?"

"Yes, please!" Bran agreed.

Rhian stood up and thought for a second.

"If you really want to find out more about your *tadcu*, have a tidy in the attic. There's bound to be something interesting up there. I don't think even Dylan has ever looked through everything that's in those chests."

"I'll do that."

"Will you come to watch the Ellylldani dance?"

Bran smiled. When he was little, he loved to observe the tiny Fire Fairies – *Salamandrae Inferiores,* as the biology teacher called them – frolic under the bathtub as the water boiled above their heads.

"I think I'm a little too old for that, *Mam*."

"Yes, of course, son."

Rhian smiled, but Bran could see sadness in her eyes.

A couple of old navy trunks of thick leather hidden away in the corner of the attic contained a treasure trove of books, scrolls and old papers, printed long before Bran's birth. Most of them were accounts of trade negotiations and maritime treaties, but there was among them a collection of fascinating reports on mysterious lands of the Far East, including a volume on Eastern dragons, long-bodied, wingless creatures that very few Western Dracologists had a chance to see and research. Bran searched through the books, trying to discover any clues on Ifor from notes on the margins, but they were all written in strange scribbly markings of some unknown Oriental script.

One early September evening, hot and muggy, he dug down all the way to the bottom of the largest trunk, hoping to find some more forgotten mementos. There was usually something interesting at the very bottom of a chest like this, some artefact from Ifor's journeys, either deliberately hidden or sunken through the papers over the years. A pile of

documents and books grew on the floor as Bran dived
farther and farther in. At last, he reached one final bunch of
yellowed, densely written pieces of paper. Apart from those,
the trunk was empty. Slightly disappointed, he picked up the
sheets and found a small box of strange material lay
underneath.

It was neither wood nor metal, smooth to the touch,
but strong like ivory, raven black with a reddish glint. On the
top was a golden emblem, a diamond shape split in four.

He lifted the box carefully and stared at it for a while,
hesitant to open.

Why had it been hidden in this chest?

It certainly seemed more precious than any of the
useless souvenirs forgotten in the attic, the unknown
material glistening mysteriously in the light of the setting sun
like polished onyx. The emblem, as far as he could tell, was
made of real gold leaf.

He opened it carefully. Inside, the box was split into
two compartments. One of them held a golden brooch of an
unusual sort, or rather a buckle tied to a slender ribbon of
silk, in the shape of an Eastern dragon coiled around an
irregular jagged hole, where a stone was missing. Bran
pressed his ring to it – the blue stone fit snugly.

In the other compartment lay a round silver medallion
with the True Image of a young woman. The woman, gazing
sadly at Bran from the thaumaturgic illustration, was unlike
any the boy had ever seen. Her skin was pale and without
blemish, her eyes child-like, almond-shaped beneath thin
straight eyebrows, her nose small and flat, her hair black and

glistening, coiffured into a tall bun intertwined with flowers and elaborate leaf-shaped ornaments.

When he touched the surface of the image, the scribbled hieroglyphs from the margin notes appeared vertically along the side of the medallion. A translation in Prydain materialised below.

Beloved Ōmon. Ifor, 51 Geo. III

Whoever the woman was, she was not Bran's grandmother. The boy remembered *mamgu* Branwen well as a decent Gwynedd woman with nothing remotely exotic about her.

The yellowed crumbling papers covering the box appeared to be the pages from Ifor's diary. Bran had found a few scattered fragments of the memoirs earlier, but these sheets had been set apart, tied together with black cord and stamped with a red ink seal of the same split diamond shape as the markings on the box.

With racing heart Bran took them to the window, where the last rays of the setting sun cast a crimson tint on the paper.

HMS Phaeton, Temasek, 48 Geo. III – he deciphered. Year Forty-Eight of the Mad King's reign.

Forty-five years ago.

It was too dark to read the rest of it, so Bran snapped his fingers and a hovering flamespark appeared over his head. In its flickering bright light, the boy continued.

HMS Phaeton, Temasek, 48 Geo. III (2561 a.u.c.), July 14

We got a new captain today. Broughton Reynolds, a brash young fellow. He's barely nineteen and has already made a name for himself with dauntless attacks on Bataavian ships. Looks like our two years' holiday is over.

THE SHADOW OF BLACK WINGS

*HMS Phaeton, East of Bashi Channel, 48 Geo. III (2561 a.u.c.),
September 23*

*We are chasing a stubborn Bataavian merchantman across the
South Qin Sea, and have now entered, on good wind, the uncharted
waters east of Ederra. The captain refuses to give up the chase. Where
is the Bataavian going, anyway? There are no ports here other than the
Qin beyond their tarian, and if he wished to cross the Ocean then we've
already missed the currents.*

*HMS Phaeton, Unknown Waters, 48 Geo. III (2561 a.u.c.),
September 30*

*The sea is like nothing I have ever seen. It's calm where we sail,
but mists and storm clouds are all around us. The Weatherman stands
on the prow and says nothing. The navigator hasn't left his room for
days. Men say his mind is going. At least the Bataavian seems to know
where he's headed, and we're still able to follow him.*

HMS Phaeton, Unknown Port, 48 Geo. III (2561 a.u.c.), October 4
*We have entered a pleasant warm bay surrounded by green hills.
A great city sprawls on all sides, with all dwellings made of dark wood
and whitewashed stone. The Bataavian anchored at a fan-shaped island
in the middle of the bay, connected with the mainland only through a
narrow bridge and a gate. There is a multitude of Qin and other ships
in the harbour, all very primitive.*

*Both the island and the city are within range of our guns. There
seem to be no proper cannons defending the bay whatsoever. We are
flying Bataavian colours.*

HMS Phaeton, Keeyo, 48 Geo. III (2561 a.u.c.), October 5
*The Bataavian officials entered the ship to inspect it. The captain
ordered them captured for hostages and to fly the Imperial Jack.*

*We've learned from our prisoners that the island is called
"Dejeema", the city is "Keeyo" and the country is that of "Yamato". I*

have sailed these oceans for the best part of my life, but I've never heard of this port. Where in Annwn are we?

The merchantman was running empty, so to gain anything from the adventure, the captain demanded the Bataavians to provide us with supplies and some silver bullion, of which we know the red-heads always keep plenty. Our Carron guns gave a warning shot and, judging from the reaction of the locals, this was the first time they had ever seen or heard such devices. The authorities of this Keeyo seem unable to stage any sort of effective defence, so it looks like the matter will be resolved only between us and the Bataavians.

HMS Phaeton, Keeyo, 48 Geo. III (2561 a.u.c.), October 6

A most unexpected development. Today a boat approached our ship and a local woman – very pretty, I must add, and wearing the finest of silks – begged to be let on board. She spoke good Bataavian. The captain took pity on her. He is now discoursing with her in his cabin. What can all this mean?

Later today another boat arrived and a local official, through an interpreter, demanded the release of the woman in a very haughty tone. We've "released" a musketful of lead shot instead, and he turned tail.

HMS Phaeton, Keeyo, 48 Geo. III (2561 a.u.c.), October 7

Out of the blue, the captain ordered us to set sail in the morning, even before we received all the supplies we asked for.

As we were about to lift the anchor, there was an explosion on the island and a raging fire spread quickly throughout the wooden buildings. The Bataavians and locals alike fled from the flames to the boats. Soon there was only one man left standing on the shore. I looked at him through the spyglass to see what manner of fool he was.

It felt like he was looking straight at me, even though the ship was by now a good half a league away from the island. He wore a flowing crimson robe, his hair was long, dark, flowing in the wind and *his eyes – I swear – gleamed like nuggets of pure gold. He raised his hand and pointed accusingly at the Phaeton.*

I shiver even now writing about this queer incident. I am glad we've left the wretched place behind.

HMS Phaeton, South Qin Sea, 48 Geo. III (2561 a.u.c.), October 10

As soon as we had left Keeyo harbour, a strong north-easterly carried us towards charted waters. We should be back in Temasek much sooner than we hoped.

Saw the Yamato girl promenading the deck with the captain. She really is the most striking beauty. Like all her kin, she seems to belong to the same race as the people of Qin or Siam, but her skin is very smooth and pale, almost glowing. We exchanged glances and she smiled.

There is sadness in her brown eyes, and she is looking sickly, as if she was carrying some heavy burden on her heart. I hope we can get her to a safe harbour soon.

That was the last page. There was no mention of the pendant or the medallion. Bran could only guess what happened next, but the inscription on the locket proved Ifor and the mysterious woman at some point had grown closer. Their happiness, however, could not last long. Dylan had been born two years after the True Image's creation, and he was definitely the son of Branwen, Ifor's first and only wife. Something must have separated Ifor from his beloved Ōmon... Perhaps she had at last succumbed to the sickness mentioned in the diary. On the other side was a rough sketch of a map. He studied it carefully, read aloud the names he had barely recognised. Where the easternmost verge of the vast Varyaga Empire met the mysterious land of Qin out in the ocean, on the other side of the globe from Dracaland, there was a red question mark signed *Yamato*.

His heart pounded madly. He looked out through the attic window, where the Sun traced scarlet the edge of a long line of dunes. Beyond the dunes lay the endless sea, the slow humming of its waves clearly audible in the twilight. He imagined himself on that sea, on a ship bound for uncharted shores, sailing to Bharata, Temasek or even Qin. The low hills and forests of his homeland appeared too familiar, boring, suffocating. Now he knew why his father - and his father's father – had abandoned the friendly plains of Prydain and sailed the wide oceans; the wanderlust stirred within him and there was no escaping its call.

Sweat streamed down Dylan's furrowed forehead in thick rivulets, even though the Chamber of Precision was always cooled to exactly sixteen point four degrees centigrade. He stared at the floating needle intently, without blinking.

The silver needle entered a tiny hole in the side of a bronze cylinder, alongside a hundred other identical needles.

The last one.

As it settled in with a barely audible click, Dylan sighed and fell back onto his leather chair.

"Fantastic work, Master Dylan." The assistant, wearing the white and blue mantle of a thaumaturgist, clapped his hands. "Without your help, assembling this lightning capacitor would have taken us a month!"

"It's nothing. I'm glad to be useful."

"There is always a use for one with such talent. If I may be so bold, why didn't you stay at the Academy, Sir?"

Dylan looked at the boy and smiled.

"How old are you, son?"

"Nineteen this year, Sir."

"Ah, you've got your baccalaureate then?"

"Just this June."

"I can see by the way you wear your coat that you are used to wielding a sword. Second faculty in Dracology?"

"My first, actually. I've only taken up thaumaturgy as an alderman, but I much prefer it here in the Tower of Research."

"Yet you still fly sometimes?"

"Oh, yes, Sir, once in a while," the boy said with a nod, "I don't have a dragon, but I borrow one from the Academy stables."

"Are you a good rider?"

"So I've been told, Sir."

"Then you understand what it's like to have a passion for one thing and ability for another. I won't give up the feeling of hot wind on my face, or the smell of the sea any less than you would give up your experiments."

The assistant's face lightened.

"To take pleasure from what you do for a living is a great gift, boy," Dylan added. "You and I are both very lucky to have it this way."

"I can't disagree with that, Sir."

Dylan nodded to himself. The boy seemed happy enough where he was. Why Bran couldn't be more like him? Dylan wished to give Bran the same simple happiness, the joy of living his life doing what he was best at but his son's lingering uncertainty irritated him.

He must grow up.

The heavy faer iron door to the Chamber of Precision hissed open and Doctor Campion entered with a bundle of notes.

"Here are the divinations you asked for, Dylan."

"Ah, excellent, give them to the gentleman here," he said, pointing to the assistant. "You know what to do with it, boy?"

"Of course, Sir, the calculations of Solar and Jovian tides are of the utmost importance to our work."

"By the by," the astrologer said, turning from the door, "I keep forgetting to tell you – about week ago I've seen your son."

"What, here?"

"Well, yes. He stumbled upon some lich dragon in the marshes and wanted to know what it was."

Dylan frowned.

"A lich dragon?"

He never said anything…

"The swamps up here are full of those remains, you know – all the monsters escaped from the Ruin of Aberteifi."

"And have you… told him?"

"About the Abominations? As much as we are allowed to divulge, yes."

Dylan scratched his scar in thought.

"Was he all right?"

"He was unscathed as far as I could tell. He is a very brave lad, Dylan. I told him not to worry."

"Did he know I was here?"

"He said he didn't wish to disturb you. That sounded like a sensible idea."

Dylan stood up abruptly and glanced first at the lightning capacitor then at the assistant.

"You'll be all right with that on your own?"

"Of course, Sir, but – "

"I'm going home. I think I need to talk to my son."

Dylan wanted to talk about the bone dragon, but Bran would hear nothing of it.

"I want to sail with you on your next voyage, Father," Bran said with a firm, unwavering voice.

Rhian put down her cup of afternoon tea noisily and looked at her two men with concern.

Out of the question! Dylan wanted to say, but only sat down and started at his son, dumbfounded. He suspected Bran's primary motive was a trip overseas and back, giving him at least a year to decide about his future.

"You've told me so many stories about your youth out at sea," argued Bran, as the silence prolonged, "but I've never been anywhere. My idea of a 'faraway land' is Glowancestre!"

"I only joined the corps after eight years in the Academy," Dylan reminded him, but there was no conviction in his voice.

He had sailed around most of the Dracaland's colonial dominion before the age of twelve, accompanying Ifor on various merchant and warships. He had witnessed all the perils and dangers of life on the open sea and hoped to shelter his son from them, but it seemed the call of blood could no longer be ignored.

"And you are certain this is what you want?"

He raised his green eyes and looked straight into Bran's to try to discern the truth.

"On my dragon's wings," the boy replied with an oath understood by every dragon rider.

"Let me talk to your mother in private."

Dylan stood up and nodded at Rhian. They disappeared into the kitchen.

"I knew it would end like this. He kept asking me about your father, he did."

"It was bound to happen. He's got the Sea in his blood. Like me."

94

"You're not thinking of letting him go with you?"

Dylan bit his lips nervously and took her by a hand.

"Is that such a bad idea? A trip like this would be a perfect opportunity for us to bond."

"He's your only son, Dylan. He should be at school. You could force this decision on him if needed be."

"Then he will despise me even more."

"Isn't it dangerous out there?" she asked.

It's not exactly safe here, either, thought Dylan, remembering the bone dragon.

"I have been sailing for almost thirty years now and no harm has ever come to me. Besides, this is just a simple diplomatic mission."

"He is not you," she said.

"He's not a *dwt* anymore – he'll be sixteen next year. His friends are already joining the army."

Rhian sat down on a stool and gazed outside the kitchen window.

"You Gwaelod folk just can't stay in one place for too long. It's that damned sea at your doorstep. I should have gotten used to it by now."

Dylan embraced her tenderly.

"Look at the boy, Rhian. I can sense his dislike. He thinks *I* dislike him! I've never taken him anywhere; I'm always late for everything. We'd be back before summer."

She gave him the look of silent, resigned disapproval he had known so well.

"I will consider it," he told Bran when they returned to the room. "I'm to sail to the land of Qin in October, so I'd suggest you learn whatever there is to learn about it. At any rate, a little knowledge never hurt anybody."

"Yes, Father," Bran said, bowing respectfully, barely containing his excitement.

He walked slowly out of the living room, but as soon as he was out through the doorway, he sprinted to the stables.

Dylan looked after him and shook his head.

"I do hope he's not planning on taking that *thing* with him..."

CHAPTER VII

Gwynedd, October, 2606 ab urbe condita

"What's that on the coast, Father?" Bran shouted over the wind.

Emrys was slowly growing tired, barely keeping up with Dylan's silver dragon. They had travelled over a hundred miles since leaving Cantre'r Gwaelod early in the morning, and were flying over the mighty Severn Barrage construction grounds – an imposing wall of faer iron and silksteel, stretching for over ten miles across the estuary, that was to provide the Dracalish mages with an inexhaustible supply of Water Elementals – when an even more unusual sight on the horizon caught the boy's attention.

"That's a city, boy!" laughed Dylan. "That's Brigstow!"

The city surpassed his boldest expectations. Neither Aberdaugleddau, a port town in southern Gwynedd he had often travelled to, nor Caerlion, the largest settlement west of the Dyke, could even compare to this immense expanse of stone, timber and tile.

Before reaching Brigstow itself, they first had to pass over a deep gorge, carved where the river raced towards the sea. A tremendous tower of gleaming white marble spiralled upwards some three hundred feet, parts of it still under construction, cranes and scaffolding climbing around crenelated walls, peaked arches and buttresses. On the other side of the gorge another smaller tower grew over a golden dome and a grandiose sandstone building. A broad bridge thrown over the gorge, suspended on silver silksteel ropes, connected the two structures.

"That's Clistane, the Tower of High Magic," explained Dylan as they circled the taller spire, "and the Brigstow Academy on the other side. Designed by the arch-thaumaturgist Brunel, himself."

Dylan's voice, used to shouting orders in the midst of battle, carried loud over the buffeting of wind above and the din of harbour below.

"And that one?" Bran mouthed, pointing to another tall ornate spire of red brick and white limestone.

It towered over a vast vaulted structure, with copper roof supported by a forest of wrought iron columns, hidden behind a turreted facade of black granite. A huge tube of imbued glass emerged from the eastern side of the building and disappeared into a nearby hillside.

"That's a terminus of the Atmospheric to Lundenburgh," his father replied. "A two-hour journey takes you straight into the heart of the capital. That's also one of Brunel's."

The city spread out for at least three miles each way, street after street of tall, massive stone houses, palaces, towers, warehouses and wharves. Bran felt as if they had travelled not only in space, but in time. A few hours before they had left their little slate house where Rhian was baking cakes for breakfast using an old iron griddle and a single fire faery. The house and the little town of Caer Wyddno – with its grey stone walls, fishermen coming from their morning catch, farmers departing to till the barley fields – seemed like something out of the Age of Unbridled Flame now as they circled over the naval harbour, a marvel of engineering and thaumaturgy, floating above the river in a series of terraced cascading docks supported on arches of wrought faer iron.

Modern, sleek, mistfire-powered ironclads prepared for their long journeys, spreading the power of the Dracalish Empire over the high seas. There were battleships and frigates, infantry transports and dragon carriers. A few airships hovered above it all, ever watchful. One of them, a streamlined chaser, approached Bran and his father menacingly, to ward them off, away from the docks. The Dracaland was always at war somewhere with somebody; it was its way and purpose.

They ascended to avoid a large glowing orb, travelling slowly in a perfectly straight line – a carrier wisp, delivering some important message to one of the ironclads. Another long line of warships piqued the boy's interest, steaming out of the harbour at full speed.

"Where are they all going?"

"There is some trouble brewing in the Scythian Sea," said Dylan. "The Varyaga and the Shahr are at each other's throats again, and Rome will not stand by idly either, when there's fighting so close to Taurica."

Bran was barely familiar with the names his father dropped so effortlessly. He knew only that the Scythian Sea was somewhere east, far beyond Midgard.

"Taurica?"

"A province of Rome on the northern coast of the Sea, stuck like a thorn in Varyaga's side. Remind me to show you the map later, if you're curious. The *koenigs* of Varyaga have been eyeing it for a long time."

"And why is our fleet involved in this?"

"The balance of power must be sustained. Rome, Varyaga and the Shahr are the most powerful nations on the continent – we can't let any of them grow any stronger."

"We will stand against all three?"

"By Owain's Sword, no!" Dylan said, laughing. "That would be our doom. Diplomacy, trade, spying - that's the great game the Dracaland plays, son. The navy will be just one of our assets."

They banked to avoid another airship emerging from beyond a steep tower. It was black and threatening, armoured with iron spiked plates.

"A Midgard delegation," said Dylan, pointing to the Fafnir insignia painted on the side of the ship, an emerald dragon over two crossed swords, volant, which served as the symbol of this militant northern nation. "I wonder what their official business is, apart from spying on our fleet. You know, I'm glad we're leaving now. Your mother worried needlessly - the East should be a much more peaceful place than here."

Bran looked down to the bustle of the streets below, overwhelmed by the immense splendour of the city. He could not believe the crowds moving along the broad pavements and boardwalks. They seemed like living creatures, giant, thousand-headed serpents slithering their way in every direction.

"How many people live in this place?"

"More than in all of Gwynedd combined!" his father yelled back over the noise of the factories, mills and mistfire plants they passed as they circled the eastern industrial district. One of the multitude of chimneys belched out a great cloud of thick, black sooty smoke. Dylan's dragon swerved right immediately, but Emrys was too slow and rushed straight through it.

Bran and his dragon hovered over the factory, both covered in soot, coughing and spluttering. The boy futilely tried to wipe the black dust from his goggles. The silver drake looked at them with scorn. Dylan stifled a laugh and sighed.

"All right, that's the end of sightseeing. I can see your dragon is too exhausted, let's get you to the hotel. There's only one in Brigstow, but it's quite decent."

"What's a hotel?"

"An inn! Of sorts."

The Brigstow Grand looked like no inn Bran had ever seen. The ground floor was shot through with giant panes of crystal glass, and there were three more rows of windows above it, dividing the yellow facade with straight stylish lines. A balcony with intricate iron balustrades spanned the length of the second floor. The roof was surrounded with a line of sculpted plaster supported by heavy stone brackets.

The valets reached for the dragons to take them away to the stables. Emrys was anxious at first, but Bran managed to placate the beast and it shuffled off, still snorting and sneezing from the dust. The boy followed his father through the entrance, a portal of crystal and wormfire-wrought steel, braided and spliced together in floral ornaments worthy of a nobleman's palace. The lobby was as big as the Great Auditorium at Llambed and lavishly decorated. Bran felt dizzy from all the excitement - and the black smoke he'd inhaled.

"See that dining hall, son?" Dylan said and pointed to another crystal and steel entrance. "Get yourself cleaned up and come down here for supper. I have to deal with a few formalities and make sure all our bags have arrived. The bellboy will take you to our room."

The "room" was an apartment, almost as big as their slate-roofed house in Caer Wyddno, with a palatial

101

bathroom, blue-tiled, with a huge enamelled bath. The water was kept hot constantly by a couple elementals trapped in the fire-stone piping.

Soaking himself in the luxurious bath, he wondered why Dylan had never taken him to a place like this before. Brigstow did not lie beyond impassable mountains and oceans, it was easily reachable by dragon or mistfire omnibus. Why had they never moved to a city? Life here seemed much more convenient than in Gwaelod - and much more interesting.

Half an hour later they were sitting by a large oak table, waiting for the main course. Dylan wore a knee-length black frock coat embroidered with golden thread, with silk-faced lapels and a grey waistcoat. His face, furrowed by age and experience like a bark of an old fir tree, was smooth-shaven and freshly powdered to conceal the scar on the left cheek and his eyes, glinting the same green as his son, shone brightly. Bran had never seen his father look so dapper before.

A human-shaped, turbaned and bearded creature of smoke and fire whooshed out of thin air by their table, with a carafe of rose wine and a bread basket.

"Who... or what... was that?" whispered Bran when the creature had disappeared in a puff of scentless smoke.

"That's a Djinni. They come from the deserts of Durrani," explained Dylan. "A few of them served as porters and interpreters in the Dracalish army and when we moved out, they chose to come with us rather than remain and be branded traitors."

"I don't know these names. We weren't taught anything about this history."

"I'm not surprised. These were Dracaland's wars, not Prydain, and not something to boast about. The Queen's armies tried to conquer the Durrani some three years after you were born, but they were decimated. They say only one dragon survived the retreat from Gandhara."

"I thought the Dracalish soldiers were invincible."

"Mm, so did they."

"Were you taking part in this war?"

"No." Dylan shook his head. "I was never in that part of the world. Durrani is inland, between Varyaga and Bharata." The tip of Dylan's finger lit up and he traced a simple map in the air. The drawing hovered for a moment before Dylan dispersed it with a wave. "Maybe one day. We will return to Durrani, eventually, it's too precious to leave it alone. The Dragon Throne always hungers for more riches."

He keeps saying we, thought Bran. He didn't like it. Although both sides of the Dyke were formally united under one crown, most of the freemen of Gwynedd prided themselves in their independence from the White Dragon Throne in Lundenburgh.

The Djinni appeared again, this time with platters of fancily prepared meats and salads. Dylan chose the dishes, as the names on the menu, all in Latin, meant nothing to Bran.

"This is duck, I believe," explained Dylan.

"How... how is this duck?"

The bits his father pointed to on the platter resembled no food he had ever seen.

"It's foamed and pressed through a cold steel tube."

"Why?"

"This is a restaurant for spoiled city folk who are bored with normal food. But that's still tasty."

"And this?"

Bran pointed to a small golden cube.

"Try it."

The boy gingerly put the cube into his mouth. At first it tasted of seared beef, but then it exploded in his mouth with a rainbow of tastes and aromas, which he barely recognised. Bran opened his eyes wide. Dylan laughed.

"The cook here is also a wizard. I'm sure there are many other surprises like this. But now, tell me, what have you managed to learn about Qin?" Dylan asked, putting a spoonful of foamed duck onto his plate.

"Not a lot," Bran admitted. "I read of the silk trade, of their wars with the Horse Khans and Toshara, and their dragons... I studied this *Boym's Travelogue* you gave me. But it looks so old! Are you sure it's up to date?"

Dylan chuckled. "I'm sure it's not. But we don't have much else. You'll find the Qin are a notoriously elusive race."

Two centuries had passed since the Venedian named Boym had travelled the length of the old Silk Route, across the great plains of southern Varyaga, the steppes of the Horse Lords and the deserts of Toshara before reaching Ta Du, the capital of the mighty Qin. In the West, the Wizardry Wars had been at their most terrible. Millions perished in battle, poverty and famine but Qin was populous, rich, peaceful and technologically advanced beyond imagining. Boym had spent a great part of the book describing the marvels of the Emperor's palace, as big as a Western city, clockwork humans that raced down the corridors with messages, walls that moved aside on their own as the guest approached, mechanical servants pouring tea and war machines that marched on legs of metal.

"I learned about the Qin dragons, *long*, at the Academy. They say you don't feel dragon fear around them but rather a dragon awe."

Dylan nodded.

"Not long after Boym's travels the Qin sealed themselves off behind a giant shield, like a country-sized *tarian,* impenetrable to outsiders. *Haijin,* they called it, the Sea Ban."

"Why would they do that?"

"You've read the books. Back then the Qin was an island of wonder in the sea of despair. There was nothing the outside world could offer them except refugees and disease."

Bran pondered the news briefly.

"You said we're sailing *to* Qin…"

Dylan smiled.

"Ten years ago we've managed to penetrate their shield by force and establish a factory. There is now decent trade flourishing between Dracaland and Qin."

"Then what are we going to do when we get there?"

"You, boy, will be mostly sightseeing and learning." Dylan pointed his fork at Bran's pouting face. "I have my mission, and that is an actual state secret, so I'm not telling you anything else. You'll read about it when the state archives open in fifty years.

"Be Sires caring for appraisal of our dessert course?" interrupted the Djinni, hovering over the table with a silver bowl. "We having offering of sherbet of hibiscus and sandalwood, or offering of pistachio halva, garnished with saffron."

"I'll have the halva," Dylan said, "the boy will have sherbet. You'll love it," he added, smiling at his son.

Bran only nodded, too busy trying to tell apart the changing flavours in his mouth.

The airships passing overhead whirred their propellers monotonously. The mistfire carriages – Bran had only seen one of the contraptions before, driven by the richest merchant in Caer Gwyddno – clinked and clanked about the broad cobbled avenues with a whistle like a boiling kettle. The omnibuses, crammed full of people, hurried between their destinations with the great roar of their elemental-powered engines, ringing of bells, screeching of geared wheels upon grooved iron tracks. The horses whinnied, the wyverns bellowed, the paperboys and greengrocers tried their best to shout over the constant din.

The streets reeked of sulphur, soot, smoke and the acrid stench of wyvern droppings flowing down the open gutters. The *tafarns* and restaurants spread the smell of burnt meat and spilt ale, the bakeries overpowered Bran's nostrils with the sweet, mouth-watering scent of freshly baked bread and moist aroma of yeast. The river, split into several canals running through the city centre, stank of silt, seaweed and something else Bran could not easily identify - an oily chemical stench. The water in the river ran brown, with rainbow stains of grease.

The people of Brigstow liked to build high. Tall towers rose on every corner, delicate spires of steel or stocky turrets of white stone. The topmost levels of the merchant residences and aristocrat mansions appeared to float in the air, supported by a thin latticework of miststeel. The rooftops peaked in a series of narrow conical turrets, almost piercing the clouds. Bran wondered how the inhabitants could enjoy climbing so high up every day, until he saw the lifts – stone platforms rising and falling noiselessly on pillars of compressed Ninth Wind. At night, the city streets were as bright as day, illuminated with blazing evertorches and glistening sparklespheres.

This place never sleeps.

Hosts of people he had never imagined could exist in one place filled out vast market squares and broad thoroughfares. The men all wore dark frocks and tall top hats, the ladies donned flounced skirts, capes and bonnets. This was a far cry from the simple country garments he was used to back in Gwynedd, or the practical uniforms of the Academy. There were more different kinds of clothes, shoes and hats to buy at the market stalls and in shops lining the main streets of the city than he had ever thought necessary. Bran's clothes all came from the same tailor in Caer Wyddno, and he only had two pairs of shoes, one for flying, one for walking.

In time, Bran began noticing other, more subtle, things. There were very few dragons. He had become used to their presence at the Academy, their smells, their sounds, the constant buzz of Farlink feeds passing through the air that his sensitive mind would inadvertently pick up on. Here only the town guards travelled regularly on dragonback, mounting purple hawk drakes, a small swift and agile race fit for chasing ruffians along the narrow alleyways. Sometimes a nobleman or army officer would soar past on an expensive thoroughbred. Ordinarily, however, even Emrys was bound to make a sensation when it landed in the middle of the market square, startling the much smaller, two-legged wyverns of the common townsfolk.

"A dragon is an expensive creature to keep in a city," explained Dylan.

They were sitting on a bench in the Empress's Square, watching the well-to-do citizens of Brigstow walking their pets. This was the only quiet part of town, although even here the honking, whistling, clacking, roaring and shouting carried over from the surrounding streets, drowning the singing of birds and wind rustling in the oaks and limes. On one side of the square the buildings were strangely ruined, abandoned, staring at the garden with black empty windows.

"You need stables, pastures… Land is too precious," Dylan continued. "You can get anywhere by omnibus or automated carriage, really, which don't need feed and freedom to roam."

"And what about mages? I haven't seen any since we arrived."

"You won't see them just wandering the streets, they're always busy." Dylan smiled. "The Brigstow wizards don't like to cause a fuss. They're just holed up in the Tower of Grand Magic and get everything they need delivered there… Brunel's the only one who regularly comes down to the city on one of his contraptions, to look after the ships and trains."

"I'm glad I didn't go for wizardry, then."

Dylan laughed loudly, startling a passing lindworm, which let out a puff of sulphuric steam. The creature's owner gave him a scornful look.

"It certainly is not as glorious a job as they present it in the Academy, but think of the advances we've made thanks to the wizards and thaumaturgists. Imagine what this place would look like without airships, mistfire, automatons…"

Bran nodded, without conviction. In the countryside where he had grown up there was little use for these novel inventions. Spark oven and Faerie laundry was all the modern magic his mother used on a regular basis. He realised how remote his father's life had become to that of his family. They were almost strangers.

"Yes, imagine if the Sun Priests got their way," Dylan added to himself, gazing vacantly at Brigstow's spiralling towers, "this place would look like Rome…"

"Have you ever been to Rome?"

The ancient Imperium was no friend to the Dracaland and travel between the two empires was rare and restricted except to the open ports of Vasconian coast.

"Only once, on a spying mission," Dylan replied without much enthusiasm. "All the palaces, temples and circuses of the top tier are still there and they're a magnificent sight, no doubt, but the squalor, the filth, the poverty... I have been the lower levels and I would never want to see it again."

He shook his head.

"Lower levels?"

"The entire city is built in seven tiers, like a giant cake. You know how obsessed the Old Faithers are about the number seven. The richer and more powerful you are, the higher you live. The Imperator's court and the Mithraeum Maximum are on the seventh tier, but the first floor is a slum bathed in perpetual darkness. Six million people in one place. Can you imagine?"

Bran couldn't. Until they came to Brigstow he didn't even know what a few hundred thousand people gathered in one place would look like. The world was far bigger and scarier than he had ever envisioned.

"Is it true they still have gladiator fights?"

"Oh, yes." Dylan nodded. "The circus for the games is perhaps the greatest building in the world, and sits right in the middle of the second tier, beneath the Imperator's palace. But they no longer fight to the death. The Romans are not barbarians, even though they are so backward. They still have the old gravity plumbing, and only the richest can afford spark ducts."

And we're still using a well for water and Faerie fire for heating, Bran thought.

A drop of water fell on Dylan's nose and he looked sharply to the clouds.

"Oh, look, I do believe it's going to rain. Finally! Let's go to the old Trow before the skies open."

By the morning a message had come from the harbour; their ship was ready to depart. Bran and Dylan packed their belongings and sent them via pneumatic courier to the harbour. Dylan insisted they took a leisurely stroll along the streets of Brigstow towards the seaport, one last time.

They walked down the canyons of tall yellow brick warehouses; sloping bridges, down which the porters rolled barrels of oil and wine, joined the two sides of the street. Iron cranes squeaked, lifting heavy crates to the top floor windows. At length they arrived at the river and moved along the bank, past the sleek yachts and copper-clad barges, until Dylan turned into an alley between another row of warehouses to their left and a great wall of black iron and steel to their right.

"When do we get to the ship?" Bran asked, by now completely lost. "I thought the quays would be somewhere around here."

Dylan smiled mysteriously, but said nothing. They reached a flight of metal steps leading to the top of the wall of steel, some fifty feet up. He silently gestured Bran to climb it.

The roof of the strange edifice was completely flat, covered with wooden planks and surrounded by silksteel railing. Brass coils, glass pipes and a row of four, tall black funnels running through the middle and six tall wooden masts protruded from the rooftop, with a white mansion-like building between the third and fourth. Dockers and seamen busied themselves around the structures, hauling goods and making some hasty repairs. The whole construction filled out a wide canal joining the main docks of the Brigstow harbour with the Afon.

"You're standing on the deck of MFS *Ladon*," Dylan announced proudly, "the largest ship ever built!"

"This can't be..."

"See for yourself!"

Dylan guided him around the deck. One of the structures on the bow hid a giant capstan, with an anchor chain the links of which were the size of an adult man. The quarterdeck boats attached to the sides of the ship were as large as the canal barges. The staircases leading to the lower decks were as deep and wide as those in the towers of Llambed.

"Can it even move? Where are the paddle wheels?" Bran asked, full of doubt, and Dylan smiled.

"Fifteen knots against a gale-force wind, son! It's another feat of Master Brunel. Come, I will show you the engines."

The engine room was built like a basilica, vast, tall, vaulted, running through the entire length of the colossal ship. The engine itself was three storeys tall, surrounded by a maintenance gallery on every level. Four giant cylinders of crystal and copper lined the floor in a row, joined by a network of pipes, valves and flanges. In the massive boiler, forming the core of the engine, hundreds of the purest Jorvik elementals rested dormant, waiting for the command from the ship's captain. A double row of piston rods, tall as tree trunks, lay in the back of the engine room around a crankshaft.

"This turns the screw which propels the ship," Dylan said, patting the massive crankshaft, "the largest piece of wrought faer iron in the world. We are now twenty feet under the waterline. Impressive, isn't she?"

Bran nodded, staring agape at the tangle of metal around him. The buzz of magic needed to keep the elementals in peace, the smell of grease and oil made his head hurt. He wanted to ask about something else, but was finding it difficult to speak.

"You're pale," Dylan noted. "Let's get you some fresh air. Come, I have something else to show you."

Bran followed his father outside up the winding metal staircase and onto the raised part of the upper deck, a large platform of reinforced wood with a broad ramp leading down into the bowels of the ship.

"This is the landing deck. And ho, they're bringing in the dragons!" cried Dylan, pointing to the sky, his eyes laughing.

Bran looked at him in surprise. Once on board a ship his father became a different man - tall, strong, bright-eyed and somehow younger and more handsome than he had ever seemed at home. Unwittingly, Bran smiled.

A squadron of Silvers and Azures landed around them. The soldiers climbed down from their beasts, unbuckling the saddlebags. Bran ran up to them. The heat of the dragon breaths made the air around the beasts shimmer.

"What unit are you?" Bran asked one of the soldiers, not recognising the winged anchor insignia on their navy blue uniforms.

The man was lanky, slim and silver-haired. When he turned to answer, his cat-like eyes glistened bright amber in the sun.

"You're *Faer Folk*!"

"And you're a rude little boy," the soldier said with a grin. "Why so surprised? Haven't you seen a Tylwyth before?"

"I didn't know you served in the army."

"Why not?" The soldier shrugged. "Even Faer Folk need money these days. You can't spend all your life hunting and singing. Not when there's no more game in the forests."

"I've seen your people… Dancing in Brycheiniog."

The Tylwyth nodded thoughtfully.

"That's where my mother comes from. They are the last to keep to the old ways."

There was among the dragons one very different from the others, a sleek, smooth-scaled bronze beast, with large, wise eyes and long, slim neck.

"Who's flying *that*?" Bran asked, admiring the beautiful creature.

"You are, son."

His father approached. The soldiers stood to attention.

"At ease, men. Soldiers, this is my son, Bran. Bran, this is the Second Dragoon Regiment of the Royal Marines. We'll be travelling together."

The soldiers saluted the boy, but Bran's attention was elsewhere.

"What did you say?"

"It's your new dragon, Bran. A bronze thoroughbred – fast, elegant and presentable as befits my son. It's the latest fashion among young riders these days, I hear."

The joyous mood perished in an instant. Bran narrowed his eyes and leaned his head forwards.

"This is *not* my dragon. Where's Emrys?"

"That old thing? I left it at the hotel. But look at this one, son! Isn't it a beauty?"

"I don't care, father. I'm going to get Emrys."

He pushed through the soldiers, passing his father by. Dylan reached out to him.

"Son, wait." There was pleading breaking through his commanding voice that made Bran stop and turn. Dylan nodded at him to step aside, away from the unloading soldiers.

"I know this is not easy for you, but it's better to do it now, before we leave."

Bran relaxed his fists and unclenched his teeth.

"I'm sorry, father. It's a beautiful mount, and I'm sure it was expensive, but I can't leave without Emrys."

"But you're too old! It's as if you'd insisted on bringing a pony! It's a danger for you – *and* for the others in the open sea. It's bound to go feral soon."

"It will stay calm as long as I'm with it."

"You can't promise that and I can't take that risk. If you want to sail with us, you must leave the dragon behind."

"Very well. I'm going back home. Maybe I can still make it to the inauguration, just like you wanted."

"It's you who wanted to come with me in the first place!" he heard as he stormed towards the metal stair.

"What happened? I've seen the boy leave the ship in a great huff."

Dylan was pretending to study the maps, too distraught to focus, when Reeve Gwenlian found him on the bridge.

"I've decided my son is not mature enough for this journey," he said, turning to her.

It'd been months since he had last seen her soft features, surrounded by a storm of jet-black hair. He almost forgot about the quarrel.

"You're letting him go back home?"

Dylan's fingers rattled on the table.

"Tell me, Gwen - at what age does a young dragon rider obtain his second mount?"

"I got mine when I was thirteen."

"And the third?"

"Ooh… seventeen I think. What is this about?"

"Bran's had his beast since he was ten. It's a Marsh Wyrm!"

"So?"

"He refuses to leave it on shore."

"Is that it?" She almost laughed. "I'm sorry, Dylan – I mean, Ardian ab Ifor – "

"It's alright, we're alone here."

"Dylan – I know you're used to tough negotiations, but the lad's your son. It was to be your first trip together. Let him be."

"You sound like the boy's mother," he scoffed, "but you're a rider yourself, you should know better. By Owain's Sword, how can I make a man of my son if I let him keep his childhood toys?"

"Looks like you've been doing a great job so far. You know what will make him even more manly? A whole another year without seeing his father."

He took a deep breath. This whole affair was taking too much of his time and nerves. The ship was about to take off and he hadn't even talked to its captain yet.

"How do you know so much about me and Bran? I don't remember telling you about my family."

"I have brothers – and I know *you*," she replied, touching his face gently. Her face lit up in one of her famous smiles.

From dragonback, Bran could appreciate the full size of the MFS *Ladon*. It was aptly named after the legendary

Broodfather of the volcanic dragons, Ladon of the Hesperides. Other vessels, even the great ocean-going warships, seemed like mere toys compared to this black floating monster. The four enormous funnels of the ship were already spewing white steam as the elementals inside the engine cauldron awoke in preparation for the voyage.

Feeling the warm Ninth Wind on his face calmed him down. He still wanted to sail – even more now that he had finally seen the ship – and the thought of coming back to school filled him with dread. But there was nothing Bran could think of that would convince Dylan to take Emrys. His reasons made sense, but Bran wished Dylan acted more like a father than a soldier. And for as long as Bran remembered, in Dylan's mind the navy had always taken precedence over the family.

If I start flying now, I should be at Abertawe before nightfall – and back home for tomorrow's lunch... Mother will be surprised.

He saw a silver shape launching from the *Ladon*'s deck. *Father?* No, the dragon was smaller and nimbler than Afreolus; but it was heading unmistakably towards him and as the beast got closer he saw an astonishingly beautiful and strong faced black-haired woman riding it.

"You must be Bran," she cried over the sound of her dragon's beating wings, "I'm your father's Reeve, Gwenlian. Ardian ab Ifor asked me to take you back to the ship."

"I'm not leaving my dragon!" he cried back.

"It's alright. You can keep it. Come, the ship is about to steam off."

As he landed, Bran could feel the entire deck humming and trembling with the tremendous power of the engine. Emrys snorted uneasily; this was unlike any surface it had landed on before.

"I will take you to your quarters," the Reeve said and smiled warmly at Bran, removing her goggles. Her eyes were dark as night. He felt his cheeks redden.

"What did you call my father? Ard..."

"Ardian - that's his rank in the Royal Marines, commander of the regiment. You may have noticed our titles are different from the other units. I'm a Reeve – equivalent of a Sergeant."

Commander of the regiment?

This meant all the riders on the ship were under his command. Bran knew Dylan must have been a high-ranking officer, but he had never suspected just quite how high.

I know nothing about him, really, he realised.

"Can I talk to him now?"

"He'll be busy at the bridge, with the ship's captain and all the steersmen. We're sailing any minute now and there are still some preparations to take care of."

"Any minute now?"

His stomach turned. He didn't feel ready yet. He looked towards the spiral towers of Brigstow. He was about to leave it behind together with Gwynedd, Dracaland, all that was familiar and safe. White smoke puffing from the ship's funnels changed to grey. Water on the aft-side boiled as the massive propeller started turning.

A couple of soldiers were standing by the railings, singing.

> *Ffarwel fo i Langyfelach lon,*
> *A'r merched ieuainc i gyd o'r bron;*
> *'Rwy'n mynd i dreio pa un sydd well,*
> *Ai'm wlad fy hun, neu'r gwledydd pell.*

THE SHADOW OF BLACK WINGS

Farewell to gay Llangyfelach,
And all the young girls;
I'm going to see which is better,
The faraway lands or my own country.

"What's that song?" he asked the Reeve.

"Farewell Langyfelach," she answered, her black eyes glinting. "It's a song of those who sail away from the shores of Gwynedd into the unknown."

CHAPTER VIII

Yamato, Winter, 6ᵗʰ year of Kaei era

The training at the *dōjō* continued throughout the winter. Six months in, only the two most talented and persevering students remained in Satō's little class of *Rangaku*.

Shōin was a son of a family of tailors and cloth merchants from Nagato, tall for his age, but thin, with his ear-long black hair always messed up and uncombed, and simple unkempt townsman clothes. Keinosuke was his opposite, an heir to a rich samurai family from Chūbu, always impeccably dressed in a black and white kimono with the crest of his clan, Sakuma, on the shoulders and back. The boy usually kept to himself unless asked directly, silently observing the world from under thick eyebrows.

In the winter months the class moved from practising in the courtyard to studying the theory of magic in a small six-mat room on the upper floor of the main hall of the Takashima mansion.

"Remind me, what did we start on after the runic alphabet?" Satō asked, checking her notes.

The boys sat at a low table covered with small scrolls of paper written over in the scribbly Yamato letters and runes of the West.

"Potentials," answered Shōin eagerly, rising slightly from his knees.

The other student just nodded.

"Ah, that's right. Answer me this, then: which is easier, encasing a boy's hand in a block of ice, or freezing a cupful of water?"

The tailor's son looked to the ground, sheepishly.

"Freezing a boy, *sensei*," he said quietly.

"And why is that?"

"Because... freezing water is True Magic not a mind trick?"

Satō shook her head.

"That's not quite it, Shōin. When you're frozen, you not only think you're frozen - that would be an Illusion. The ice is real, it melts and leaves puddles on the ground. Keinosuke, do you know why?"

The other boy raised his eyes as if surprised that somebody would mention his name.

"Water... is not alive. It is fixed in form, unchangeable. It has no, er... potential," the boy replied, struggling.

Satō smiled and nodded.

"Every living thing, from a tree to a samurai, has the potential to change itself and its nearest environment. The Bataavians call it *mogelijkheid*. That's how it's written." She presented them with a piece of paper with the new word inscribed in decorative runes, and waited for a minute until the boys scribbled it clumsily to their notepads. "This is what makes living things grow and transform, from a single bean to a beanstalk, from an egg to a sea-hawk – and that's what a magic user taps into if he wants to enchant something that is alive."

"So our nature is actually making it easier for you to enchant us?" asked Shōin. "That doesn't seem fair."

"It may seem unfair," Satō agreed, "and if there was no power other than *mogelijkheid* involved, wizards would be truly terrifying people, once they'd reach their full power. However, as you grow up, your resistance to enchantments grows also. Without realising it, you become more and more resilient to magic, even if it's beneficial to you. That's why it's so hard to heal adult men, compared with children."

"Is this why the Spirit healers have to use *sakaki* wands and boiled rice to heal old men, but prayer and touch is enough for us?" Shōin guessed.

She nodded. "Eventually, even the power of *kami* cannot heal the injuries or extend life for infinity. Some say if it wasn't for this natural resistance, we could be immortal."

"Is it also something we have no influence over, like *mogelijkheid*?"

"You can train it, to some extent. Your resilience will grow as you become more attuned to your magic talent."

"Can you train yourself to become completely immune to magic?" Keinosuke asked softly and unexpectedly.

"There... there are legends of such feats, usually achieved by powerful priests or demi-Gods in ancient time. They were called *Hanryū*, Half-Dragons. Can you guess why?"

"Because the *ryū* are immune to magic?"

"The *ryū* were said to be immune to magic. But it may just be a legend - nobody has seen one in Yamato for hundreds of years. Anyway, going back to the lesson... Now, to easily freeze a cup of water, which is, as you said, fixed in state and has no *mogelijkheid* of its own, you need to use one of the two methods. The first one the Bataavians call *thaumaturgie*, or wonderwork. That's the most difficult and complicated school of *Rangaku*, and I doubt you'll ever need to concern yourself with it. It's the art of transforming lifeless matter. Look at this sparkleball."

Satō produced a round object the size of a large orange, which glittered and sparkled in all colours of the rainbow. Colourful flames travelled over the surface of the ball, sparkles formed random flowery patterns. It was impossible to tell what the ball was made of. It was cold and firm to touch, its edges blurred by all the glittering points of light.

"This is what young thaumaturgists practise on," said Satō. "They take a round polished stone and change it into this - it's called *twinkelbal* in Bataavian - forever. It will never cease to sparkle, it is Truly transformed."

"Does Takashima-*sama* know any thau... wonderwork?" Shōin asked.

Satō shook her head.

"Only very little. It's most difficult to perform in Yamato. From what I understand, when many people start using magic in one place, a field of *mogelijkheid* grows into which one can tap. The Bataavians call it *morfisch veld*. However, since we have so few wizards in Yamato, our field is very weak. Do you understand?"

The boys nodded, but their expressions were blank.

"Still..." Satō continued, "that's thaumaturgy, but there is another way to freeze water, and that's to use the elemental magic - wizardry. This is something not only the *Rangaku* use - the shamans of the Northern Tribes know it, and priests of the mountain temples use it in their purification rituals, even if they don't understand how it works. It may well be the oldest magic known to men. Through it, we use the potential of the Earth itself, the *mogelijkheid* of Nature, of elements. This is the power of water drilling through the rock, of wind eroding a mountain. Now, our scholars recognise five basic elements, but the Westerners only concern themselves with four – Are you writing this down, Shōin?" she interrupted.

122

"Of course, h-here it is!" the tailor's boy stammered, and presented his notepad.

There were several words written on it in the runic alphabet, full of spelling mistakes, and a doodle of a sparkleball.

Satō sighed. After a few months of performing teacher's duties she had learned she couldn't really expect thirteen-year-old boys to absorb that much knowledge all in one go. Even Nagomi often got bored when Satō became too involved in describing some peculiar aspect of an enchantment.

The wizardess looked out through the window, the black frame cutting a serene painting out of the city landscape. A thin blanket of pure snow covered the roof of a nearby house and the boardwalk of the street visible beyond. It was a rare occasion in Kiyō. The snow fell in soft gentle flakes and the world outside was silent and calm. Only a lone hotpot vendor praised the qualities of his dishes into the empty streets.

She knew it was her duty as an heir to teach the boys – but she wasn't an heir yet. Until her father officially passed the inheritance, was she truly obliged to do anything for the *dōjō*?

Of course you are. Heir or no heir, you're still a Takashima.

"Just remember about the four Great Elements - earth, fire, air and water," she told the boys, "you can write it down in normal characters, not runes - *Chi, ka, fuu, sui*." She paused and waited as they struggled with their calligraphy. "Like our *Butsu* scholars, the *Rangakusha* don't count the Void, *ku*, as a Great Element."

The boys stared at her blankly. *They have no idea what I'm talking about.* She cleared her throat.

123

"We'll get back to that next week. You don't have to remember it all yet. It's too nice outside to stay indoors," she concluded, "that's it for today."

Shōin jumped up immediately. He bowed fast, picked up his notebook and brush, and ran off before the other boy had even managed to reach for his bundle.

Keinosuke bowed slowly and deliberately.

Satō finished rolling up her scrolls and noticed the boy was still in the room.

"What is it?"

"Takashima-*sensei*, do you have any books or writings about dragons - or *hanryū*?"

"Keinosuke... this knowledge is forbidden. I'm not even sure I should have told you about those legends."

"I see."

The boy seemed dejected.

"I'm sorry, but my family is in trouble as it is. Even the Bataavians aren't keen to mention these matters openly. Maybe one day you'll get to talk to one of them about the dragons... but you're way too young for it now."

"Yes, *sensei*, but..."

"What else?"

"You didn't say you don't have the books."

How does he ...?

"The class is over," she said abruptly, and slid the door open, "see you next week."

The samurai son bowed again, unsuccessfully concealing a satisfied smirk, and left without a word. Satō followed him down the stairs, made sure he put on his winter sandals and watched him walk past the guards at the gates. Returning to the upper floor, she entered her father's library. She knew Shūhan would still be in the elemental laboratory he had set up on the other side of the residence,

124

across the courtyard, far away from his precious books. A tall, Bataavian-made bookcase stood in the corner. Satō rose on her toes and reached to the top-most shelf with an effort. From among many identical leather-bound tomes she chose one without hesitation, wiped the dust and spoke a magic word. Crimson fiery letters appeared, burning upon the leather cover.

She did not know the language of the book - it was some Western tongue, but not Bataavian - but she knew what the letters said, for the smuggler who had brought it from Dejima had told her father as she listened through a hole in the floor, hiding upstairs while the men talked in hushed, rasping voices one moonless night.

The fiery letters spelled the long, mystic title: *Applied Dracology, Student's Handbook, Year One. Property of Llambed Academy, Ceredigion, Gwynedd.*

Satō did not open the book, just gazed at it admiringly. She did not understand many of the foreign words of the title, but still it invoked in her mind an image of a great hall filled with books of lore and magic scrolls, a tall tower of stone - as she had seen in a Bataavian painting once - around which dragons of all shapes and colours soared, and a crowd of wizards practising their powerful spells on wide bright courtyards. This image appeared in her dreams ever since she had first heard of the "Llambed Academy", dreams full of mysterious words like "Ceredigion" and "Gwynedd" and of majestic winged, serpentine creatures, spewing fire and lightning.

Keinosuke's words made her uneasy. How could the boy possibly have known the secrets of the Takashima library? Had he been spying on her? But how? The residence was guarded, surrounded by tall walls… she shook her head. He was just a kid! It must have been something else. Maybe

125

she had blabbed something unwise in improper company…
Or maybe he had overheard Shūhan talk about the book
with his father. Master Sakuma was a renowned *Rangaku*
scholar in his own right, and as frequent visitor to the
Takashima mansion as the conditions of Shūhan's house
arrest allowed. Yes, that must have been it.

*I hope the kid knows how to keep his mouth shut. His family
would also get in trouble if they were caught dabbling in dragon lore.*

She heard familiar steps on the squeaking stairs.
Quickly, she slid the book back among the others and
sneaked out of the library.

CHAPTER IX

Off the coast of Yoruba, West Africa, December, 2606 ab urbe condita

A deafening broadside roared over the beach, startling a flock of parakeets that fluttered away in a green cloud. The shower of cannonballs brushed the tops of the palms and disappeared into the jungle beyond.

As soon as the ringing in his ears quietened, Bran heard his father speak in the commanding tone he had always assumed when talking to other soldiers.

"Still no reaction, Banneret?"

Dylan, wearing the gallant uniform of a Royal Marines Ardian, scarlet with golden Aberffraw lions on cuffs and buttons, turned to the Tylwyth standing beside him. Edern lowered the brass telescope and shook his silver-haired head.

"Nothing, Sir."

"I told you, Ardian, Tinubu will not give up easily," a third man spoke, rubbing the back of his neck. His dark bronze skin stood out against the white linen of his navy shirt.

"Don't worry, *Oba* Akintoye," replied Dylan, "we'll get you back on the throne today. The navy always keeps its promise."

It was not the first time the ship had to turn from its course towards Qin to play a part in some local skirmish or influence a diplomatic stalemate one way or another. The *Ladon's* course had been plotted deliberately so that the ship would pass near as many of the empire's troubled colonies as possible. A month had passed since the *Ladon* had set sail from Brigstow and they had been barely half-way to the Cape.

The bronze-skinned man was, as Bran had learned, some native pretender whose claim to the throne the Dracaland had decided to support. The reason did not matter; the orders from Lundenburgh rarely divulged more than the details necessary for a particular mission.

"Banneret, aim at the fort, and load the wall-breakers," ordered Dylan.

"Aye-aye, Sir."

Edern's cat-like eyes glinted in anticipation. The smooth-bores lowered in preparation for another salvo. The striped banner of the incumbent ruler Tinubu flew proudly over the fort's stone ramparts.

Bran noticed something on the horizon, a square of white in the sea of azure.

"Another ship, father?" he asked. Dylan looked to where he was pointing.

"Well spotted, son. Edern, what is it?"

The Banneret did not even need to raise the spyglass. The Tylwyth were famed for their keen eyesight.

"They're flying Napolion's Eagle, sir. That's a Vasconian man-o'-war if I've ever seen one."

Romans!

Bran had never seen a Roman ship before. Of all the many nations inhabiting the Imperium only Vasconians, from the northern coast of Iberia, were an ocean-going race – although their sail-driven ships could not dream of matching the mistfire ironclads of the northern nations.

128

"They dare not intervene," Dylan said. "They're just here to observe. Fire at will, Banneret!"

The guns bellowed again and this time the shells struck the limestone walls with a terrifying force. The rolling thunder of repeated explosions shook the small island, and a thick pall of black smoke hid the beach from sight.

"The wall's been breached, sir," the Banneret reported, when the echoing rumble had passed and the smoke rose in the wind, revealing the scene of destruction. The officer's words were something of an understatement: the fort's sea-side ramparts were reduced to a smouldering pile of rubble. Still the striped banner flapped defiantly in the wind over the tall sandstone turret, in the middle of the stronghold.

"Right," said Dylan with a sigh. "I don't have time for this. Scramble up, we're coming in."

"Careful, Master Dylan!" Akintoye said, "Tinubu knows many tricks!"

"So do we, *Oba* Akintoye," Dylan said, laughing.

"Father, *look*!"

Bran pointed at the sea between the island and the ship. The waters bubbled and frothed, and the rolling waves parted, revealing the head of a giant hissing serpent. Its emerald-scaled body, most of its coils still hidden in the water, was easily as big as a frigate. The snake rose from the sea and sped towards the ship.

The Royal Marines dragons, which were waiting impatiently for their turn to take part in the battle on the landing deck, were now shaking their neck frills and snorting boiling steam from their nostrils. Their metallic silver scales glinted blindingly in the tropical sun.

"*Damballah*! I told you, Ardian! I warned you!" cried Akintoye.

For a brief moment Dylan gazed at the creature unfazed.

"Shall we launch the torpedoes, Sir?" Edern asked, glancing nervously at the approaching serpent. It was not big enough to threaten the *Ladon*, but it could still do some costly damage on deck.

"No, Edern," Dylan replied, "the time for trinkets is over."

He turned to his son.

"You'd better step away from the railings. This may get nasty."

As the dragons flew past the bridge of the *Ladon* like two silver bullets, Bran shouted and waved. He was certain his father did not see him, but at the last moment Dylan turned in the saddle and waved back – seconds before his dragon and the giant serpent struck against each other with tooth, flame and claw.

The parade processed down the main broad street of the town, rising clouds of yellow sand billowing into the sky so bright and pale blue it seemed almost white. Crowds of natives lined both sides of the road cheering and dancing, throwing wreaths of flowers, beads and bird feathers under the feet of the marching soldiers.

Ekō. That's the name of this hovel, Dylan remembered. He had lost count of how many towns like this he had helped conquer, liberate or destroy. For a moment he pondered why the Dracaland's complex interests required the previous ruler toppled – *Tinubu, was it?* – but he quickly decided he didn't really care. He did not expect this new *Oba* to last any longer than the Dragon Throne's interest required.

Dylan was riding Afreolus in front of the marching Marines. The silver dragon ambled onwards awkwardly, grunting unhappily, unused to walking for such long distances. Bran was sitting behind him on the dragon's back. One dragon was more than enough for the small parade.

"Are people always so glad to see us?" asked Bran.

Dylan let out a short laugh.

"They have no idea why they're here, or who we are. The local king ordered them to cheer. See how well dressed they all are? This is all just for show."

The locals forming the crowd were all wearing their finest clothes, loose-fitting, wide-sleeved robes of purple, crimson or white silk, embroidered with golden thread, and long colourful headscarves. Many wore jewellery, silver chains and small gem-studded rings, pearls and glass beads.

The cavalcade reached the steps of the palace of the *Oba*. It was not a grand building by any measure, a single storey high, with yellow thatch and white-washed walls covered in black ink paintings and bas-relief, damaged in places by the recent battle, but it stood out from the mud-brick houses around it enough to give its owner sufficient prestige. A hastily sewn standard of the old reinstated clan replaced that of the abolished one over a single square turret. A fountain in the courtyard provided a little respite from the overwhelming heat, even if not from the stifling humidity. Several remarkably life-like bronze statues of previous kings and queens decorated the square. Miraculously, they all seemed to have survived the fighting unscathed.

Those bronzes would have been worth thousands at an auction in Lundenburgh, Dylan thought briefly.

The marines positioned themselves in a half-circle around the courtyard, Bran among them in the first row. Local soldiers, armed with ceremonial spears and antique muskets, stood in front of the main entrance. Dylan, along with two other men – the Captain of the *Ladon* and the representative of Dracaland trade companies – moved forwards, to be greeted personally by the *Oba* Akintoye himself.

The reinstated ruler of Ekō stepped out of his throne room almost unrecognisable in his dazzling coronation robes. He walked magnanimously, the tails of his kaftan supported by two squires in silk loincloths. In his right hand he held a bronze spear tied with beaded string. He raised his left hand and Dylan bowed before this gesture. Others followed his example.

The *Oba* gave a short speech in his native language – although he spoke perfect Seaxe – thanking the Dracalish Empress for assisting him in regaining his rightful place on the throne.

He speaks as if he was Victoria's equal, Dylan thought. *His entire kingdom would fit into* Ladon*'s holds with room to spare.*

The three men were each given a large heavy necklace of gold and jewels. Dylan knew that the trade representative valued ink and paper over gold, but the treaties had to wait. Once the rewards were given out, Dylan stepped back, making way for others – local allies of the *Oba*, spies and traitors. Every one of them demanded praise and reward.

How many will live to see tomorrow?

The ceremony was coming to an end. One last ritual remained – the blessing of the ancestors over the new king, a renewal of contract with the Spirits.

The low droning of drums started, slowly at first, and the dancing shaman, *Egungun,* wearing a loose kaftan stitched of a thousand different patches of cloth, emerged onto the courtyard. White heron feathers, lining his mask and scarf, shook with every movement. He was already in a trance, spinning, jumping and howling. The drums picked up the pace and the dancer moved faster still, always a step ahead of the rhythm, as if anticipating the musicians' strokes.

The dancer neared the *Oba* and performed a series of complicated gestures and leaps. He took out a bunch of parrot feathers from the pocket of his kaftan and threw it over the king's head. They perished in a flash. The king bowed, smiling. The Spirits were approving.

This should have been the end of the ritual, but the *Egungun* dance did not stop. He looked around the courtyard from under the heron mask, as if searching for something. Dylan frowned when he noticed the direction in which the dancer headed. The shaman whirled towards the row of marines, where Bran stood. For everyone else it must have seemed a harmless extension of the ceremony. The dancer stopped in front of his son, screeching wildly. Suddenly something long and metallic glistened in his hand. Dylan launched forwards, but even as he started moving he knew he would be too late. The dancer dropped his arms down on Bran's head. Gwenlian, standing beside the boy, raised her hand at the last moment…

By the time Dylan reached the place where Bran stood, everything was settled. The dancer was lying on the courtyard floor clutching a broken arm, the piece of metal beside him. Bran was breathing hard, but was otherwise unharmed.

"Take him away," Dylan commanded sharply. "Hide him in a safe place."

Gwenlian grabbed Bran and pulled him towards the harbour. Dylan crouched by the injured shaman to examine the item with which he believed his son had been threatened.

I promised Rhian there would be no risk, he thought. *I should have left him on the ship.*

The bit of metal was shaped like a long chisel with a short handle, it was blunt and rather harmless-looking - a mere ceremonial weapon. The shaman started explaining something in an agitated voice. Dylan stood up and looked at the *Oba* quizzically.

"What is he saying?"

"This is a Spirit dagger," explained Akintoye, "it destroys all evil."

"Why did he attack my son?" Dylan enquired, allowing himself to sound angry.

"Not the boy, but the evil that is to befall him. It is a great honour."

Dylan frowned.

"Great honour? How so?"

"The *Egungun* deemed the boy worthy of their blessing. Rarely does one of no royal blood deserve the power of the daggers. I assure you the shaman meant no harm to your son."

Dylan nodded and helped the dancer to stand up.

A blessing dagger. Of course.

He remembered he had seen this sort of harmless "weapon" before.

"Tell the shaman I'm sorry for what happened. I'll send the ship's doctor to treat his arm."

According to the ship's calendar it was the middle of the winter, but Bran had never been so hot and sweaty. He was finding it very difficult to concentrate, and he needed all the attention he could spare. He was playing *tafl*, the King's Table, with Samuel, the ship's doctor. He had never played the game before boarding the *Ladon*, although the Seaxe boys at the Academy had been spending hours at a time pondering the movements of the black and white figures.

After a few weeks of Samuel's tuition it had quickly become his favourite pastime.

"This is like a dream," he said, trying to turn the doctor's attention from a particularly bad move he made with his Archwizard. "I never imagined the world was so vast and beautiful."

Samuel nodded, moving one of the Priests along the diagonal.

"And you've only seen a fragment of it."

"I think I understand now why father so rarely comes home. There's just so much to see. I can hardly remember Gwynedd now."

"Believe me, you will always remember your home. Now watch your Wizards, boy. You've completely exposed yourself with that move."

"It's this damn heat. Will it never end?"

"The weather rarely changes in these parts, so close to the equator," Samuel explained. "Only the wind can grow weaker or stronger."

As if in confirmation of his words, a gust of wind bent the palms on the beach low to the ground - a finger of a winter storm they were holding out in Goa, a Vasconian outpost on the coast of Bharata. The proud golden eagle of Rome spun on its mast like a weathervane.

By the evening the wind lessened and a small black ship steamed into the harbour, adding its grey banner with a strange black sigil of a horned circle to a multitude of colours already gathered in what was the only neutral port for days. Not long after its arrival, shouts of joy and gun salutes roared all along the *Ladon*. The agitated dragons buzzed with excitement in their holds under the deck.

Bran wanted to ask his father about the sudden celebration, but he was nowhere to be found. This was not unusual; Dylan rarely kept himself idle. There was always some errand he could run for the Empire, even without direct orders. Instead, the boy stumbled onto Edern.

"What's going on? Who sails that ship?"

"The ship is Gorllewin – don't you recognise their crest? It doesn't matter. What matters is the news they bring: the war with Arakan is over!"

"What's Arakan?"

"A kingdom on the other side of Bharata. We had some nasty border dispute with them."

"But why so much celebration?" Bran said as another of *Ladon's* guns thundered joyously.

"Had the war continued, we would have to join the fighting. And Arakan is a terrible place to do battle: hot, wet, fever-ridden jungles full of monsters and hostile natives. It would also have meant at least another month of delay. Now we can sail straight past Temasek, the shortest route possible."

The soldiers of the Second Dragoons prepared a great feast on board the *Ladon*. Dylan, having at last returned to the ship, ordered signal flags thrown from the masts inviting everyone in the harbour to celebrate the victory. The Breizh and Bataavian sailors came first, with song and wine. Their nations may have had their differences with Dracaland, but here in the colonies all Northerners were allies. The Vasconian rulers of the outpost were at first reluctant to bask in the glory of a competing imperial power, but then they saw barrels of prime grog being rolled out onto the deck and quickly changed their minds.

As dusk fell, a group of silent men in grey hooded robes entered the ship: the Gorllewin delegation. They stood on the side, in shadows, everyone giving them a wide berth.

"Come, Bran," said Edern, winking. He held a jug of grog in one hand and a chunk of cheese in the other. "I bet you haven't talked to a Grey Hood yet."

The two of them came up to the grim figures. One of the silent men came forward and cast down his hood. He was bald shaven, and had a horned, crossed circle tattooed on his forehead. His eyes were black as night, but his face lit up with a gentle smile.

"You have brought us joyous tidings, friends," said Edern, presenting him with the jug, "you should come closer, join the festivities."

The man nodded. "Thank you for the invitation, Arthur's Kin, but we are tired with the journey. We came here hoping we might speak with your Commander."

"Oh, Ardian ab Ifor? He's over there, on the bridge," Edern said, waving his cheese-arm.

"Why did he call you Arthur's Kin?" Bran asked when the hooded men shuffled off.

"Because that's what we are. Your king Arthur was of our people. Who's been teaching you history?"

"Miss Farnham," Bran said. Edern chuckled.

"Yes, I remember her. She wasn't too keen on the history of the Faer Folk."

A firework shot up from a Congreve rocket launcher and lit the sky up with red, white and blue, the colours of Dracaland Empire. At this signal, several dragon riders took to the air in a show of acrobatics. Chasing after them a bright green shape emerged from the holds..

"Emrys!" Bran cried. He focused on the Farlink connection to command his dragon back, but the distance and excitement coming from the beast were too big.

"Who let it out?" he asked, angrily.

"We thought your pet could use some fresh air," said Edern. "Look at it fly!"

The celadon-scaled dragon fumbled comically in an attempt to match the silvers and azures aerial prowess. It tumbled over itself chasing after the larger dragons.

Edern laughed.

"I can see why you like it so much. That's just priceless!"

"It's really a good beast," Bran said quietly. "It's just... not used to the life at sea, that's all."

"I'm sure it will grow up into a decent dragon."

"It is grown up!" the boy blurted, "I've had it for six years now."

"*Duw!* A six-year-old Swamper that's not gone feral yet?"

"Is that so strange?"

Despite Dylan's warnings, Bran had not seriously considered the likelihood of his mount turning against him. It was the eventual fate of every dragon rider and Bran knew how to deal with it, but unlike Afroleus and many other military dragons he had known, Emrys had never yet shown any signs of rebellion. In time, Bran had all but forgotten about the risk.

"Aye. Our silvers can last ten years, but they've been bred for loyalty. I've never heard of one of the lesser races take more than five years to turn wild. I take everything back, that's a fine specimen you've got there!"

"Father doesn't seem to think so," Bran looked at the bridge, where Dylan turned for a moment from his conversation with the Grey Hoods to look at his son. Bran could not see his face clearly but was certain it was filled with disdain as always when Emrys was around. Edern coughed.

"I'm sure Ardian ap Ifor does whatever he thinks is in your best interest."

"It's what's in *his* interest that concerns him most."

"I believe you're being unfair. He sounds worried whenever he talks about you…"

"I wish he talked less *about* me and more *with* me."

To that the lieutenant found no answer.

Whatever was left of the grog after the feast at Goa was now shared among small party of the crew and the soldiers in Bran's honour. It was the boy's sixteenth birthday. The Ardian's son was sitting at the top of a long table in the officers' mess, in a neatly ironed blue uniform. After the squadron's piper finished his celebratory ditty, Samuel stood up and rubbed the back of his bald head. Everyone looked at him expectantly. He presented the boy with a set of ivory-carved Staunton *tafl* pieces, where the blacks were Sun Priests and whites, the Wizards and a small spyglass, richly ornamented with brass lions and copper elephants he had picked up at a market in Temasek.

"It is a most precise instrument," he explained, "and I trust you will take good care of it. The barrel was wrought on the island of Kilwa in Zangibar, the iron came from the secret mines of Motapa. The glass is Bataavian, of Walcheren, enchanted at Delft. The case is made of grey selkie skin from Brendan's Island, so that it never sinks when dropped into the sea."

Samuel was delighted to see sparks of recognition light up in the boy's eyes as he listed the exotic place names. Over the last six months he had witnessed Bran's transformation from a country bumpkin, a landlubber, into a true traveller.

It reminded Samuel of his own humble beginnings in the navy. Son of a *mohel* from Bethnal, he had known nothing of the world outside the dark, narrow stinking streets of eastern Lundenburgh until he had boarded his first ship as a surgeon's apprentice. That very first voyage had taken him through lands of myth and legend, through oceans and continents he had only ever read or dreamt of. He had seen monsters and Gods, and ancient magic hidden in the jungles and deserts - and he never wished to go back home again.

It must have been the same for Bran. Any journey with Ardian Dylan and his dragoons was bound to be filled with adventures and excitement. On Brendan's Island they had flown over active volcanoes, assisting a group of Dracologists in their research. At Oyo they went with the embassy to the Yoruban King, who had treated them to a show of horsemanship and archery. Past the Skeleton Coast they'd sailed through mist so thick one could not see the end of an outstretched arm. On a south-westerly gale they'd passed the whitewashed, many-pillared walls of Zangibar and tall-spired fire-temples of Pemba, past the islands of sea coconuts until they reached the jungles of Bharata. From Goa the *Ladon* hurried across the Bangla Sea, past Temasek, due east, towards Qin.

Along the way Bran had become acquainted with most of the crew and the marines on board. The soldiers let him join their training in fencing and lancing. Samuel watched these bouts with slight concern at first. The army issue swords and cutlasses were larger and heavier than what Bran was used to, and their Soul Lances were solid flexible shafts of energy, a full nine feet of length, as befitted trained soldiers. The boy had to build up some muscle before he could think of matching their skill. The physical effort made wonders for his mood. Even Emrys eventually earned the crew's sympathy as the ship's informal mascot.

140

Among all the new friends and in all the excitement of the journey, Bran must have felt even more acutely the neglect with which his father seemed to have been treating him throughout the journey. The first few weeks of the voyage had been exemplary. Dylan was showing his son around the ship, introducing him to the crew, spending as much time with the boy as he could, trying to rectify the years of abandonment. The two had spent an entire day together on Brendan's Island and then another on the Rock; but the idyll had ended once the *Ladon* moved into the colonial waters. The commander of a Royal Dragoons regiment was rarely at rest. The dragons were too precious to idle for several months at sea.

Dylan was noticeably absent at his birthday party. At last, when the brief celebration was almost over and there was no fruitcake left, the Ardian appeared in the mess with an apologetic look on his face and a small bundle in his hands.

"Happy Birthday, son," Dylan said sheepishly, "I'm sorry I'm late."

"It's all right - work. I understand."

Bran waved his hand generously, although his voice was cold.

"It's only a little something…" Dylan presented the parcel. "I got it from a Bataavian physician we picked up on Birkenhead and thought of you. I hope it's to your liking."

"Thank you," Bran said quietly, unwrapping the gift.

Father and son shook hands. Every show of affection between the two always seemed awkward, as if they weren't sure how to go about it, but Samuel could see sincere concern in Dylan's eyes. Bran, on the other hand, seemed much more interested in the present, a small dragon figurine, its red surface glistening with a reddish tint in the lamplight.

"Thank you, Father," the boy repeated, and gently placed the statuette into his satchel, along with Samuel's spyglass.

Samuel smiled to himself. The night before the Ardian had arrived at his cabin, visibly distressed.

"I don't have a gift for my son. I never had the time to go to the market at Temasek. I know you spend a lot of time with Bran – I need your help, Samuel."

The doctor nodded and thought for a moment.

"I have just the thing."

He reached into a drawer of his desk and took out a small figurine of a dragon, intricately carved in red oriental resin. The serpentine creature resembled those of the Qin race, but was longer, more slender and sported two large leathery wings not unlike those of the Western beasts. The wide open mouth was surrounded by long whiskers and beard, two sharp horns split into antlers protruded from its head and the tail was on fire. In one of its three-clawed paws it held an orb. On the base were carved initials, in Roman alphabet: "P.F.V.S.".

"Bran is obsessed with the Eastern dragons, he should like it."

On the morning after his birthday Bran stood by the starboard railings, wrapped in a storm cloak of thick oily krakenhide. A cold eastern wind blew across the deck. The *Ladon* was passing a small harbour town clumped around a steep mountain. Through his new spyglass he observed a cluster of off-white buildings disappearing behind a rocky outcrop, warehouses, trade factories, merchant houses and the rising spire of a wizard tower. Some of the buildings had odd roofs that resembled peaked hats with up-curved brims, but most of them would not have been out of place in any town in the west. Dracaland Jacks fluttered in the breeze above the docks and on the masts of many merchant ships moving to and fro among large gaff-sailed junks of the Qin. The same imperial flag – red, white and blue dragon heads on green - was hoisted on a tall mast atop the summit of the mountain.

"Ah, Fragrant Harbour!"

A sudden voice jerked Bran out of his pensive observations. Dylan came up to his side, looking wistfully at the town.

"Ten years have passed since I last saw its piers and storehouses. How it has grown!" He sighed like a proud parent observing his child. "It was barely a fishing village when we got it from the Qin. It may well become the greatest merchant port these seas have seen, one day."

"And what's that over there?" Bran pointed to the west, where, farther away, a similar cluster of houses clung to a tiny island. He couldn't see the design on the flag through the spyglass.

"Vasconians."

"They seem to be everywhere."

"They've been here for much longer than us. Still, now the Qin prefer to make trade with the Dracaland. I suppose we're more reliable than Sun worshippers," Dylan scoffed.

"We're not coming to port here?" enquired Bran as the ship made no indication of changing its course.

"No, our duty is elsewhere this time. We go farther up the river."

"Why, what's up the river?"

"Fan Yu, the Great Harbour! A Southern trade centre for all of the empire. Now brace yourself, we are passing through to Qin territory!"

Dylan pointed to the blue sky in front of the great ship. Squinting, Bran noticed a slight shimmering in the air some two miles ahead. As they moved closer, the shimmering grew to a visible distortion, a pinkish hue added to the blue of the sky, like misty dawn. The air around the ship turned noticeably colder and the waters of the delta, still and calm until now, rose in a windless storm. The *Ladon* started to heave fore and aft over the waves.

Lightning cracked from a cloudless sky and, in its light, Bran saw the full size of the magical barrier. It stretched endlessly from east to west, separating the islands of the delta from the mainland, and rose straight up for at least a mile before starting to gently curve inland.

"How do we get around *that*?" Bran cried out in disbelief.

Dylan smiled.

"That, my son, is what we fought a war for."

Just as the ship's bow was about to hit the barrier, Dylan raised his arms and bellowed in a deep voice, an incantation in a language Bran had never heard before. His hands flared up with golden light. More lightning streaked right above the deck and a round portal, bound in blue and green dazzle, opened before them. On that signal the engines of the *Ladon* pushed one last time and the ship surged forwards, passing the barrier. With a loud whoosh and a pop, the magic door closed behind them. The sea became calm and quiet again and the ship chugged along merrily like a packet steamer on a summer morning.

CHAPTER X

Fan Yu, Qin, March, 2607 ab urbe condita

The ship passed the whitewashed watchtowers guarding the entrance to the harbour, and Bran saw, spreading before him, the vast imperial metropolis of Fan Yu. It was almost a country of its own, sprawling over hills, terraces and islands of the delta for miles. Boats of all shapes and sizes, coal barges, tea junks, fishing sampans, dinghies, ketches and yawls passed in all directions, like grain carts on the busiest of market days. The *Ladon* had to move slowly in this maze of vessels, careful not to crush the boats beneath its powerful iron-plated bow. The riverside was lined with facades of the many-roofed, clay-tiled houses of the townsfolk, suspended on wooden pillars over the water. Further upstream the dwellings of the rich and powerful encroached on the rising banks. Tall, tiered temple towers, the red and yellow walls of monasteries, ancient gold-plated palaces of local magnates and new, Western-styled marble facades of trade princes' houses.

It was all designed to awe the passengers of the vessels passing towards the harbour, but all this magnificence, all this splendour was marred by signs of destruction and misery. Walls were pocked with shot marks, wooden pillars splintered, shutters broken to pieces. Paint was peeling off in patches, and of the gold leaf on the sculptures and carvings only sad remnants remained. A layer of dust covered the rooftops and gutters. The damage seemed old, as if the city was in a constant state of disrepair, slowly eaten by some creeping war with no beginning and no end in sight.

It took *Ladon* half a day to navigate from the shanty outskirts of the town to its centre, where Thirteen Factories stamped their heavy colonial mark on the oriental surface of the city centre: a collection of western-style buildings, two and three storeys tall, fresh, new and magnificent. The colonnaded facades of purest white marble shone brightly in the sun like polished ivory, as did the zinc-covered roofs. Flags of the colonial powers and trade corporations flapped in the wind on tall masts of cedar wood, the Dracaland Jack flying between the banners of Midgard and Bataave. A small aerostat floated in the air, moored to a landing mast, which also served as a receiver for carrier wisps.

There was no pier big enough for the *Ladon*, so the ship was forced to stand at anchor a little off the harbour. A few of the crew, Bran and his father among them, boarded a cutter and made landing near the mouth of a small creek, by the customs station.

The Imperial Factory was the greatest of all, a three-storey edifice, with a row of blue-shuttered windows above a sculpted architrave showing the greatest triumphs of the Dracalish and Prydain might. Bran strained his memory trying to recall all the wars and battles he had always paid little attention to. He easily identified Arthur's march into Rome and the defeat of Norsemen at Crug Mawr, for that was part of Gwynedd's history too. It took him considerably more effort to name the siege of Ar Roc'hell during the Wizardry Wars and a more recent sea battle of Cape Spartel, where the dreaded Kyrnosian Imperator's invasion fleet was vanquished. The conquest of the northern Bharata he

146

recognised from the stories told by some of the elder soldiers. But the last scene he could not remember at all: an ironclad battleship sailing into a walled harbour with all guns blazing.

There was a warehouse on the lower level of the factory, full of tea bricks and bales of fresh golden silk piled in pyramids on one side, and large unmarked crates of red wood on the other. A group of Qin workers emerged with another cartload of tea, and it was the first time Bran had seen these mysterious people in the flesh, with their narrow eyes, flat noses and long braided ponytails under round cloth caps. They moved about silently, like automatons, their emotionless faces grey with fatigue. Their vacant eyes glanced through Bran as if he was invisible, as they proceeded to unload the cart onto the warehouse floor.

The meal they were served was, somewhat disappointingly, what one would expect to eat in any dining room of the Dracaland. Only the surroundings made it feel exotic. There was white fish with roast vegetables, imported all the way from the West but, not having survived the journey well, everything was withered and bland.

Bran wondered why anyone would go through so much effort when the land around the city seemed fertile and plentiful. He chewed the badly seasoned fish in silence, sitting at one end of a long table, his father at the opposite end already discussing some important local matters with a gentleman in a black magisterial robe. They talked in hushed voices, sometimes slipping into some sort of code, and Bran could not make much sense of the conversation. Prices of rice and silk were mentioned, and army movements, weather forecasts and geomantic divinations. Bran wiped his lips with a serviette, coughed and excused himself to leave the dining room.

Dylan paused the conversation and turned to his son. "Yes?"

"I thought I might do some sightseeing in the harbour."

Dylan thought for a brief moment then nodded.

"Yes, I suppose."

He snapped his fingers, whispering a spell. Bran felt a tinge of protective magic field surrounding him.

"Just don't go out too far. There's not much to see outside the Factories anyway, and you won't be allowed past the walls of the city proper on your own." Dylan lowered his voice. "The locals..."

"What about them?"

"Well, they rarely speak our language, that's all." He smiled and patted Bran on the shoulder. "Off you go. There's a boat dwellers' village to the west - that might be of some interest. Be back by supper. Don't get into trouble."

"Yes, father."

"Good lad," said Dylan and turned back to the man in black robe. "I'm sorry, *tai-pan*, you mentioned Xiuquan's new policies..."

Bran walked the long narrow lane at the back of the factories. There were no magnificent facades here, clean white plaster replaced by plain practical wood and low-fired brick, but it was still a neat and well-kept area. He passed dozens of natives, construction workers, dockers and porters, carrying their goods on bamboo poles. There were very few Westerners here, mostly foremen or guards. A few loud drunk sailors stumbled from a tavern on Hogs Lane, noticed they were in the wrong part of the city and swayed back. Among themselves, the Qin walked straight, talked and laughed, but when Bran or any other Westerner approached they all fell quiet, turned their eyes away and dispersed, skulking. All except one man, resting under the eaves of a tea house, looking the passing men straight in the face in silence. His hair was uncut, his eyes bright and on his forearm was carved a tattoo of a black lotus flower. Bran nodded at him lightly and the man's lips curved in a wry, mocking smile.

The dragon rider turned left towards the riverside, past the anchorages of long narrow boats covered with thick canvas, and noticed an opening in the fence surrounding the Factories, through which some workers sneaked with sacks of rice and construction materials. Curious, he decided to follow them.

Past the fence lay a different, more native area. The houses here were low, but densely packed, with blue-tiled overhanging roofs. The wooden and clay walls were painted in bright colours, the windows and doors opened out onto the loosely cobbled streets and narrow canals filled with stale smelly water. People lived here, not only worked. Old women sat outside spinning yarn or milling grain, children played with their funny little dogs. That much was the same as in every village in every part of the world. Here the women and children looked at him curiously and without apprehension. He saw a few girls who resembled the image in Ifor's medallion but their faces were grimy and their teeth had fallen out.

But there was something else, odd, disturbing. On the constricted alleyways, along the canal shores and gutters lay half-naked emaciated men with blank eyes, smoking long wooden pipes attached to some copper contraptions. The men looked straight at him and through him as if in a daydream. The whole district was filled with the sweet and sickly scent of the strange smoke.

The farther into the village Bran went, the more of these strange people he saw, gathered around their copper pots and clay pipes, huddling together, shivering despite the heat. He noticed some of them sitting on top of red unmarked crates, the same as the ones he had seen in the factory warehouse. These were darker, more sinister alleyways. The houses here were poor, dirty, half ruined, in disrepair, just like the ones along the river. Again he found markings of some past war, never fixed, and there were people wounded or maimed by sword and bullet, in rags, hauling buckets of water or pots of rice to their desperate households. The children were running naked amongst the rubbish and rubble strewn on the streets and, what somehow seemed the most ominous about the area, there were no dogs here. Bran instinctively touched his shoulder where the unseen Seal of Llambed buzzed patiently, and hoped his father's protection spell worked.

Some of the younger children approached him with outstretched hands, begging. He had nothing of value to give and tried to wave them away, but they saw his rich clothes and his pink skin and followed him. More came like scared goats to a shepherd, all crying:

"*Tai-pan, tai-pan!*"

He started to feel uneasy. The men paid no attention to him, deep in their narcotic daydream, and the women passed him by too busy with their ceaseless chores to notice. But the children were now coming from all the nooks and alleyways, demanding gifts now, not begging.

He raised his hand and they shushed. He fluttered his fingers and cast a simple illusion, a kid's toy spell, one of the first any student of magic would learn.

"*Pili-pala!*"

A dozen rainbow-coloured butterflies flew from his palm.

The children gasped in delight.

"*Blodeuyn!*"

The flowers followed, whole and petals, falling from the sky. The little ones tried to grab them, disappointed when they proved no more solid than soap bubbles. Bran continued his show with some fireworks and little birds, but by now he had caught the attention of the grown-ups. A few of the less drug-addled men were looking at him now, their brows furrowed over narrow eyes. One of them stood up heavily, swaying, raising his hand and shouting something.

Bran felt strangely tired. The simple spells were much more exhausting than they should have been. He wondered if it was the effect of the Barrier. It was time to return to the Factories. He bowed to his audience, spread some more bubbles from his fingers as an encore, then turned around and froze. A small mob of tall burly men was standing across the narrow bridge, looking angry. They were dressed in rags and loincloths, but they stood straight and their eyes were not as milky and blurry as of those lying in the gutters about the village. The men murmured at him in their strange tongue.

"I... I don't understand," he answered, trying to sound apologetic.

Still they approached, waving their hands and talking with loud voices, agitated. A small stone thrown by an unseen hand buzzed off the shield surrounding Bran and fell at his feet. He stepped backwards, but behind him there was a crowd of children, still eagerly waiting for more entertainment and to his sides – only the murky waters of the canal. He drew the sword by few inches to show he meant to defend himself. The runes on the blade and the eyes of the dragon on the hilt lit up with a bluish glow. Somewhere in the *Ladon*'s stables his mount raised a scaly head and Bran felt a familiar surge of power.

"I don't want to hurt you," he said, now with a threat in his voice.

The men in front of the group halted and let a few others pass from behind. These new adversaries carried wooden clubs and some broken farming tools. A couple more stones whizzed past Bran's head.

Suddenly one of the men reeled back in terror, pointing at something in the sky above Bran. He felt his energy coming back. The boy looked up and saw a great silver dragon hovering above the bridge, its wings rising clouds of yellow dust, dispersing the sweetly scented smoke. The men who threatened him disappeared in an instant, scurrying into the shadowy alleyways.

"*Bran*! What are you doing here?" Reeve Gwenlian cried, her long black hair billowing in the wind. "This is not a place for a Western boy. Hop on, I'll take you back to the Factory."

Bran did not see much of his father for the next few days. Dylan scarcely left the confines of the Imperial Factory's boardrooms, where he discussed matters of national importance with the *tai-pans* – chiefs of trading companies – and other officials.

After his misadventure beyond the fence, he was cautious not to venture beyond the walls of the Western settlement again. Bran could fly his dragon along the length of the Pearl River, from the harbour to the sea, as long as he took care not to land on or fly over the riverbank. Whenever he got too close to the city walls, Qin aerial patrols, flying on hand-crank whirligigs, scrambled to frighten him off with flares and fireworks. Although Emrys could blow the fragile bamboo vehicles out of the sky with one breath, Bran was not too keen on starting a war on his account, and dutifully obeyed the warnings.

Bran sensed that Emrys disliked the whole experience, dizzy and uncomfortable whenever they flew too high or too far from the Factories. There were powerful enchantments, remnants of old spells and forgotten curses woven across this ancient land for generations after generations, which the creature felt with its entire self. The currents and updrafts of the Ninth Wind, which gave the dragon wings their lift, were treacherous and unstable. At least the river, being so close to the great sea and used by foreign traders and travellers for millennia, was more or less clear of these dense influences.

The boy soon found that the people of the boat anchorages, the Tanka, were much friendlier and more hospitable than the town dwellers. They were not afraid of his magic, minor illusions he cast as thanks for small gifts and snacks they gave him as he hopped from one canvas-covered boat to another. A few of their tradesmen, who delivered fresh fish and mussels to the dining rooms of the Thirteen Factories, even spoke a little Seaxe. Bran befriended one of them, Bou, a small happy man with a bald head, which he usually covered with a garishly-coloured scarf. Bou volunteered to be his guide around the anchorages, gaining visible satisfaction from the fact he could be seen accompanying a rich child of the foreigners.

Bou was equally curious and asked a lot of questions, and the boy obliged him with all the information, glad to have somebody eager to talk to. In exchange, Bou tried to respond to all Bran's enquiries in a mixture of broken Seaxe and mime.

"What are they singing about?" asked Bran one evening as they sat on Bou's merchant boat, watching the sun set over the mountains.

They were munching on some sticky rice balls covered in sesame. Bran loved these new unknown tastes, and often snuck out to the Tanka anchorage at dinner time, to avoid the bland "Genuine Dracaland" canned food served at the factories.

The boatmen sang a long-vowelled, wailing, trilling melody without any recognisable words.

"Fish… and women. Most important in man's life," said a grinning Bou.

"I suppose the women sing about fish and men then," Bran guessed, nodding towards a group of fishermen's wives cleaning oysters on a nearby boat.

"No." Bou shook his head. "Women sing about *you*."

"*Me?*" Bran almost dropped his rice ball, his ears reddening. "Why me?"

"You're a new, curious thing - Western boy with power - not often among the boat people. Worth singing about."

"I don't understand. Why is my magic so curious? I can sense the power running through the bones of this country. The Barrier is like nothing I have seen before – you must have had tremendously powerful wizards… and yet, wherever I cast the simplest of tricks, a crowd gathers."

"The boat people - never much trade in Words of Power." Bou shrugged. "We are simple folk, fresh fish and peace from typhoons are all we need, but the town-dwellers, they many-many witch, long time ago, before the Cursed Weed."

"The Cursed Weed?"

Bou nodded again.

"It muddles thoughts... makes one forget what's real. It... eats your power and your pride."

"Is that what they smoke, the sweet scent? But... why? I can't imagine anything I would wish to give up my Power for..."

"The Cursed Weed asks no questions. It just is. It gives all he wants and takes all he cares. This not a happy land, only the Weed makes happy."

The sad expression did not fit Bou's round wrinkled face.

"Where did it come from? What is the Cursed Weed?"

Bou turned to Bran and looked him straight in the eyes, which was rare even among the Tanka.

"Ask your father, boy with Power. Not my tale to tell."

Bran opened his mouth to answer, but something else caught his attention. A white dot appeared over the hills to the west, approaching quickly.

"What's that?"

"*Long*," Bou answered piously, standing up, "the Heavenly One."

It took Bran a moment to realise what the man had said. A Qin dragon! At last!

"Run to your people, boy," said Bou, pointing towards Reeve Gwenlian, who was heading for Bran with concern on her face.

The silver dot turned towards the Factories.

"The war is near."

"*War*? What war?"

"There always war in Qin," the little merchant said sadly.

The dragon came fast like the hurricane, its alabaster scales glowing crimson in the setting sun. The elongated serpentine

155

body coiled among the clouds as it soared on the Ninth Wind without the aid of wings. The silver antlers on its head glistened brightly, and the tip of the long tail blazed with a red flame. The rider, a tiny black figure, could barely be seen on the dragon's jagged back.

One of the town guard whirligigs tried to get near the splendid creature, shooting its usual red and blue flares to frighten it away. The dragon opened its wide mouth and a powerful stream of water gushed from it like from a fountain. In an instant, the thin bamboo and paper structure of the flying vehicle shattered into splinters and the hapless guard plummeted to his death with a bloodcurdling cry.

The soldiers of the Second Dragoons observed the dragon in silence at first, admiring its beauty, but when it attacked the guard, they immediately sprang into action. A wing of three Silvers scrambled off the deck of the *Ladon*. They were smaller than the graceful flying serpent, but more muscular and aggressive. The Qin dragon was almost within range of the dragoons' lances when its rider decided to turn tail. The beast spat a dense puff of protective mist and disappeared into the thick grey clouds above.

Dylan watched the skirmish from the balcony of the Imperial Factory, stern-faced. As soon as the white dragon vanished he ran down to the stables and mounted Afreolus.

He came back two days later and, without even changing his clothes or washing himself, called a meeting in the dining hall between himself, the *tai-pans*, superintendent of the port and captains of the royal troops. Before long, a decision was made.

Dylan paced the deck of the *Ladon* observing the ceaseless commotion around him. The carrier wisps travelling back and forth between the ship, the Factory and Fragrant

Harbour. The soldiers armed with pneumatic rifles, glass air tanks strapped to their backs, standing watchful as the Qin porters filled the hauls to the brim with rice, grain, dragon fodder, dried fruit and Bangla rum. Weapons hauled up from their hidden compartments onto the gun deck. The armament was all state-of-the-art, as modern as the ship itself. Four huge mistfire-powered autoguns of Brezhon design, each with four rotating barrels, were winched onto the top deck, aft and fore; smaller smooth-bore cannons firing explosive shells lined the broadside. A battery of Congreve's rocket launchers was mounted on the foredeck. A lightning thrower, complicated coiled apparatus capable of hurling electric bolts over vast distances, was assembled in the machine hold and connected to the copper-gilded rods of the main mast with rubber cables. Magic amplifiers hummed in glass canopies along the sides.

He climbed onto the landing deck, where Gwenllian was briefing the stable masters. Even with all the magical arsenal the dragons were the ship's main weapon, and their comfort on the journey was of utmost importance.

"Have you seen my son somewhere?" he asked her after they exchanged greetings.

"He went to see the Gorllewin steamer. Do you want me to bring him?"

"No, no, you're busy. I need to talk to him myself."

He flew back over the Fan Yu harbour. He easily guessed what had intrigued Bran about the ship of the Grey Hoods. Many vessels were arming themselves with guns, canons and other machines of war in expectation of conflict, but only one was carrying dragons: a broad black steamer with four of the snow white beasts on the landing deck.

He found Bran observing the ship from the end of the pier.

"Surprised? I know I was."

"You didn't know the Grey Hoods keep dragons?"

Dylan shook his head. "Not until recently. We still know little about what they're up to. The Gorllewin have appeared in these waters only a few years ago, keeping themselves neutral from all the conflicts."

"These dragons were not bred for fighting," said Bran. The white beasts were squat, heavy and slow. They paid little attention to their surroundings, dozing off on the landing deck in the afternoon sun.

"Oh, a *Snaellander* can be fierce if it is roused. But you're right, they're not much of a threat. Not sure why bring them all the way here..."

One of the dragons raised its head and yawned lazily.

"We're moving out tomorrow," said Dylan.

"Where to?"

"We sail north, to Huating and then Jiankang. It's the southern capital of Qin, and it's about to be besieged. The viceroy requested our help."

"Besieged? By whom?"

"There was a major rebellion not far from here. That's what's causing all this... ruckus."

Dylan waved his hand around the harbour.

"You feared the rebels would march on Fan Yu?"

"Yes, but we managed to... *convince* them we're not worth the trouble."

A year's worth of unmarked crates it cost us, he remembered.

"The court at Ta Du is their target and enemy."

"And now we go to help that court against the rebels, even though they left us in peace?"

"The Dragon Throne's interests are diverse," said Dylan, the corner of his lips raised in a faint smile.

We need to recoup our losses after all.

"I'll go get myself ready."

"*You* are staying in Fan Yu."

The boy stared at his father in silence.

"I promised your mother you would stay safe. The ship is moving to a war zone, that's no place for you."

"Father, don't you even – "

"I'm serious. Fan Yu is safe. In Jiankang there will be a real battle, real death. I will not dare losing you to a stray bullet or arrow."

"Or do you think that I will not manage, that I will shame you with my toy dragon?"

"By Owain's sword, don't be ridiculous!"

"Do you think I have not noticed the way you kept shunning me, the way you've always looked at Emrys with contempt? Would you have let me go if I rode that bronze you wanted to give me? Is that it?"

Bronze – ? Ohh, that thing. He still remembers.

Dylan scratched his forehead, sighed deeply, sat down on a bollard and loosened a button in the collar of his uniform.

"Look, Bran, I had no idea… I didn't even remember – "

"Why not just send me back on the first ship to Dracaland? I'm obviously of no use to you here."

"What would you have me do? You're my only son. You're just a boy…"

"I know you've almost managed to forget it, but I just had my *sixteenth* birthday," Bran reminded his father dryly. "I could just go to the quartermaster and volunteer myself to join the regiment."

Bran was right - past sixteen, he was free to sign up to the army if he so wished. Of course as the regimental commander, Dylan had a final say in who got accepted but he knew the refusal would only further antagonise his son.

He closed his eyes and clasped his furrowed forehead in his fingers.

"Right," said Bran, turning around, "I'm off to enlist."

"*Wait!*" Dylan grabbed him by the arm and sighed deeply. "Promise me… promise me you won't be doing anything foolish," he said at last.

"Father!"

"Promise!" Dylan cried impatiently. Bran pulled back in fright.

What am I doing?

"If you want to be treated like an adult, behave like one," he said, calming down. "In the army you have to listen to your superior's orders. Well, on board the *Ladon* you will listen to me. This is my order."

"I promise, Father."

"And not a word about this to your mother. She would skin me alive."

CHAPTER XI

Fan Yu, Qin, April, 2607 ab urbe condita

The large dining hall on the top floor of the Imperial Factory had been turned into a war room. A great geomantic map of Qin was spread out on a surface made of several dinner tables. The map did not show the physical or administrative layout of the country, but was a diagram of ley lines, hot spots and power points that were known or detected by the map makers. Sacred and Cursed Grounds were painted white and black, while crucial nexii were marked with red wax seals. The entire land was divided into sixteen regions, each signed with one of the geomantic tetragrams. Dozens of tokens and markers were spread throughout the map. Some obvious, like miniature cinnabar pagodas where temples and monasteries were known to exist, others obscure, like a small turtle of black clay, which moved a little bit every evening on its journey from north to south towards the centre of the map, where a large yellow Qin dragon was painted, sleeping.

Dylan stood over the map, observing intently the changing colourful lines and flickering flaming dots lighting and extinguishing, seemingly at random. He scratched his scar in distress. Once the rebel army had passed through the province, his precious network of spies and scouts became dispersed, communications broken. He had to rely on divinations and geomancy to track the movement of enemy armies, and it troubled him. One could never depend fully on magic in this ancient, tormented land.

"The ship is ready, Father."

Dylan turned around, surprised. Bran was standing in the doorway looking at the map curiously. He was wearing his blue cadet's uniform.

"And they've sent you to tell me this?"

"I... volunteered, Father. Is that the map of Qin?"

"Yes. See, we are here." He pointed at a bright dot on the Southern coast and the runes *Fan Yu* lit up. "We sail north-west – Ederra Strait is still out of bounds for our ships – to here, the port of Huating. I've never seen it before – that's a new one for me," he said, smiling.

Bran studied the map for a while, trying to make sense of the moving lines, lights and symbols.

"There's always war in Qin," he murmured.

"What did you say?"

"It's something the Tanka people said."

"Mhm. Yes, I suppose some of these townsfolk can't even remember a time before all the wars and rebellions..."

"The Qin I read about was a mighty, rich, beautiful empire, a land of fairy tale. But all this... is nothing but a shadow. What's happened to this place?"

Dylan scratched his beard, covered with a three-day stubble. Lately he was so busy it was getting difficult to maintain the regulation clean shave.

"Stagnation," he replied after a while. "Inability to deal with new threats."

"What new threats?"

"Us."

"You mean the Cursed Weed?"

Dylan glanced at the boy sharply.

162

"I see you haven't been spending time idly. What do you know about it?"

Bran shrugged.

"I have seen what it does to people. The boat people told me to seek answers from you. Did we bring the Weed to Qin?"

"It's not quite like that. The Qin have always grown and consumed the plant, and so have we, for medicine. You may have heard of laudanum?"

"Some sort of an analgesic," Bran recalled.

"The same plant. The Emperor of Qin had the Weed banned over a hundred years ago and it has become much more desirable and expensive since, as with all things forbidden. This is where we – rather, the Dracaland trade companies - came in. They have flooded the land with the cheap product grown in the plantations of Bharata."

"The unmarked crates?" Bran guessed.

"Yes. We bribe the authorities to overlook them in our warehouses."

"It's shameful."

"It's good business," said Dylan, shrugging, "and what our Empire is built upon. Without the Cursed Weed money you would have no tea for breakfast."

"*Our* Empire? This is the Dracalish way, not Gwynedd."

"There is one crown on both sides of the Dyke," reminded Dylan, feeling increasingly uneasy about the way the conversation was progressing.

"But you're still a freeman of Gwynedd. You don't have to be doing this."

"I don't deal with the Weed trade. I just... know about it."

"So you just close your eyes and let things happen around you."

Dylan sighed.

Yes, sometimes I have to close my eyes to stay sane, he thought.

He remembered himself, on his first assignment in the Imperial Navy, sent to fight in the Cursed Weed war. Corruption, smuggling, assassinations, blackmails... There was nothing decent or just about the way Dracaland waged its wars. But, that was a long time ago and he had since learned to accept the harsh realities of the war and diplomacy. He knew Bran would too, one day.

"Why aren't the rebels attacking us?" Bran asked.

"We manage to funnel their wrath at the Emperor."

"We then get paid for helping him to deal with the rebels?"

"You grasp it quickly."

"We're behaving no better than Warwick," his son said through clenched teeth.

"*Warwick?*"

Dylan frowned at the sound of a familiar name. The old Warwick was his persecutor at the Academy. Did he have a son?

So that's why you didn't want to go back.

He put his hand on Bran's shoulder and looked him in the eyes.

"You're no longer at school, Bran. Adults don't live in a fairy tale. The Qin are not innocent themselves. They have also conquered nations in the past, and they did it with might and subterfuge, not morals and good deeds. They were a brutal, atrocious race while they were yet strong. Who knows, they still might be, one day..."

"And now we are the strong ones? Is that your lesson, Father? Power prevails?"

164

"No, Bran…" Dylan grew exasperated. "Listen –"

"What would Grandpa say to all this?"

"Ifor?" Dylan blinked.

What is he on about?

"He was a decent, straight-forward man. I'm sure he would disagree with all this subterfuge and deception."

Dylan almost burst out laughing.

"Who told you that? I'm sorry, but there was nothing straight-forward about that man. Your grandfather left my mother, left all of us when we most needed him, chasing after some long lost dream, disappearing into Sun knows where. If *he* dared to talk to *me* about morals, I'd laugh in his face. Look, you don't know – "

"I know enough. Leave me alone."

The boy shrugged his father's hand off his shoulder.

"Your soldiers are waiting," Bran said, then turned around and stormed out of the room.

It had taken the *Ladon* a full week to navigate around the island of Ederra and along the eastern shore of Qin towards the Chang River delta.

Bran's excitement grew as the ship sailed north. They were now in the waters mentioned in Ifor's diary, sailing past the Tagalogs out onto the open ocean where the big red question mark had been scribbled on his grandfather's map. Plenty had changed since HMS *Phaeton* ventured through these straits. The sea was now properly charted, the Qin coast accessible to Western shipping in several places. None of the crew, however, made any mention of the mysterious land of Yamato as if Bran was the only person on board aware of its existence. It wasn't even on any of the navigational charts at the bridge.

The *Ladon* was to wait about a hundred miles offshore for the Qin official guide-ship that would lead them past the small, but swiftly growing, port of Huating deeper into the delta where Jiankang lay.

Dylan walked the length of the ship back and forth, checking the equipment and weaponry in preparation for another Barrier crossing. There was now a great deal of delicate and precise equipment on board, so everything had to be carefully taken care of. Bran followed, trying to learn as much as he could from observing his father's meticulous craftsmanship. They may have had their differences, but Dylan's skill was next to none and it would be unwise – and childish, Bran reminded himself – to ignore the opportunity to study.

By evening they reached the foredeck, where Dylan hunched over the launching pad for Congreve's rockets. He examined it and grimaced.

"What the…? This has not been properly locked. Help me with that wrench."

"Why do you have to do it yourself? This ship has got an army of technicians."

"I need to know the position of every screw and bolt on this vessel if I want to weave them all into the Passing Spell."

Despite himself, Bran glanced at his father with admiration. He could hardly imagine the mental strain caused by such a complex enchantment. He tightened a few bolts in the base of the machinery as instructed. His father, with some effort, pulled out a coiled copper wire from inside the launch pad, held it in a clenched fist and murmured a few words of a Binding Spell.

"That should do it." He pushed the wire back, closed the hatch and stood up, stretching his back and arms. "That

166

was the last thing. I'd say we're good to go." He stood for a while, looking longingly over the bow at the waves below. He spoke at last. "I remember sailing these seas with my father – before he settled down - the best years of my life. I should've brought you here earlier, son, when the world was much safer."

"To show me how you help enslave some other people?"

Dylan shook his head.

"There's more to the world than Dracaland's wars, son. I can show you so many beautiful things..."

"Can you show me *Dejeema*?" asked Bran.

Dylan stared at the boy.

"Where have you heard this name?"

"I... overheard Bataavian merchants in the harbour. I haven't seen it on any maps."

"They must have been most careless." Dylan licked his lips. "The very existence of this place is one of their best kept secrets."

"What is it, then?"

"Some four hundred miles that way," Dylan said, pointing to the east, "lie the islands of Yamato. Dejeema is where their main harbour is – so I've heard."

"So you've never been there?"

"No. No Western ship can sail there, except Bataavians." Dylan shook his head. "Who knows how they've managed to do it."

"*Can't* sail? With all this power?" Bran asked, waving his hand around the *Ladon*.

"There are powerful storms and currents along the way, like an ocean maze. The navigation tools become useless. Even the clocks run in a strange way. In a way it's even more effective than the Qin Barrier. I've heard rumours of a

Dracalish captain once forcing his way into Dejeema, but that was long before you or I were born."

There was some shouting coming from the port side of the ship. Dylan broke his tale and turned in the direction of the noise.

"That will be the Qin boat. I must welcome it."

He walked off leaving Bran alone. So Dylan didn't know his own father had been to Yamato… The boy stared towards the eastern horizon, trying futilely to see the distant harbour of *Keeyo*, but there was nothing but grey clouds.

He took his grandfather's box and the dragon figurine from the satchel. Bran wondered if the dragon, too, had come from Yamato; both things were made of the same smooth, glistening material. The medallion lay inside peacefully, but there seemed to be a faint azure glow within the blue stone of the ring, which Bran had been keeping inside throughout the journey, near the golden brooch from which the stone was taken. He raised the jewel to the sun. The gem was no longer translucent, but slightly cloudy, as if it had begun stirring back to life.

The Qin pilot arrived in a small junk with three square red sails, tiger eyes painted on the bow and a band of gold and enamel running along the broadside. Two bronze cannons adorned the foredeck, more decorations than real weapons.

The pilot and his entourage, all dressed in rich dark yellow robes, were shown around the *Ladon*. Their faces showed no sign of emotion as they examined the advanced weaponry and technology of the ship. They listened to the interpreter's explanations and nodded in unison. Eventually they were led to the mess hall where dinner awaited.

As soon as the second course was served, Bran slipped outside. As he would most nights when the ship was in the open sea and he didn't play *tafl* with Samuel, he went to the stables on the second deck, untied his dragon and led it outside via a large ramp leading astern.

Emrys would only want to fly for a few minutes each night, just enough to straighten its wings. It was still afraid of the open ocean, even after so many months at sea. If the weather was less than clement, the dragon loathed even to leave the stable for too long, but it enjoyed strolling the width and breadth of the top deck, breathing the salty air while Bran looked at the stars through the spyglass, marking subtle changes in their positions in his notepad as the ship moved through latitudes.

The dragon fell asleep on the foredeck, and Bran put the spyglass back into the satchel and took out a book on *tafl* rules he had borrowed from Samuel. These were his favourite moments; the dark silent nights. There was nobody outside except for a couple of watchmen on extreme points of the ship, each far away from where he sat. Some noise was coming from the mess hall where the Qin pilot and the crew still banqueted, but it was muffled and easily ignored. Apart from that, only the soft lapping of the waves and gentle ringing of the rigging in the breeze disrupted the quietness. With a snap of his fingers, Bran conjured a floating flamespark and settled himself among the coiled ropes with the book.

The lookout on the bow cried out. The portside searchlights lit up, their beams setting the sky ablaze, and all the bells and sirens rang out in alarm. Three long whistles meant they were being attacked from the air.

Emrys stirred and woke up uneasily. The boy jumped up, but could not yet see anything in the night sky. Unlike the lookouts, he did not have the naval Farfinder device that could spot danger for miles, at night, in storm or in fog.

Within seconds the soldiers and crew started appearing on deck. Bran had seen them train the battle alarm countless times before, but now, at last, it was the real thing. The great hatch opened, the ramps lowered and the dragons were led by the stable hands out onto the landing deck, one by one. Their riders poured from the forecastle cabins, strapping swords to their belts and donning flight hauberks and wind goggles. The gunners ran to the fore and aft turrets. Smaller rapid guns, six of them clustered on the aft side, were the first to howl. The operators, always on watch, appeared inside the glass turrets moments after the alert rang, propelled from their cabins under the aftercastle by mistfire lifts. The smooth-bore broadsides were useless against an aerial attack, but the quadruple barrels of the great self-repeating cannons could be winched to a high enough angle to wreak havoc in the sky above the ship.

Dylan was already on deck, shouting orders and peering into the darkness, paying no attention to Bran. At last the enemy was in plain sight. A whole skein of Qin *Long*, twelve at least. They were glorious to behold; long coiling bodies surrounded by a haze of mist and lightning, scales glinting with all colours of the rainbow in the beams of the searchlights.

"*Mount up!*" cried one of the marines. Bran recognised Banneret Edern by his silver hair, eyes burning brightly as they always did when he was agitated.

"*Scramble the Silvers!*"

"Gunners, protect the pilot boat," ordered Dylan, "and prepare Afreolus, I will lead the first squadron mys – *Bran!*" He noticed the boy at last, somewhat surprised. "What are you doing?"

170

Bran had finished preparing the saddle by now and was ready to mount Emrys and join *Ladon's* defenders.

"What are your orders, Ardian?" the boy asked solemnly, putting on his flying goggles.

"I order you to stay here where it's safe. You are not a soldier yet."

"Father, I'm more than capable –"

"We're in a war zone now. Do me a favour and just keep quiet," Dylan snapped. The Qin dragons were almost upon them. "You'd only get in the way."

"So that's what you really think of me?"

"Boy, I have no time for your quarrels now!"

"Then just let me –"

"*By the Red Dragon's Breath*, just stay here and wait!"

Dylan pointed at Bran and spoke Binding Words. The boy felt himself freeze, his entire body paralysed by the powerful enchantment. Amazingly, the spell was strong enough to even to stun his dragon. Bran could only speak – barely more than a whisper – but his father would not listen anymore.

Dylan spread the palm of his right hand and summoned his Soul Lance. This was the first time Bran had seen his father's weapon. It was unique; as bright as the sun, a twelve foot long shaft of solidified golden light, slightly curved and broadened at the end, like the blade of a cavalry sword. Dylan grabbed the lance firmly, mounted his great silver dragon and launched into the air, followed by other soldiers of the Second Dragoons.

With his fists still clenched the way they were when he was Bound by the spell, and heart burning with rage, Bran could only observe the battle in the night sky, illuminated by searchlights, flares and blasts of the guns. The Qin dragons were swift and agile, and there was a whole flock of them now swarming over the ship. They were blue, red and yellow, spewing dense mist, spouting streams of boiling water from their maws and shooting lightning from their antlers.

Ridden by skilled men, these would be formidable opponents, but their riders were nowhere near as well trained or experienced as the Dracalish soldiers and were soon overwhelmed by the *Ladon*'s squadron. Dragonflame of the Silvers proved a terrible weapon against the beasts of Qin. Even before the marines closed in for a melee with their brightly shining lances, the first of the Qin *Longs* fell, burning, spilling golden blood as it tumbled towards the dark sea, still coiling like a silk ribbon in the wind. Seconds later another followed. At last the others started breaking off. The marines followed them in hot pursuit, swiftly disappearing beyond the range of *Ladon*'s lights.

Silence fell upon the ship as the fighting dragons departed towards the western horizon. Bran could only wait for them to return, still paralysed by his father's spell as if he was a child.

He felt a presence. Somebody was sneaking along the line of coiled ropes and toolboxes. A man crept out from the shadows and looked the boy straight in the eyes. It was a Qin man. Bran recognised him by the black lotus tattoo on the forearm: one of the gaffers from the Fan Yu harbour; the quiet one.

He was holding a large tube of soft iron. Bran felt cold sweat trickling down his forehead as he realised what it was – the warhead of Congreve's rocket, a hollow chamber filled with potent explosives.

Bran struggled to speak.

"What... what are you doing?"

The man grinned.

"What do you *think* I'm doing, boy?" the Qinese answered in surprisingly fluent Seaxe.

"You're going to b-blow us up!" Bran stuttered.

Big though the ship was, there was enough ordnance, magical and otherwise, in the munitions hold to split the *Ladon* in two, and a lot of it was now brought up to the upper decks in preparation for the battle.

"So the dragons were just a ruse! You are a rebel saboteur!"

"I don't care one way or the other for the rebels - or the court. My cause is older than any of them."

"What do you mean?"

The Qinese looked sharply at the boy.

"What's it to you? You don't know me, I don't know you, and I'm certain it's the last time we will see each other. You better make ready to meet your ancestors."

The man grinned again. It seemed to Bran that his eyes glinted gold for a moment, but it had to be a trick of the light, a reflection of an evertorch. He bowed mockingly and sneaked away, clutching the piece of rocket in his hands.

Bran remained where he was, still unable to move. One long terrible minute passed then another. Emrys struggled against the Binding Words. Groggy and dazed, the beast tried to shrug the enchantment off its wings, lift its head and open its jaws. It managed to nudge Bran's shoulder with its snout and sniffed around, sensing danger.

The dragon rider dared not think he would die there and then, but, unwittingly, his thoughts went back to the red walls of his home, his favourite beach on the shore of Cantre'r Gwaelod, his mother's dark eyes. For a brief moment he evoked the tattooed, sad-eyed face of Eithne and recalled the day of the Graddio ceremony... Then, he remembered. Llambed's Seal! Of course, he only had to...

THE SHADOW OF BLACK WINGS

A low, loud rumble went through the ship spreading from the centre to the edges. A long second later a tremendous explosion burst through the hull from deep in the cargo hold with a deafening blast, showering the main deck with rubble and shrapnel. The blast did not simply make a hole in the ship – it broke it apart. The middle section, with the bridge, vaporised in an instant. The stern and the bow rose to the sky and the two parts started sinking within moments.

The eruption swept Bran several feet into the air and he was struck dumb. When he came to, the foredeck he and Emrys were on was already sinking into the water at a sharp angle. With a deafening creak, shatter and hiss, the massive boiler came loose from its bolts and smashed into the dark ocean. The released elementals turned the water into white steaming foam. The men in the water screamed in terrible agony. Others still held on to various bits and pieces on the bow as it sank fast into the deep.

By a stroke of luck, the force of the explosion broke Bran free from the Binding. He managed to grab onto some hatch handle firmly attached to the deck. His dragon was shrieking in panic, beating wings and jumping chaotically in place. It still could not fly away. Sliding towards the water, Emrys scratched the deck boards in desperation as the foaming and hissing surface of the boiling sea got ever nearer. Bran, his consciousness slowly slipping away from him, tried to dispel Dylan's enchantment on the dragon. It wasn't easy. With his True Sight he could see the individual strands forming the magical net. In the surrounding chaos, Bran had to focus on the one crucial strand and either dissolve it or snap it in two.

"Hounds of *Annwn*, I'm not a wizard!" he cursed in despair, as the dragon continued to flail about. Bran could

174

feel its fear and confusion through the Farlink and it did not make things any easier for him. At last he found it, a single thread glowing bright gold, Dylan's signature colour. He reached towards it with his free hand and made a pulling gesture as if he tugged on an invisible rope.

"*Chwalu!*" he cried at the top of his lungs.

The Binding Spell unravelled in an instant. Suddenly released, Emrys leapt forwards with a single beat of wings into the starry darkness and disappeared out of Bran's sight.

With an effort, the boy turned his head and looked to the western sky – he could faintly see the first dragons of the Second Dragoons speeding back towards the sinking ship. They were flying fast, but it was too late. Below, the waters fumed and boiled as the ship slipped inexorably into the scalding deep. Bran felt his grip on the hatch handle slip.

With the last glimpse of awareness, he invoked the Seal of Llambed. At first nothing happened and the boy gave in to despair. So this was how it would all end, his short uneventful life. At least he had managed to see a little of the world before he died…

He then felt a burning sensation on his right shoulder and saw a pillar of blinding bright light envelop him. The raging sea, the sinking ship, the dragon regiment, all disappeared in the radiance. The last thing he saw was a silhouette of a great white eagle, swooping towards him from the sky.

CHAPTER XII

Yamato, Spring, 7th year of Kaei era

The shrine gardens overflowed with sweetly-scented blossom bursting from the branches in waterfalls of white, overhanging the gravelled pathways, showering the lawns and ponds with heart-shaped petals.

Watching the cherry trees bloom was something best done in company.

Nagomi wore the plain clothes of a shrine maiden, a white *haori* jacket and red split *hakama* skirt. Her long hair was pale strawberry blonde, as if the whiteness of the cherry blossom reflected in its gleam had weakened the mysterious hue. She stood at the top of the three hundred steps leading to the main entrance of the Suwa Shrine and watched her friend run up from the riverside, past a pair of stone-carved lion-dog guardians, by granite lanterns and under a row of stone *torii* gates. The wizardess clutched a bamboo leaf box in her hand.

"I brought pink sea bream," she said, catching her breath, "and pumpkin *mochi*."

"My favourite!" said Nagomi, smiling. "Let's go to the turtle pond, you can see the whole harbour from there."

"Is your father still away?" Satō asked, sipping from a cup of a salty, but refreshing, drink of pickled cherry petals.

"Yes," Nagomi replied, "and now Mom decided to pay him a visit. The house is all on Ine's head."

"He's not coming back soon then?"

"Doesn't look like it. The pox is still very bad in Ōwari and my father can only produce so much vaccine. It's difficult to obtain all the equipment he needs in Nagoya."

"If only the *Taikun* would let my father travel," said Satō with a sigh. "The Bataavians have been filling our house with all sorts of glass and copper apparatus that I'm sure Keisuke-*sama* could use in his laboratory."

"Have the rules of arrest been relaxed then?"

"Yes but only a little. The Overwizard is keen to have as close a relationship with my father as possible without attracting too much attention, so we are now being showered with more gifts than we know what to do with." Satō laughed. "Blueprints, equipment, exotic ingredients… My old man rarely ever steps out of the laboratory these days."

"And how are the boys?"

"The students? Not as annoying as they used to be, that's for certain. Keinosuke can still be scary when he sits silently for an entire lesson and then comes up with some random question... but I think he knows now I'm not going to tell him anything really important or secret. He's much too young for that!"

"Must be his father's influence - you said Sakuma-*dono* is a great scholar."

"He is," Satō replied, nodding, "perhaps the greatest alive, or so my father says. He also says it will all end badly for him and his family one day."

"That may be. The times are dangerous." Nagomi bit her lip. "That's what Kazuko-*hime* told me. The Waters of Scrying are shrouded in shadow – " she stopped abruptly.

Not even your friends…

It was difficult to keep secrets from Satō, even more than it had been from her family. They had been the closest of friends for as long as she remembered. Satō was the only kid in the neighbourhood who hadn't mocked the colour of her hair, and their friendship had grown ever closer since then. This was the first time she couldn't tell the wizardess about something important.

"*Not until we know more,*" the High Priestess had told her, "*not until we're certain you're safe.*"

A sudden breeze from the sea shook the branches and the white flowers fell like fresh snow. The girls were both silent and solemn for a while, but then Nagomi giggled.

"What is it?" Satō asked.

"I just imagined… You're the only daughter of the finest teacher of *Rangaku*, and Keinosuke is the only son of the greatest scholar in Kiyō… Isn't that a perfect match?"

"Don't be absurd!" Satō was genuinely flabbergasted. "He's three years younger than me – *and* a precocious little brat!"

"But you have to admit, he does come from a great family, and your father's *dōjō* –"

"*I* will inherit the *dōjō*, not some arrogant idiot. Just because he's a boy, doesn't mean… *Ugh*, I can't even think about it!"

"I was only joking…"

"It's easy for *you* to joke, you don't have to worry about getting married to some random fool."

"I won't be a maiden forever, you know. Priests can marry too."

"Yes, but only if they want to."

"I'm sorry, I didn't mean to upset you."

"It's all right," Satō said, calming down, "I should not have lashed out like that. It does not behove a samurai to lose temper so easily."

"Have you gotten any further with the book?" Nagomi asked, quickly changing the subject.

There could only have been one book she meant. Ever since Satō had discovered the Dragon Book in her father's library, she spent every free moment trying to decipher as much of it as she could.

"I'm barely past the first few pages. The language is somewhat similar to Bataavian, but not enough. I'm not even sure I'm doing it right." She shook her head. "I'm getting an odd word here and there, but really, I could be wrong all the time. Oh, but the drawings! They come alive on touch, the scales start to glint in the lamplight, the wings flap, the flames burst from the page, scarlet and golden..." Satō's eyes burned with passion. "I have never seen anything like it. The drawings made by our chroniclers, when the Vasconians first brought the *dorako* – they might as well have been lizards and dried up newts. Oh, I'd give anything to see a real *dorako*..."

"Can't you get one from Dejima?" asked Nagomi.

She did not share the wizardess's fascination with the strange Western creatures. In truth, she was barely aware what they looked like. For all she knew, they were just big lizards.

"Do you think these are chickens?" Satō was taken aback by her friend's ignorance. "A grown-up *dorako* is as big as a merchant's ship, and Bataavians would never dare to bring one to Yamato. They would be banned from Kiyō in an instant if they so much as mentioned the beasts."

"I didn't know..."

"No, of course, all this is secret knowledge. There are only a few scholars in the country who claim to know anything about these creatures."

"And none of them has a book like yours," added Nagomi.

"No, I don't think they do," Satō said with a grin. "That's what makes the whole thing so great; this feeling of exploring a whole new uncharted land, a journey into the unknown."

"I'm happy for you."

The apprentice felt a pang of guilt. Satō had no qualms about divulging forbidden knowledge, yet Nagomi could share none of her secrets in exchange.

"And how about your apprenticeship?" asked the wizardess, biting off a piece of chewy, rubbery *mochi* cake.

"Kazuko-*hime* said I'm making good progress," said Nagomi. "I have already tried some Scrying under supervision."

Should I have said even that much?

"That's great, that's really great." Satō smiled brightly. "I've always known you'd make a great priestess."

Nagomi turned her eyes to the horizon, her cheeks suddenly hot.

"It's nothing."

"What are you talking about?" Satō protested. "You're fifteen and already a skilled healer. You can commune with the Spirits, and that's something I could never do. I can only banish them to the Otherworld."

"Any other girl in the shrine can do what I can do," Nagomi said, shaking her head.

"You're better than any of them, I'm sure. Here, have another drink – to the two best girls in all of Kiyō!"

Satō raised the cup with blossom water in a toast. Nagomi joined her, but turned her face towards the harbour to hide the tears welling up in her eyes.

The wind picked up, once more showering them with the rain of white petals. The sun drifted beyond the mountain tops. The lunch box was empty. Satō rose and cast one last look at the sea.

"I need to go back; I bet the old man forgot to eat his supper again."

A streak of bright white light appeared high over the horizon for a brief moment, like distant lightning. A shooting star crossed the sky, but it was unlike any shooting star Nagomi had ever seen. It fell straight down, silently, towards the city, eventually disappearing somewhere in the harbour area, beyond the warehouses lining the bay north of Dejima's fan-shaped island.

"*Did you see that?*" Satō exclaimed.

"Yes..." whispered Nagomi piously. "It fell from Heavens..."

"Let's go see what it is."

"But—"

"We won't be long. It's just by the beach. *Come on!*"

"What now?" asked Nagomi, catching her breath after the long run.

They were at the open beach near the fishermen huts, having just run down the streets of the magistrate quarter, through the harbour, and past the quays and wharves full of foreign goods, fishing nets and crab pots. The sailors and workers watched them in surprise.

What a sight we must be, she thought. *A shrine maiden and a samurai among the filthy warehouses and muddy alleyways. And my hair…*

Some superstitious fishermen crooked their fingers and clapped their hands to repel evil, but none dared approach them.

The tide was coming in, but the beach was yet wide - and empty.

"Look! Near the mackerel pier."

Satō pointed at something in the water beside bundles of old fishing nets. There was a faint glow, receding fast, barely discernible now, like the fluorescence in a boat's wake.

Before they reached it the glow was gone, but now they could easily see a shape lying at the edge of the water, half-submerged and tangled in the nets. Satō stumbled across the wet sand towards the puzzling object, dark now in the quickly falling twilight, and knelt down to examine it.

"It's a *person*!"

It was indeed a human being, face down in the sand, wearing odd foreign clothes, blue jacket and a shirt that was once white, all tattered and singed, and a buckled leather bag was slung over the shoulder. A strap with two round pieces of glass hung around his neck.

The girls turned the castaway onto his back.

"*Gaikokujin*!" Nagomi gasped. "A Westerner!"

"A soldier," said Satō, frowning. "Look at that sword!"

Attached to the leather belt was a sword in a broad scabbard, with a sculpted hilt in the shape of a winged golden *dorako*. The foreigner seemed to be about their age. He had a gently hooked nose and deeply set eyes under thin brows. His short black hair was clumped with mud, his square face pale and bruised. Up close, his skin was still radiating a faint glow.

"I thought they all had yellow or red hair like you," remarked Satō, "or maybe he's a Vasconian…"

The apprentice put her head to the boy's chest.

"He's alive," she whispered, "what do we do?"

"We need to take him away from here first. He'll drown in the tide."

Nagomi waddled into the water and picked up the boy's legs, clad in thick cloth trousers. Satō did the same with his arms. The sword dragged a deep line through the wet sand. Heaving, they carried their load into the shadow of the willow trees by the fishing pier.

"I have to get my father, or, or Ine." Satō stood up and paced about in confused excitement. "We need to hide him from the authorities. You stay here, I'll get help."

"You are leaving me alone with him?"

Satō handed Nagomi a dagger.

"Use this if he tries anything."

"I didn't mean that…Go now, but be quick."

The wizardess' feet thumped on the sand as she disappeared into the darkness.

Nagomi leaned over the boy, studying his face in the light of the Spirit flame she always carried in a small clay beaker. There were some cuts and bruises on his skin, which she cleaned up with water from a nearby stream, but there were no major injuries visible. The boy didn't seem to need her healing. Where did he come from, and why? The sword by his side showed he was a soldier, but of what army?

A will-o'-the-wisp of a lantern appeared on the beach. Nagomi stood up at first, thinking it was Satō returning with help, but the light moved towards the waterline then hopped along the waves. Nagomi hid farther into the shadow of the pier, blowing out the Spirit light. She could now see two men searching the beach. They wore brown vests with the city crest on their shoulders.

The magistrate officials!

The girls obviously weren't the only ones who had seen the falling star…

The boy stirred and moaned.

No! Not now!

Nagomi knelt down by the stranger. It would be a disaster if they were found out. The law was clear – no foreigners were allowed on the sacred soil of Yamato without permission. The punishment for trespassing was death by beheading. Even the castaways were not exempt.

In desperation, she cradled the boy's head in her arms, trying to muffle his groans with the sleeve of her kimono. The magistrate men were now very close. One stray sound and they would notice the apprentice and her secret. Nagomi prayed silently to all the Gods she could remember. The boy's breath was distractingly warm against her hand.

The men passed her by and the light of their lantern bobbed away. She sighed with relief. The boy stirred more strongly and Nagomi had to let go of his head. He opened his eyes slowly and painfully, squinting with effort. At that moment, the moon came out from behind the clouds and lit up the boy's face. In a reflex, he reached out his hand trying to touch her hair, glistening red gold in the moonlight.

"Eithne," the boy whispered, and the strain caused him to lose consciousness again.

His hand fell to the sand limply. Nagomi sat silent, awestruck. The boy's eyes were as green as jade – as green as the jewel she had seen in the Waters of Scrying.

CHAPTER XIII

Yamato, Spring, 7th year of Kaei era

Old Yoshō, the white-haired servant of the Takashimas, arrived at the Itō's house in the middle of the night, requesting a palanquin. Doctor Itō Keisuke had sometimes been using one to bring in the sick from outside the city.

"Did something happen to Shūhan-*dono*?" Ine enquired, looking worried, "or Satō-*sama*?"

"The master and yun' missus are in no danger," the old servant mumbled a reply through toothless lips. "They ax'd me to fetch the palanquin to the beach."

Ine dispatched the old man with two of her porters and waited anxiously.

"Who's that?" she asked when, half an hour later, the porters brought out an unconscious boy with a face wrapped in bandages made of what Ine identified as cotton torn off the under-kimono.

"I dun' know nothing", Ine-*shiama*," the old servant mumbled. "Nagomi-*shiama* tol'me to bring the boy and not touch the bandages."

"And where *is* my dear little sister?"

"She's gon' back to the shrine, Ine-*shiama*, she said she'll come in the mornin'."

Ine frowned. Of all the annoyances her sister's overt benevolence caused, this one was the most peculiar. Nagomi was like a misguidedly generous cat, constantly bringing dead mice and birds to the house as unwanted gifts – only *her* gifts were sick children, poor cripples, dying old men she kept finding on the streets of the deprived outer districts of Kiyō.

"What do you expect me to do with all these people?" their father despaired. "We have no means to help everyone in need, and they are scaring away the paying customers."

But it was enough for the girl to look at Keisuke with her eyes of a doe and the doctor's heart melted. He had dedicated a separate room in the attic for the treatment of Nagomi's "strays", and – to prevent them from mingling with the richer clientele – had a separate entrance and stairway built at the back of the house. Despite Keisuke and Ine's best efforts, most of them never survived, and had to be carried away through the same entrance, preferably out of Nagomi's sight.

It was to this entrance that the porters now brought the mysterious boy. He seemed like none of the usual foundlings. The briny smell of seawater permeated his thick clothes. Underneath a blue jacket she noticed the bulge in the shape of a sword. In an instant Ine realised whom he was.

"Bring him up, quick. *Hurry.*"

She could only hope the porters failed to recognise the obvious. The boy was a castaway, a foreigner, a *Gaikokujin* soldier. This was too much.

Damn that girl! What was Nagomi thinking? Why bring him here? If the authorities found out they were harbouring a castaway, their family would be finished. They would be happy to get away with exile.

It was too late to do anything now. If Yoshō was sent to bring the foreigner, it meant that Master Takashima himself was aware of the situation. Ine had to trust the old

188

wizard's judgement. Perhaps it was only for one night. Perhaps tomorrow somebody from Dejima would appear and take the dangerous guest away.

The boy moaned as the servants put him on the floor. Ine waved them away and unwound the bandages from around his face. Cleaned up, he even looked quite handsome, for a Westerner, with symmetrical well-defined features and prominent cheekbones. He smelled faintly of butter and meat, like all of his kind, but not as much as most Ine had met. He had a sharp-edged, olive-coloured face, not a pale round one like those of the Bataavians, which always reminded Ine of a full moon. His chin was strong and slightly jutting, his lips wide and thin. His skin was covered with tiny splinter wounds, as if he had head-butted through a wooden plank, though they were all sealed up. His breath was regular and blood had returned to his face.

She took his dirty clothes – the shirt and trousers almost fell apart in her hands, soaked and tattered – and covered him with a warm blanket.

Bran opened his eyes slowly, achingly. For a moment he couldn't see anything as his sight adjusted to the darkness. He was strangely weary. His bones ached, his head thumped and his entire skin burned with a myriad of tiny pinpricks.

What an odd dream, he thought. The enormous mistfire ship, a long journey, the city of the narrow-eyed people...

I must tell Mother about it in the morning.

He turned on his side. A thin mattress filled with some hard husks or chaff rustled when he moved. There was no bed underneath, just soft floor. He realised he was naked, wrapped in a warm blanket.

This is not my bed. This is not my house. How did I get here? What's going on?

189

He remembered. The ship was real. It was called MFS *Ladon*, and Bran had spent the last few months aboard it, sailing across half the world towards the land of Qin. Now they were on their way to some city to... He struggled to recall – fight the rebels, that's it.

I must've bumped myself on the head, he guessed, massaging his throbbing temples, *and they put me in the infirmary*.

The room smelled strongly of medicaments and rubbing alcohol, but there was also another odour, a strange, nauseatingly sweet scent, like damp straw in the barn after the rain.

He was hungry and thirsty. How long had he been out? His lips were parched, his eyelids glued together with sleep. He blinked repeatedly and lifted himself up onto one elbow, his head spinning. He was starting to see shadows and edges in the darkness, in the faint moonlight seeping through a window. Something was odd.

It couldn't have been the ship. The floor was solid, unmoving, there was no trace of the familiar swaying he had become accustomed to over the months. No room on the *Ladon* was this big, not even the captain's cabin. Certainly not that empty. He was in a house, on land, but where? Why? He closed his eyes, trying to recall the last thing he could remember before waking up.

The visit of the Qin pilot... The attack of the dragons... The rebel spy lurking in the shadows... The explosion...

Bran opened his eyes wide in terror. The *Ladon* was no more, obliterated in the blast, sunk with everyone on board - Doctor Samuel, the old Weatherman, the cooks, the mechanics, all his new found friends in the crew. All dead, except those men and women of the Second Dragoons who were in the air at the time.

He was still alive, seemingly unharmed, not counting the headache and overall state of exhaustion. The magic of the Seal must have saved him and bring him here, wherever *here* was. He had no idea how powerful the Seal was, or how it chose its destination. Most likely he was somewhere in Qin. If so, his father would no doubt…

Father…

It had all been Dylan's fault, Bran remembered, gritting his teeth at the memory. If he hadn't pointlessly Bound the boy like a spoiled brat, Bran could've stopped the Qin rebel. Everyone would be alive now. Everything would have been all right.

Bran punched the floor in anger. Somewhere in the corner of the room something clanked metallically. He stared in the direction of the sound, trying to penetrate the gloom. There was a little moonlight in the room, but it was strangely dimmed, as if filtered through gauze. Under the wall he made out a bundle on the floor. Slowly, Bran unwrapped himself from the blanket and crept across the soft floor towards the bundle. His bones and joints pained with every movement, but it was no more than how he would have felt on the morning after a tough training session.

He touched the bundle with his fingers – it was a neatly folded pack of clothes, but not his old ones. They were alien, made of very fine smooth cotton, almost silk-like. He felt farther and his fingers found the cold touch of a scabbard and a dragon-shaped hilt.

My sword!

Probing on, he found his flying goggles and a leather satchel lying beside it. He tried to unbuckle the bag to see if all his treasure was inside, but sudden weakness overwhelmed him.

Bran realised he was shivering with cold, his teeth chattering. It was an early spring night, he was naked and a chilly draught was blowing in through some crack in the wall. He crawled back to the blanket and managed to wrap himself back up before succumbing to deep dreamless sleep…

When he awoke again it was already light. He lay still with his eyes open, trying to get his bearings. The room was not as big as he had first thought in the darkness, but very neat, impeccably clean, with walls of light wood covered with grey paper on one side of the room and a lattice of black slats and white translucent paper on the other. The bundle of clothes still lay in the corner, as did his sword and the bag. Everything in the was divided with straight lines – the floor made of large mats of packed straw, lined with dark material, the walls and windows segmented by planks and slates into asymmetrical rectangles. There was a small cupboard in the corner with what looked like medical instruments, but no other furniture – no chair, no table, no bed. The room was made to look like a prison cell or a hospital ward.

The latticed wall slid apart and a Qin woman came in, carrying some towels and a porcelain bowl filled with steaming hot water. She was wearing a white flowing robe with wide sleeves, as clean and sterile as the room, tied with a wide grey sash at the waist. Her hair was tamed in a threefold bun, with an ivory comb stuck through, a hairstyle that seemed oddly familiar. Her feet moved in tiny measured steps. She knelt by his bedding and noticed Bran was awake. She let out a quiet gasp, but composed herself momentarily and put the bowl and towels by his bedding. Then bowed, rose and left, sliding the latticed door behind her.

Bran raised himself up on his elbows and waited until the spinning in his head subsided. He was about to move towards the water bowl when the door slid open again. The woman had a clay cup in her left hand and a small bowl of rice and a pair of chopsticks in her right.
She knelt down again and watched him intently. The cup was filled with some greenish brew. He took a sip, but it was yet too hot for his parched lips. He looked at the rice. He had seen locals using chopsticks in Fan Yu, but never got around to learning how to use them. He didn't want to seem barbarian, but was too hungry to pretend, so started eating the sticky rice with his fingers. The woman smiled approvingly, as if she was familiar with dealing with strangers. By the time he had emptied the bowl, the brew in the cup was cold enough. He drank it in one gulp, it was bitter and savoury.

"Thank you," he said, trying to convey the feeling of gratitude in his words as best as he could. "*Xiexie*," he added in Qin.

The woman smiled again and nodded. She brought in a large clay pot and a lidded black box then disappeared again, this time for good. Bran investigated the contents of the vessels - more rice and more of the green brew. The rice was bland, unseasoned, but it filled his stomach pleasantly and there was enough liquid to quench his most immediate thirst. He felt the energy and warmth slowly returning to his body.

He managed to carefully wash himself with a wet towel, hissing with the pain radiating from taut muscles. He tried to stand and, after a few attempts, managed not to tumble back down onto the bedding. He picked up the clothes. There was a long strip of linen cloth the purpose of which he could not identify, but after not finding anything else resembling an undergarment he decided it had to be the kind of loincloth the porters wore in Fan Yu. He wrapped it clumsily around his waist and between his legs then put on a loose indigo-dyed gown and tied it over with a broad sash made of thickly spun silk. The clothes were comfortable and pleasant to touch, almost luxurious. The fine cloth felt cool against his skin.

He sat down, leaning against the wall, and opened the satchel. All the contents were there. The spyglass lay untouched in its selkie skin case, beside the small notepad and the precious Keswick pencil. The tip of his lucky *tafl* wizard was broken off, but the dragon figurine had survived unscathed, as had the black box. He held the spyglass in his hand, remembering poor Doctor Samuel, his sallow gentle face and wise dark brown eyes. Did he have a family of his own? Bran had never heard him mention anything about it; all he knew was that the Doctor's ancestors had arrived in Dracaland at the end of the Wizardry Wars. And now he was buried at sea, along with so many others.

Bran reached for the sword, and the warmth of its wyvern-hide grip reassured him. He shook off despair and suppressed the tears welling up in his eyes. There would be a better time to mourn. For now, he had to gather his racing thoughts and assess the situation.

He was alive and healthy, but alone in a strange, possibly hostile place, maybe even imprisoned. He was now certain the Seal had brought him back to the land of Qin. The locals looked like Qin, ate rice like them and drank a hot brew with their meals, although slightly different in taste to what he had become used to in Fan Yu.

He could still feel a faint delicate link to Emrys, which meant that his dragon was also still alive, somewhere. He remembered the beast desperately flying away into the starry night sky. This thought relaxed him. Things weren't as bleak as they might have been, all things considered. The house he was in was probably somewhere near the coast... His father would be searching for him, others too, and the local authorities were no doubt already alarmed to the presence of a Western boy. It was surely only a matter of days before he'd be rescued.

The moment he stood up supporting himself on the sword, the door slid open once more. The woman aided him back to the bed. He could smell the faint scent of flowers on her hair and clothes as she laid him back onto the floor. She brought incense, a cone of pressed powder sitting on a pile of ash in a clay bowl. The room quickly filled with the aroma of plum blossom.

The woman offered him some more rice with an encouraging smile, but he declined as politely as he could, already feeling full and warm. He found the blanket snug and cosy, and suddenly felt very tired again. He laid his head on the thin mattress.

The Seal's magic must have drained my energy, was his last conscious thought as a quiet dreamless sleep enveloped him.

The girls came at noon, their faces beaming with excitement. Ine led them hurriedly to a room at the back where she was certain nobody could hear them.

"Perhaps you wish to explain what exactly were you planning to do with this… *stray*," she asked Nagomi.

"We couldn't have just let him drown in the tide, could we?"

"When he's alright, we'll just send word to Dejima," said Satō.

"*When he's alright?* How long do you think I can keep him here?"

"I don't think he comes from Dejima... He fell from Heavens, not from a ship," said Nagomi.

"Fell from Heavens?" Ine raised an eyebrow.

"He was cast down to the beach on a beam of white light," Nagomi said.

"Some kind of Western magic," Satō added. "Father already used his contacts to ask around. There were no boys of his age on Dejima this year. And he doesn't look like one of the Red Hairs."

"Whoever he is, the Bataavians need to take him away," said Ine.

"Won't they report him to the authorities, though? You know how concerned they are with observing our laws," said Nagomi, worried.

"Not if my father asks them not to," replied Satō, "they owe him too many favours."

"Good," Ine said with a nod, "he's awake now, so he can be moved somewhere more suitable. This is a respectable infirmary, not a smugglers' den."

"*Eeh*! He's *awake*? Why didn't you tell us sooner?"

Nagomi and Satō started down the corridor to the infirmary room, but Ine stopped them with a single sharp word. She had learned this assertiveness the hard way, running the infirmary single-handedly whenever Keisuke was away. The patients rarely believed a woman could, or indeed should, know enough to be a scholar of medicine. They often objected to the treatments they deemed too bizarre or expensive, but Ine did not care for their protests. Once inside her infirmary, regardless of class or wealth, they were hers to command. Illness made everyone equal, this much she had learned from her father. For the treatment to be effective, all her patients had to be obedient, peasant and samurai alike.

"He needs rest. He's still disoriented and weak."

"Is he saying anything?" Satō asked, her fingers tapping on the hilt of her sword.

"No, he's mostly asleep. Whatever happened to him must have been exhausting. He did eat some rice, though. You can come in, but be quiet."

Ine slid the door a bit to see if the stranger was still sleeping. He was sitting cross-legged on the floor, examining the many straps of his new clothes. She had explained to him before, in mime, how to put on the paper-lined *kosode* robe and tie it with a broad sash. Ine nodded to the girls, and stepped into the room.

The door slid open and a girl and a boy entered, along with the woman who took care of him. He faintly remembered seeing the girl when he awoke for the very first time, but the boy was a new guest. His haircut was odd, neatly and close cut all over except a ponytail at the back. His face was smoothly shaven, soft and handsome. The girl's shiny copper hair was tied in a long braid falling down her back, almost reaching her waist. They were both rather short and Bran found it difficult to tell what age they were, although the girl seemed younger.

The pair sat down under the wall, staring at him curiously. Bran gazed back at them, especially the fiery-haired girl. He had no idea the Qin could have hair like this, glinting almost like dragonflame in the light of the sun seeping through the paper-covered window. Her locks were redder even than Eithne's, almost orange, like fox hide. He remembered a student at Llambed with similar hair, a wizard named Willem, from Bataave.

The girl wore a billowing, pleated vermillion skirt and jacket of thick white cloth, pure and immaculate like freshly fallen snow, as was everything Bran had seen in this place so far. She was quite pretty, he assessed, in an innocent childish way. Why were these two youngsters here at all?

The elder woman sat down in front of him and looked intently in his eyes.

Biting her lower lip, Ine managed to recall the first words of Bataavian she had ever learned.

"*Spreekt u Bataafs?*"

The foreigner thought for a moment then shook his head.

"Seaxe? *Latina?* Brezhoneg," he replied instead. "Umm… *Ne Hao?*"

"No, not Qin," she replied, but the boy didn't understand her.

As almost anyone of importance in Kiyō, Ine knew some Bataavian, but she was only vaguely aware of other Western nations, much less of how they spoke. They had to revert to more primitive means of communication. She pointed at herself.

"I-ne. Ine."

"Ine," repeated the boy. "Bran," he added.

She struggled.

"Bu-ran?"

He smiled and nodded.

"What is *Bu-ran?* Is that his name, nationality or profession?" Satō asked from the back.

"His name, I think," Ine answered. "Be quiet. I need to teach him a few basic words, we can't communicate with signs all the time. Luckily it seems he's got his wits about him."

"*Go-han. Gohan,*" she said, continuing the lesson, pointing to the bowl of rice.

He nodded, uncertain.

"*Ha-shi. Hashi,*" Ine said, picking up the bamboo chopsticks, still clean and unused.

"He's not a Bataavian." Nagomi whispered.

"I know!" replied Satō. "Isn't this exciting?"

"Where could he be from?"

"Well, he's definitely not from Dejima. They wouldn't let in anyone who doesn't speak their language. He's looking at you again. Maybe he fancies you," said Satō and giggled.

Ine noticed the boy's gaze and turned around to see Nagomi look away in embarrassment, her cheeks flushing red. Her little sister wasn't used to men paying attention to her. Of the two sisters, Ine was always the pretty one. She had the same black braids, dark eyes and flat nose as any other girl in Kiyō. She did have a hint of something eccentrically exotic in her features, but it made her seem only more attractive to the Yamato men. In contrast, they looked at Nagomi with barely hidden disgust. This was unfair; both girls knew there was little difference in looks between them other than the colour of their hair.

But there was no repulsion in this boy's eyes.

Of course, Ine reminded herself, *in the West people's hair and eye colours varied.*

They could have hair of copper, bronze or gold, their eyes could be brown, green, grey or blue. He did not see anything out of the ordinary in Nagomi's auburn tresses.

Satō interrupted her thoughts.

"What's he saying now?"

The boy raised his hand as if to ask about something important.

"Qin?" he asked again, making a wide gesture.

Ine sighed and shook her head. She spoke slowly and precisely.

"*Dat is niet* Qin. Ya-ma-to."

"Yama…"

The boy collapsed, his head hitting the pillow with a thud.

"Yamato…" he repeated.

Ine was disturbed by his sudden weakness. Obviously this was not the answer he had expected. She wiped his forehead with a damp cloth.

"What is it?" Nagomi asked, "what's wrong?"

"Our conversation must have tired him," Ine replied, "it's best we leave. Satō, please open that window before you go. He needs fresh air. This attic gets stuffy in the evenings."

CHAPTER XIV

Yamato, April, 2607 ab urbe condita

"Dat is niet Qin."

He didn't know Bataavian, but this sentence was easy to understand. His head started spinning again, and he had to lie back on the floor.

This is not Qin.

This was Yamato; a strange uncharted country, the land of his grandfather's mysterious adventure, the land of the black box. There would be no Westerners here, except a few cunning Bataavian merchants. Nobody else knew how to get here. His father would not be coming to his rescue. He was all alone, far away from home and from anyone who could save him.

The woman and the two younglings left the room. Bran's thoughts raced. Why did the magic of the Seal bring him to this strange land? The last thing he remembered thinking about, on the deck of the disappearing *Ladon*, was his family and friends. Mother, father, the Academy... The spell must have brought him to the closest place that had some ties to his home in Gwynedd, or maybe one of the items in his satchel resonated with the Seal's magic?

Yamato...

THE SHADOW OF BLACK WINGS

The large wooden orb covered with blue paper, darkened black with age, was affixed to a brass stand at the poles. The golden stains of continents had turned grey, and very few symbols could still be deciphered.

Satō strained her eyes by the light of the oil lamp. Biting the tip of her tongue, she traced the lines of islands and continents with black ink on a sheet of rice paper. She could only hope the boy – *Bran*, she remembered – would understand what she had copied from the old Vasconian globe. She tried her best to replicate as many distinctive features as she could – the few meandering rivers, a couple of cities marked with clusters of houses – she could only name two of them, Rome and Noviomagus, and she wasn't very certain which was which. There were also animal symbols, the meaning of which she was not aware – a two-headed bear drawn on the northern wastes of Varyaga, a man with an elephant's head in what must have been Bharata, in the south, and three dragon heads on the westernmost tip of the great continent. She copied them all, just in case.

There was some noise outside in the corridor, and loud voices. Satō hid the paper in her kimono and slid the door panel just enough to peek out.

Two magistrate officials stood before her father, angry and suspicious.

"You know the rules, Takashima-*sama*," said one of them. "You have to let us do the search otherwise we'll have reasons to suspect you of harbouring fugitives."

Satō stifled a curse.

"Of course, I have nothing to hide," replied Shūhan, "but you must allow me to welcome you as befits your position. Won't you sit down for a couple of cups first? I just got a flask of saké from Fushimi."

"You can afford such treats?" The official eyed the old wizard suspiciously. "We may have to look into the conditions of your arrest."

"It's a gift from an old friend that I will gladly share with you. Please, have a seat in the main room. You must be tired; it's a long way here from the magistrate office."

"Well…" the official grumbled, "I don't see how it can hurt. You men," he turned to his guards, "stay here, keep a lookout."

Guiding the men to the main hall, Shūhan cast a glance towards Satō's room. Their eyes met. She nodded reassuringly, letting him know he had nothing to worry about. She knew the routine. While the officials drank their saké, she would quickly run around the house and hide anything that could be deemed strange, suspicious, or simply too extravagant, starting with the old Vasconian globe.

When he woke up, the woman called Ine was sitting beside his bedding, waiting. From the amount of light falling through the paper windows he guessed it was evening or dawn. It had become cold again, but he was now getting used to it.

She bowed and gestured him to rise, helping him to put on the indigo gown. When she had made sure he could stand straight, she went out of the room, nodding at him. Hesitantly, the boy followed. She was just like any Western doctor he knew: her commands simply had to be obeyed.

She led him down a narrow corridor, its floor lined with dark squeaking planks and walls built of the already familiar wood and paper lattice, down the stairs, creaking with every step, until they reached another small room smelling of soap, steam and cleanliness.

"*Oyuu*," she said, motioning him inside.

203

There was a square wooden tub in the corner of the room, small but deep, with steam rising from under the board cover, several low stools and a shallow bucket. Bran rejoiced. Although he had washed himself several times already with a wet towel and bowl of water, the sterility of the house made him shamefully aware of his own dishevelled state. He welcomed the chance of having a hot bath with great enthusiasm.

The boy looked at the woman, but she had no intention of leaving him alone. She indicated him to take off the gown. After a moment's hesitation, he did what was asked.

She's just a nurse, he told himself, *she must have seen naked men before*. She *had* seen him naked, he remembered, when she had put him to bed for the first time.

The nurse gestured him to sit on the stool.

"No bath?" he asked, jokingly, but the woman did not reply.

She disappeared from his sight for a moment, he heard the wooden cover pulled back, something splashed and, with no warning, a stream of hot water poured onto his back from a bucket. He yowled and jumped up from the stool, but her strong arm pushed him back down. For a moment a startling thought raced through his head: he was going to be tortured with boiling water! But then he felt a sponge rubbing lye soap into his back and shoulders with care, and he felt his tense muscles relax.

It was a pleasant feeling, not unlike being washed by his mother when he had been a child. Just as he started to unwind and drift off, another bucket of scalding water woke him up violently. The nurse started massaging his scalp, rubbing a lather smelling of raw egg and ash into his hair. Another splash of hot water made him shudder. He forgot all about the cold evening breeze - his skin was now turning a healthy shade of pink.

His head and back clean, the woman laid the sponge and soap container before him on the stones. He scrubbed the rest of his body then poured water from the bucket over his head. It felt great to finally wash. Unlike some of their neighbours, the Prydain prided themselves on their cleanliness. Were it not the Prydain who had invented soap? On *Ladon* there was always a dearth of clean fresh water. He lived in fear of getting lice in his hair or fleas on his body, like most sailors. Luckily, as the son of an officer, he had priority access to the scarce bathing water. The Factory in Fan Yu was run primarily by the Seaxe who did not pay much attention to matters of hygiene, so he had to make do with bathing in the Pearl River. He was glad to find the Yamato appeared as concerned with the purity of their bodies as his own people.

As his ablutions finished, she removed the cover from the tub completely and helped him climb inside. The water was pleasantly hot and crystal clear.

How clever to wash oneself before coming in, he thought.

Soaking himself in silence, Bran saw the woman's perpetual smile disappear as she drifted off into her thoughts. He wondered what she was thinking. He needed to know more about his situation. That he was not yet dead was good news, but what was his status here? A prisoner of war? The house did not seem like a military establishment and there were youths here, but he knew nothing of the strange customs of these people. Perhaps they were trained to watch the prisoners die, or perhaps he was simply kept here until he was well enough to stand before a court...

There had to be a way to communicate. He knew of only one place in Yamato. It was a long shot, but worth a try.

"De... Dejima?" he ventured.

The woman blinked and nodded enthusiastically. She motioned him to get up. After he had dried and clothed himself, she led him up the stairs to the top floor and up a rickety ladder-like steep staircase to the roof. She opened a hatch leading outside and a waft of fresh cold air almost made him fall over. He looked out and saw a sprawling city of wooden, clay-tiled, white-walled homes. The house he was in had to be on the slope of a hill, for he could see far ahead. The city was vast, neatly organised, spreading in straight lines of streets along a narrow river towards a thin blue line of the sea on the horizon. The bay was attractive, wide, surrounded by tall green hills, sheltered from winds and storms, a perfect harbour. Just like in his grandfather's diary.

She climbed after him and they sat together on the tiled roof, looking at the city and the harbour below. The setting sun was shining straight at them, and the air was surprisingly warm for the time of day – warmer than inside the house. The woman stretched out her hand, pointing at some area of the shoreline, and said:

"*Dejima!*"

Bran squinted, wishing he remembered to bring the spyglass from his bag, and saw two islands in the middle of the bay, one square, one fan-shaped, connected by a single bridge to the rest of the land. An unmistakably spiralling tower of wizardry rose above the fan-shaped one, topped with a minuscule dot of an orange flag fluttering in the breeze. So he had guessed correctly. Of all the places in Yamato the Seal brought him almost directly to the only one he knew about. Looking to the horizon it was easy to imagine a ship of the line standing at anchor, its cannons aimed menacingly at the wooden buildings of the city. The vessels he could make out in the harbour were all, as far as he could tell, small and insignificant compared to a full size Western frigate. The arrival of HMS *Phaeton* must have been a shock to these people.

The island was closer than he had hoped, and so were the Bataavians. He only needed to reach them and explain his situation.

They heard shouting from below, and the woman gestured him to come down. When they reached Bran's room, the red-haired girl and her friend were already waiting for them, impatient and anxious.

"Sister, what are you doing?" Nagomi asked with a raised voice. "Somebody could see him! *We* saw him! Do you forget what would happen if he was reported to the authorities?"

"Quieten down, Nagomi." Ine raised her hand. "Your yelling will raise more alarm than us sitting on the roof. From a distance, nobody can tell him from a Yamato boy when he's wearing these clothes."

"What were you doing there, anyway?" asked Satō. "Is he all right to go outside like that?"

"He's perfectly fine now. He mentioned Dejima, so I wanted to show it to him. Now at least he knows where he is."

"He knows of Dejima? So maybe he is from there after all." Satō sulked.

Ine noticed a rolled-up piece of paper the wizardess held in her left hand.

"What do you have there?"

"I drew the map of the West from my father's globe. We want to see where Bran-*sama* is from."

"All right, you can come in, just don't be noisy. He still needs to rest."

"Of course we won't be *noisy*, we're not kids, sister." Nagomi pouted.

"Can we give him some rice balls?"

Satō pulled out a bamboo box.

"He's a boy, not a monkey! Besides, I'm not sure if he'll like them. You know how Westerners are about our food. You'd do better to fetch something from the Qin quarter next time, or one of the bakers at the harbour."

"Nagomi," the apprentice introduced herself. "Satō," she said, pointing at her friend.

"Saato," he repeated.

She corrected his accent. He repeated again and she nodded approvingly.

They presented him with a small box made of dark red lacquer. Inside were three balls of sticky rice wrapped in dried seaweed. The boy gobbled them up, nodded and smiled. They smiled back.

Satō unrolled her map. The boy's eyes lit up with recognition. He studied the drawing for a while, his brow furrowed in deep thought, before pointing to an amorphous blob near where she had tried her best to duplicate the three dragon heads. Satō's eyes widened.

"*Dorako?*" she asked to make sure.

"Draigg, *hai*," the boy answered, pointing at himself.

Satō's sat back for a moment, not saying anything, her heart racing. Then, on an impulse, she reached into her sash, producing another bundle of crumbled papers - her notes from the Dragon Book.

The boy looked through them, perplexed. Suddenly he cried something out and started speaking fast, waving the pieces of paper. Satō looked at him not understanding anything he said. He pointed to the paper at the runes and then to himself.

"*Dragon Rider*," he read the letters aloud and stretched out his arms imitating a dragon in flight.

"*Doragon Raidaa…*" the wizardess repeated. It sounded just like the Bataavian word "*rijder*".

"What does it mean?" asked Nagomi, silent until now.

"I… I think he means he rides dragons, like in the book. That would certainly explain the sword."

"But he's so young!"

"Maybe he's only training to… wait, he's saying something else."

The boy raised his finger. The girls fell silent in anticipation. He reached for his satchel and unbuckled it. Satō watched him take out a small lacquer figurine of a serpentine dragon. There followed a black lacquer box with a crest of four diamonds on the top. The boy opened it and took out a small flat medallion, a golden buckle on a silk ribbon and a golden ring with a strangely cut jagged stone, blue and translucent. Once out of the box, the jewel suddenly sparked with bluish light within, surprising even the boy, who almost dropped it.

"What are all these things?" Nagomi asked quietly.

"I don't know... That one's definitely a *ryū*," Satō said, giving the figurine a cursory glance, "something you would buy at a souvenir stall in the harbour... The box is from Yamato, too – I wonder what family's crest this is. And this – this is an *obi* buckle, isn't it?"

She traced the scaled coils of the golden dragon with her finger.

"I think so. I've never seen one that elaborate before."

"A very rich lady must have worn it once… That ring looks Western, I'm sure. My father might know more. What's this?"

The wizardess picked up the medallion. As she touched its dark surface it glowed, showing a picture of a noblewoman in a red kimono, more vivid and truthful than any painting. A thaumaturgic True Image! She knew about these things – a piece of imbued glass transformed to hold the image forever – but had never held one. A string of characters showed along the side of the image.

Nagomi let out a gasp. "She's beautiful!"

"My love, Ōmon. Bunka year five," deciphered Satō. "Hold on, I know that date. That's the year of the foreign ship incident."

"What does all this mean?" Nagomi asked. "He is from Dejima after all, or a spy?"

"If he is a spy, he would at least know Bataavian. There is something more going on here…"

Nagomi noticed the boy's uncomprehending expression. She turned to him, pointing to the figurine.

"Um… Bataave?" she asked.

He nodded. She then picked up the medallion.

"You wouldn't remember the name of that ship from years ago?" she asked Satō.

"Of course I do, it's my father's favourite story. It was *Feeton*."

"*Feeton*?" Nagomi repeated.

The boy thought for a moment then confirmed her guess enthusiastically and spoke a few more words in his strange language.

"What about the ring?" Satō asked, touching the glowing gem.

The boy understood the question, but they could not understand his answer.

"*Phaeton*," he repeated at last, shrugging.

The door opened. Ine looked sternly at the girls.

"Are you still interrogating my patient? You're worse than the magistrate officers!" she scolded them. "He's still tired. Leave him be."

"Of course, sister."

Nagomi stood up, bowed and bid the boy farewell. He tried to repeat her gesture and words – a clumsy effort, but it made her smile.

"We need to find a way to communicate with him," said Satō. They were walking the cherry tree lined street back to Takashima mansion. "We have to know what all those items in his bag mean."

"Isn't there anyone in Kiyō who would understand his speech? What about Bataavians?"

"There aren't that many of them on Dejima at the moment. All the merchant ships have gone for the winter and won't be back for at least a month. I asked Father, but he said it would be very difficult. You know the Bataavians can't just go around visiting random houses as they wish. The gates to the island are shut when there's no trade. There will be papers to fill out, questions to answer... and the magistrate is already snooping around our house."

"But we do have to do something about him. I can tell Ine is growing inpatient." They reached a crossroads. "I need to go to the shrine now. See you tomorrow."

Nagomi turned towards the shrine mountain. Satō headed home along the wide empty street then she started to run. She stretched out her arms and roared. Tonight, she was a dragon rider.

CHAPTER XV

Yamato, April, 2607 ab urbe condita

He sat leaning against the wall of the infirmary room, eyes closed, meditating. On his left hand he was wearing his ring; the stone radiated a warm blue light. It had been glowing like this ever since Bran had taken it out of the black box. He wondered what unseen currents of magic it was picking up on. He was trying to clear his mind, to establish contact with his dragon, to learn where it was and what had been happening to it. It wasn't an easy task.

Questions raced through his head. The notes he had been shown were from a book he knew all too well – the Llambed *Dracology* textbook, first year. Where did they get it, halfway across the globe? That map was badly copied, but definitely from an accurate enough source. From the little he had known about them, he had imagined the Yamato as a backward people, secretive, hiding away, cut off from any civilisation beyond their sea maze. It seemed they were anything but…

The jewel heated up and Bran's mind was transported away from the small room. He was inside the dragon's head now. The beast was very tired and hungry. Bran could feel the dragon's exhaustion overwhelm his own body. Emrys was resting, lying on some rocks, dormant after a great effort. It could not gather its bearings, having flown over

213

nothing but empty featureless ocean. It was unhurt, as far as Bran could tell, just weak, confused and weary, too weary to respond to the Farlink beacon. Slowly the vision faded as the blue gem cooled down.

Bran was troubled. They had never been so far apart. What if they were separated for so long that the dragon turned feral? He could not bear the thought. He had to leave the strange house and try to get to Dejima on his own. From the roof it did not seem far at all. Days had passed and he still wasn't contacted by anyone of authority, only those two kids and the nurse woman. There had to be someone else who could help him.

He woke up screaming.

His body was covered in cold sweat. The traces of the nightmare were vanishing fast from his mind, but the feeling of terror still lingered. The cries of the *Ladon*'s crewmen, dying in the burning ocean, ringed in his ears. He shook his head and took a couple of deep breaths.

He waited for a while to see if anyone would come to check on him but the house was sound asleep. He stood up and snapped his fingers. A flamespark appeared in the air. The familiar flickering light comforted him.

He grabbed his bag and the sword and reached for the door. It was unlocked - in fact, he couldn't find any lock on it at all. It slid open noiselessly. Encouraged, he walked down the narrow musty corridor. The floorboards creaked with his every step. It was hard to be stealthy in this old wooden house.

He reached the small vestibule before the front door. The wooden floor descended in two steps onto a stone pavement. There was an umbrella stand here and many shoes of various types, mostly sandals and straw slippers, all quite small. Bran hesitated for a moment. There was no guard, nobody rushed to stop him from going outside. It felt like he was betraying someone's trust by running away.

The stones radiated coldness. He looked down at his bare feet. They seemed big compared with the tiny sandals on the floor. He stepped down and gasped. The pavement was slick and icy. Dew froze on it after sunset. He dared make one more step then another, and reached the door, a dense weave of reed on a wooden frame. He found a shallow indentation in the frame where a doorknob would normally be, and slid the door wide open. A tiny bell hanging from the beam tinkled in the wind, startling the boy for a moment. Still nobody came. He stepped outside underneath a rectangle of cloth hanging across the doorway and found himself on the street under the broad eaves of the house.

The city was utterly quiet. A single cat meowed in the distance and then he could hear no other noise except the wind blowing under the eaves and a faint rush of the sea somewhere far away. The narrow street, running steeply downhill, smelled of wet wood and stone, and rainwater. None of the usual city smells were present, none of the sounds. It felt as if the town had been deserted for a long time.

Bran walked down the hill for a bit. The main street mingled into a myriad crossroads below, all lined with the same rows of low, dainty wooden houses, one barely distinguishable from another in the moonlight, walls washed white or covered with vertical wooden slats. The air was fresh and crisp. Bran shivered and the cold sobered him. He was alone in an unfamiliar city, trying to get to a place of which he was barely aware. The streets and houses seemed identical, featureless in the darkness. If he became lost he would wander around the same district for hours. For all he knew, he may have been safer inside than out. Perhaps the only friendly people in the city were in the house he had just left. He had already learned that the people of the Orient did not necessarily take kindly to users of Power. What if the Yamato were as hostile as the people of Fan Yu?

He climbed back up, but did not enter the house. He let the tranquillity of the night soothe him. He extinguished the flamespark and was instantly wrapped in complete darkness. The moon hid behind a thick cloud and the city was now just sounds and smells. He listened to the calming distant rush of the waves, to the whistling of the wind dancing over the roof tiles. He breathed in the gentle aroma of fresh moist wood and cold slate. Deep within he could faintly feel Emrys. The dragon was bewildered, confused, alone. Bran tried to placate it through the Farlink, but it was futile.

He heard a shuffle. Somewhere near, somebody or something was trying to sneak past him. Bran slid out his sword from the sheath as quietly as he could and crept in the direction of the sound. Barefooted, he made as little noise as a cat. As a faint ray of moonlight pierced the clouds he saw a shadow, a silhouette against the wooden wall. Bran leapt, lighting the flamespark again with a blinding flash, his sword pointing towards the shadow. He saw a little boy huddling, pinned against the wall. The boy was covering his eyes from the flash, looking for a getaway. Bran instinctively raised his sword threateningly and grabbed the boy by the coat.

The boy twisted his fingers into a rune and cried out: "*Bevries!*"

The freezing spell fizzled out without effect, but Bran was thrown off guard by what he recognised, without a shade of doubt, as Western magic. The boy slipped out of his grasp, leaving only the outer coat in Bran's hand, and disappeared into the darkness.

216

The commotion finally awakened the household. A servant ran out with a lit lantern and was now staring at Bran with a puzzled expression. Ine appeared a moment later, hastily tying up her kimono. She grunted something to the servant and took his lantern away. She looked carefully around and motioned Bran to come back inside.

She took the captured piece of clothing from him and frowned at the large round crest on the back then she looked outside once again and closed the door shut. This time she put a heavy crossbar against it from the inside. She followed Bran as he went back up to his room then showed him how to lock his door too. It wasn't much of a fortress - the walls of the infirmary looked as if they could easily be kicked through - but the house was filled with a sense of insecurity, as if some pact with the outside world had just been broken.

The wizardess burst into her father's study, beaming.

"Father! Guess what?"

Shūhan lifted tired eyes from a piece of paper he held in his hand.

"What is it, dear?"

"The *Gaikokujin* – he's a *dorako* rider!"

"He started speaking then?"

"No. Well, sort of. We don't know what language he speaks, but I showed him the map and he – " She paused, not wishing to admit to her knowledge about the Dragon Book. "He's from Dracaland, and showed us the rest in mime… What's wrong?"

"Nothing, dear, that's… interesting."

Shūhan pretended to smile, but Satō could tell he was scowling underneath.

"You are worried."

The wizard sighed deeply.

"There have been too many of these 'accidental visits' lately. First the Varyaga castaways then that foreigner who looked like one of us –" he hung his voice trying to remember the name.

"Black Raven," she said. She was too young to have met the mysterious stranger before his sudden disappearance, but the story of how he had been brought to Kiyō from the far north and kept in a cage for the amusement of the Magistrate, like a monkey, was as famous as it was shameful.

"That's right. I wonder what happened to him. And now this... It's as Curzius-*sama* said – the Westerners are encroaching on Yamato on all sides. Soon they will find a way across the Divine Winds, like they broke the Qin Barrier…"

"Father, I don't understand... Why are you concerned about this? Isn't opening Yamato what we've always wanted? Isn't it good that Dejima's monopoly is broken, and other Westerners are forcing their way in, at last? You've always said we're only being fed scraps from the Bataavian table…"

Shūhan scratched his neck, as he always did when he was uncertain of something.

"It is always better to control than to be controlled. Yes, I would love nothing more than if the *Taikun* relaxed his anti-foreign laws and established more trading posts, but I wouldn't want him to do it at sword-point. It's what the Dracalish have done in Qin, and we have heard of nothing but calamities and disaster since."

"Bran-*sama* is not like them. Besides, he's just a boy..."

"He's a soldier. You told me he carries a sword, and now we learn he rides dragons. Who knows where he's coming from? Perhaps there's a Dracalish fleet waiting for a message from him beyond the horizon..."

218

"He would make a rubbish spy – he doesn't even know Bataavian!" protested Satō.

Shūhan chuckled and nodded.

"Maybe you're right. I'm being too mistrustful. Sometimes I forget the outside world is not full of spies and traitors, like Yamato. It's because of this letter here," he waved the piece of paper in his hand, "it's a message from Curzius-*sama*, from Edo."

"Bad news?" asked Satō.

She was acutely aware of the distrust with which her father treated the conservative officials at the Edo court. The feeling was mutual.

"The government is fractured. The courtiers are quarrelling and bickering with each other. The *Taikun* barely had time to see him between one meeting and another. It's as if a stone's been thrown into the hornets' nest. They can all sense the oncoming storm, and there are always people who want to profit from chaos."

"Do you think there will be a war?" Satō asked with a grave face.

There had been peace in Yamato for over two hundred years. The threat of war seemed as distant and mythical as the tales of Gods, demons and dragons, but it had always loomed somewhere on the horizon, like a storm brewing slowly in the distance or a quietly rumbling volcano.

"War?" Shūhan looked at her with surprise. "No, I don't think so. There would have to be armies for there to be a war, and only the *Taikun* has an army. No, a war is out of the question, but a coup would not surprise me… One minister is replaced by another, one daimyo is exalted while the other is humbled, that sort of thing."

Stricken by a sudden thought, the old wizard stood up, put his hand on Satō's shoulder and looked into her eyes with concern. It frightened her.

"The courtly intrigues, the rumours of war, the treaties and spies," he said, "in the long run, all this is not important. What matters most in life are good health and a happy family. Do you understand this?"

"I do," she replied, nodding obediently.

"Remember this, then: should anything happen to me because of all we've talked about today – you *must* keep yourself safe."

"Father, I'm sure – "

"No, listen." He raised his hand to silence her protests. "We have friends who will not abandon us. Our family is well known, our name will always open certain doors even in times of trouble. If you ever have to look for help, go south, always south - Kumamoto, Kagoshima... The farther you are from Edo, the safer. If I could, I would take you away from Yamato altogether."

It's my fault Father is worried. I brought the danger to our house.

"South, I understand," she said, trying to sound as reassuring as possible.

Shūhan's face wrinkled with a relieved smile.

"Forgive an old man's talk," he said dismissively. "I'm sure this will all blow over in a few months and everything will be back to normal. It is normal, as far as we're concerned. We mustn't let some distant gossip change our way of life. We still have students to train, a household to run. Nothing changes."

"Yes, Father."

"Now, if you could boil some water for me, dear. I need to go back to my experiments, and let's forget all about this conversation for now."

"Yes, Father."

She met Nagomi in front of the Itō house.

"Did Ine send for you too?" the red-haired apprentice asked. She was out of breath, having run all the way from Tamazono Mountain.

"Yes, she said it's urgent. I hope Bran-*sama* is fine..."

Nagomi's older sister awaited them in their father's office. The longest wall was lined with rows of small wooden drawers filled with Qin herbs and Bataavian medicinal ingredients. The room smelled sweetly of crushed spices and molasses, as Ine was in the middle of preparing some mixture in a large mortar. She put away the pestle when the girls entered.

"Good, you're both here. Sit down. Things have taken a rather nasty turn." She opened a drawer and took out the cloak. "Do either of you recognise this crest?"

Satō drew a sharp breath when she saw three horizontal stripes, the symbol of the Sakuma clan.

"It's Keinosuke's, one of my students," she explained, "where did you find it?"

"Bran-*sama* caught him spying around the house at night."

"What was he doing outside?"

"He walked out," Ine said dismissively. "I told you before, this house is a hospital not a prison. I cannot close the door for the night; everyone in the neighbourhood knows they can visit me at any hour if there is an emergency. What worries me most," she pointed at the cloak, "the boy saw the *Gaikokujin* and ran away. If I know little boys, half the town will know of our secret by dinner."

"You don't know this boy." Satō grimaced. "He's... peculiar. I would expect him to bargain something from us for the knowledge."

"The Book?" Nagomi guessed.

Satō nodded.

"He's been more and more persistent about it lately. I'm sure your house was not the only one he's been spying around."

"There is one more thing," Ine added, "not that it makes the situation much worse, but I believe the boy is a wizard."

"*What?*"

"I saw him use magic - in the middle of the street, no less."

"We had no idea..."

"This place is not safe anymore," said Ine authoritatively. "I've brought the boy back to health because it was my duty as a physician, but now he must leave."

"I understand," said Satō, "he will be gone before nightfall."

The two girls descended to the small square garden at the back of the house, separated from the street by a high clay wall. The bamboo rocker was silenced in the rainless weather. Cherry blossom petals floated on top of the stone basin, naked cherry tree branches reflected in the water. The short blooming season was almost over, so now green leaves were sprouting from the black twigs and spring proper would start. A single hydrangea bush in the corner was also turning green.

They sat on the edge of the veranda. Nagomi dangled her short legs over the edge, not quite reaching the ground. Satō started contemplating the day's news. A wizard – of course! It made sense. Dragons were no ordinary creatures, and to ride one would require extraordinary skills.

At least now it's definite he was brought by magic, not by divine intervention, she thought with surprising satisfaction.

The fact that the boy was a wizard changed everything. Even if Satō might have considered giving him away to the authorities this was out of the question now. Nobody would believe Shūhan had nothing to do with the sudden appearance of a fellow magic user. It was now even more imperative to keep Bran-*sama's* presence a secret. They were making a very shoddy job of it. Keinosuke she might hope to deal with – he was just a kid, after all, nobody would believe his word against hers and that of the entire Itō household, but if anyone else caught wind of the foreigner… She had found and saved the boy, so it was up to her to make the decision.

"What should I do? I can't bring him to our house," Satō said, moping. She did not wish to involve her father any more. "And without the Overwizard present, nobody at Dejima wants to take any responsibility for the castaway."

"We might transport Bran-*sama* to the Shrine," replied Nagomi.

Satō looked up at her.

"Kazuko-*hime* mentioned she'd like to see him."

What part of "keeping a secret" does she fail to understand? thought the wizardess angrily, but then calmed down. With Nagomi's parents constantly away, Lady Kazuko had become a surrogate parent to the girl. If Satō told her father about the boy, there was no reason for the apprentice to not discuss it with the High Priestess. Still, the speed at which the news was spreading throughout the city was worrying.

"I suppose it's the best idea we have," Satō said at last. "It's not far from here, and he could go all the way in a palanquin... but how safe would he be in the shrine?"

"Safer than anywhere else," Nagomi reassured her. "We'd put him in the private quarters, where even the Magistrate's men can't reach without a permit. The Suwa Shrine is under *Taikun*'s direct protection."

"Good. I will yet consult my father, but I'm sure he will accept this plan," decided Satō.

Maybe the Gods of Suwa will help us where men can't, she thought.

These were the greatest trees he had ever seen. Ancient and primeval, they rose into the clouds like mountains of timber, their trunks straight, broad as houses, their roots interconnected into an imperceptibly vast network of gnarled, moss-covered limbs. The forest was shrouded in a thick mist, filled with sounds of the jungle – screeching of monkeys, whistling of birds, deafening buzz of cicadas.

He was starving and worn out, growing drowsy and irritated with hunger. He hadn't eaten for days, flying from one rocky outcrop to another over a vast featureless ocean. At last he had reached this island covered with dense vegetation. He found water, roaring waterfalls and calm mountain springs, but where was food? It'd been so long since he last ate... The fires in his belly were nearly extinguished.

Something stirred in the undergrowth. A scared tiny deer, no bigger than a dog, jumped out of the ferns. With a snap of powerful jaws he swallowed it in one gulp. Sustenance at last. But he needed more if he wanted to fly any further. Much more.

There was a knock on the door and Bran snapped out of his meditation. The jewel on his finger darkened, the Farlink vanished.

"Yes?" he said, before remembering where he was. "*Hai?*" he repeated in the language of the locals.

The door slid open and a familiar face appeared in the gap – the boy in the black and orange clothes. Bran bowed and greeted him in his own tongue.

The boy said something and gestured him to follow outside. Bran struggled for a moment with the straps of his clothes, and started to move towards the door, but his guide pointed to the bundle of his meagre belongings under the wall. Apparently they were going outside.

"Another lesson in geography?" he joked, though the boy would not understand, "or maybe history?"

He strapped on the sword belt, put on a blue short-sleeved cotton jacket, slung the satchel over his shoulder and the two walked out along the dark corridor, down the steps, through what Bran recognised as the kitchen, to a back exit. It led onto a small paved courtyard hidden away from the street, with a narrow gateway leading outside. Straw sandals, a few sizes too small, waited for him on the stone pedestal. In the middle of the courtyard stood a kind of a litter, or a covered sedan chair, a black and red ornate box. A heavy cloth embroidered with a clover-like insignia covered its entrance, the same crest that was moulded onto the roof tiles around the courtyard and painted on the cloth rectangles over the doors.

The Yamato boy looked nervously around before leading Bran into the litter. The dragon rider climbed in, bending his legs and back in a most uncomfortable position. The cloth cover fell down and he became enveloped in stuffy darkness, his legs cramped in the tight space. For a fleeting moment the curtain parted and the boy looked inside. He covered his mouth, then disappeared and it was blackness again.

The litter rocked, heaved and rose up into the air. Bran found a horizontal slit in the curtain through which he could peep outside. He saw the bare back of one of the porters. It was the first time he had been in a vehicle not powered by magic, mechanics or animal muscles, but by a human being. The box hobbled out through the gate, out onto the cobbled streets of the city. He could see it for the first time in daylight, up close. He hoped they were taking him to Dejima at last, but he could not tell – by day, all the streets looked the same as well.

The litter was – deliberately, he guessed – carried along the less attended alleyways at the backs of long wooden townhouses, shops and inns. There were mostly porters here, unloading their wares, store workers in blue jackets with large white Qin characters on their backs, merchants counting their stock, servants cleaning up the cobblestones and sweeping pavements. Some wore straw sandals or wooden clogs, but most walked around barefoot. The servants wore only loincloths, and scarves wrapped around their heads. It was a warm day and they did not seem at all uncomfortable.

Bran quickly learned to recognise which of the people on the street were of a lower rank; they stood with their heads bowed down, or even prostrated themselves on the ground when the palanquin passed them by. Others paid no attention to him. There were nobles and commoners in his homeland, of course, and the divisions were stronger east of the Dyke, but even the Seaxe peasants were not obliged to kneel or fall face down in the dirt whenever a nobleman's carriage passed by.

226

There were no unpleasant odours, even in the back alleys. The streets were immaculately clean. Brigstow, he recalled, had stunk mostly of mistfire fumes and wyvern dung; Goa, the Vasconian outpost in Bharata, was filled with humid vapours from a nearby jungle and the salty odour of the open ocean. The aroma of Fan Yu was that of food, fried, dried, cooked in a myriad of ways, meat, fish and cabbage, mixed with the brackish smell of the waters of Pearl River, but Kiyō smelled only of the wood and stone of which it had been built.

Sometimes, when a servant woman poured cold water onto the pavement before her store, a waft of fresh moistness entered the palanquin. Other times they passed a cherry tree still in bloom, sweetly fragrant. The whole neighbourhood around a tea store, before which the porters paused for a short rest, was infused with the bitter scent of the brew, but these were only brief accidental occurrences, pleasantly accentuating the freshness and spotlessness of the city. There was a bluish tint of sea mist and dew about everything, and the air was humid, although not as unpleasantly as in Goa or Éko. Seen from the roof, Kiyō sprawled vastly in all directions, an area as large as any city Bran had seen so far. On the street level the houses were all small and inexpensively built. They were delicate, thin-walled, more garden gazebos or elaborate sheds than sturdy homes of stone or bales. This was a city built to a human scale, with convenience rather than boastfulness in mind. There were no excessive noises, no vehicles or mounts - everyone moved about on foot. People passed each other in polite silence, only the street vendors cried out advertising their colourful stands.

The palanquin stopped abruptly. Bran peeped through the slit carefully. They were on a broader street now, leading uphill. The aroma of alcohol and tobacco lingered faintly in the air. Two men were standing in the middle of the road shouting and pointing at each other, their faces fierce and flushed red. They were both wearing dark, sleeveless vest-like tunics with prominent shoulders, embroidered with circular crests, and the pleated skirts with which Bran was already familiar. They wore tight topknots on top of neatly combed heads. Each had two, long straight swords in plain black scabbards stuck into their sashes. The passers-by stopped, observing the scene from a safe distance.

In the blink of an eye, one of the men drew his sword and cut across the other's chest. Blood spurted in a wide crimson stream. The victim staggered back, trying yet to draw his own sword for a second then fell, thrashing briefly in death throes.

The first warrior grunted, satisfied with the result, put the sword back into the sheath and drunkenly swayed back into the establishment from which he had emerged. The crowd moved on, unperturbed. A pool of blood blossomed on the clean sand. Bran's palanquin carriers also lifted the vehicle and passed by the body as if nothing had happened.

Bran's fingers let go of the slit in the curtain and he stared into the darkness of the palanquin blankly. This was not just another drunken brawl – having spent time in harbours all over the world by now, Bran had seen what sailors and soldiers would get up to when they had consumed too much rum. *This was a murder* – no, an execution, swift, cold death...

The vehicle left the shadows of the backstreets and emerged onto a broad avenue lined with weeping cherries no longer in bloom. The crowds were thicker here. He spotted a few palanquins, but mostly men on foot, wearing the same style clothes as the two drunken brawlers, all carrying

228

swords, sometimes with a second shorter one beside them. Women accompanied them in long flowery robes, bound with wide sashes. Some covered their heads under hoods, walking slowly and majestically behind the men, always silent; others showed off intricate hairstyles and gaudy make-up, and accompanied the men side by side, laughing and flirting. A multitude of children and babies, half-naked or naked, raced all over the thoroughfare undisturbed. Commoners mingled among the crowds wearing straw, mushroom-shaped hats, simple cotton coats and knee-length pantaloons.

The carriers paused and, encouraging themselves with a shout, heaved the litter higher above their shoulders. They started to climb a large set of stone stairs lined with lanterns and trees. Two great slim pillars of granite, connected with a double crossbeam slab, formed an entrance to this stairway. This was not the way to Dejima, Bran guessed – he remembered no hill between the infirmary and the sea.

After a long climb, the palanquin passed through a richly decorated gateway onto a lush garden courtyard surrounded by low wooden buildings, the roofs tiled grey, gables undulating softly like sea waves. The trees here were sprouting fresh green buds. The grass was the colour of rich spring. Bran's palanquin carriers moved deftly through the crowd of visitors, across a long and narrow pond, down a gravel path flanked by rose bushes, under another smaller gateway and onto another, empty courtyard. The litter stopped in front of a latticed doorway.

Bran heard the porters dismissed by a familiar voice - the red-haired girl. When they had gone she unveiled the palanquin and helped him alight. Quickly, not giving him time to stretch his cramped limbs, she gestured him to take the sandals off and led him, barefoot, inside the wooden building. He walked through the labyrinth of narrow corridors, squeaking wooden floors and sliding doors. Finally they reached a small square room. She pointed to the door at the far end of the corridor.

"*Oyuu.*"

He nodded, already more than familiar with the Yamato word for bath. The girl waved her hands around the room. This was where he was supposed to live from now on. He nodded again and she smiled.

He stepped inside and began to undo his sword belt. When he turned around, she had already gone.

The room had a window overlooking the gardens and other buildings of the complex. He gathered he was either in some palace or a temple, as the layout and architecture were somewhat similar to the temples he had seen at Fan Yu. Round wooden pillars supported the roofs covered with long tiles of bluish stone, the eaves were richly carved and gilded or painted with floral decorations. Perhaps at last he would speak to someone of authority.

He breathed in the fresh air with a still lingering aroma of cherry blossom, so delightful and easy on his lungs after an hour spent in the stuffy interior of the palanquin. A stream trickled across the meadow lined with white-blooming magnolias, and birds chirped in the trees. The sun was some three-quarters down on its way towards the western horizon.

Bran stretched, yawned and looked around his room. There was a small cupboard under one of the walls, with a clay pot and a cup. One of the walls slid away to reveal a wardrobe with a rolled-up mattress and bed linen. A narrow strip of paper hung on the opposite side, with a sublime painting of a kingfisher perched on a branch, in black ink. This was all the furniture in the room, yet somehow it seemed just right, as if adding anything, another table, another cupboard, another pillow, would break the invisible harmony. Bran realised the lack of furnishings was not a result of austerity, but a deliberate choice. Like the city below, this room was built with nothing but the convenience and inner peace of the guests in mind.

There was a knock on the door. He opened it and saw a girl he hadn't seen before, in the same white and vermillion outfit he had seen the red-head wearing.

"*Dōzo.*"

She gestured towards the end of the corridor. He smiled and nodded, but she did not smile back. Her eyes were milky-white.

THE SHADOW OF BLACK WINGS

CHAPTER XVI

Yamato, Spring, 7th year of Kaei era

Tokojiro poured himself another cup of shōchū and gulped it down in one go. The warmth spread through his body. The liquor was poor, but cheap and strong, and this was all he needed.

He picked up a thin brush, held it over a stained piece of paper then put it back onto the table. His mind was empty, unfocused, as it had been every day for the last few weeks. His work on the Seaxe grammar progressed ever more slowly until it halted. He could see no point in struggling with it anymore.

Nobody in Kiyō needed a Seaxe interpreter. All the books and reports from abroad were written in or already translated into Bataavian. Study of other languages was forbidden. Tokojiro's work was nothing but an expensive and exhausting hobby. He could not hope to ever sell his book, not as long as Yamato's only contact with the outside world was through the narrow bridge to Dejima.

Why had he allowed himself to be convinced by that strange barbarian to study the wretched language instead of Qinese or Bataavian like everyone else? What good was his knowledge now?

He could curse at the owner of the inn in perfect Seaxe.

"*Damn you man, bring me more ale!*" he yelled. "Don't you understand? Of course you don't. Nobody does. The nearest people who would understand me live three thousand *ri* across the Great Sea. Black Raven, where have you gone, eh?"

He stood up and swayed. The innkeeper approached him cautiously.

"What do you want?" Tokojiro reached for his sword. "You want to throw me out?"

"Perhaps guest-*sama* would like to cool his head," the innkeeper replied, bowing and pointing to the open door.

"*Cur! Knave! Rascal!*"

Tokojiro spewed more Seaxe obscenities. He wasn't drunk enough not to see his presence at the inn was no longer welcome – not least because he had not paid yet for anything he had drunk since morning.

The interpreter headed outside, but in the doorway bumped into a young bald priest.

"Ah! A *shaved head!*" he exclaimed. "*I'm sorry.* Excuse me."

He tried to walk around the priest, but the youth stopped him and dragged him gently aside.

"You must be Tokojiro-*sama*," he whispered, "I was told I could find you here."

"You're looking for me?" the interpreter cried out, but the priest's hand on his mouth silenced him. "Looking for *me?*" he repeated, quietly. "I don't recall borrowing anything from the shaved heads. Well, maybe that one time…"

"Your talents and services are required at the Suwa Shrine. The High Priestess herself requests it."

"My services…?"

It took Tokojiro a while to realise what the priest meant.

"A Seaxe interpreter is needed urgently, although I suppose we can wait until you bathe yourself."

The priest sniffed in disgust.

"Why are we whispering?"

"The High Priestess counts on your loyalty and discretion. Remember how we helped you after Black Raven's disappearance?"

"You don't need to remind me." Tokojiro straightened himself, trying to recover some of his dignity. "I will come at once."

"The High Priestess awaits you in her quarters. Make sure you look… presentable."

Lady Kazuko's audience chamber was known as the "Crane Room" and it was easy to see why. Its walls were covered with white paper and adorned with paintings of cranes, in black and red ink, standing amidst a winter garden. A low table made from a heavy slab of dark wood, carved intricately with serpentine coils of Qin dragons, stood in the middle. Lady Kazuko was sitting at one end in an official robe of yellow and emerald, with a chain of gold and jade around her neck and a flower ornament in her greying hair tied in a bun.

Tokojiro wore the best clothes he could find; a long, tan pleated *hakama* skirt and brown cloak embroidered with white flower crests on the shoulders. He had his two swords at his side. It was important to him to show that he still had both of them, that he did not yet fall low enough to pawn his weapons for saké. His long narrow face was shaven smoothly for the first time in weeks, and his hair tied neatly.

This was his moment.

"The boy is a castaway," Lady Kazuko explained, after swearing Tokojiro to secrecy at the shrine's altar, "and speaks no Bataavian or Qin. I believe he speaks the language of your *sensei*, although I can't be certain."

"Why hasn't he been reported to the authorities yet?"

"It is my decision and responsibility to conceal his presence. I hope that is answer enough."

"Of course," he answered, although it was far from enough.

"*Let him in*," the priestess commanded loudly.

The door to the Crane Room slid open, and in came a boy, black-haired and green-eyed, slightly scared, wearing a dark purple kimono.

"Good morning, Sir," the interpreter said as he stood up and bowed. "I am Namikoshi Tokojiro, and I will attempt to translate your words to Yamato, and Lady Kazuko's to Seaxe. Please excuse any faults in my speech."

He looked at the boy expectantly. What if he got it wrong? It had been so long since he had practised the language with a native speaker... The boy let out a sigh of relief and bowed back stiffly.

"A pleasure to meet you, Sir, my name is Bran ap Dylan."

It worked. Black Raven, wherever you are, I hope you're proud.
He could still speak good Seaxe.

"I am the High Priestess of this shrine, the Suwa," Lady Kazuko said, and waited for Tokojiro to translate. "First of all, are you well? Do you need anything urgently?"

"I am fine, Lady," the boy replied swiftly, "I have been well taken care of."

"No doubt you have many questions. I shall try to answer them for you and then ask a few of my own. How does that sound to you?"

The boy agreed. Lady Kazuko smiled at him invitingly.

"I... um," he stumbled falteringly, before continuing. "That first house, with the infirmary – how did I get there?"

"I only know what Nagomi – the copper-haired girl – told me. She said you were seen brought down to a beach near Dejima on a beam of light - take it as you will. She and Satō then transported you to the Itō residence."

"Itō?"

"Nagomi's family. The nurse, Ine-*sama*, is her older sister."

"Can't I simply go to Dejima now and find myself a boat home?"

"It's not that easy," Lady Kazuko said, shaking her head, "otherwise we'd have already arranged this. We really do not wish to keep you here against your will. There are no ocean-going ships at Dejima at this time of year, and even if there were... The island is surrounded by a high wall, with only one Gate leading through it. It's heavily guarded and everyone and everything coming in or out must be checked by the magistrate. Every foreigner on the island is listed and registered with the daimyo's office. If an unknown Westerner was to appear out of nowhere, on Yamato side of the gate... A wizard, no less...!"

"I'm not a wizard," the boy protested, "just a dragon rider."

"A… a dragon?" Tokojiro hesitated. "I'm sorry, Sir, do you mean *long* – a Qin dragon or *ryū* – a Yamato one?"

"I mean a Western dragon," replied Bran.

The interpreter paused, startled.

A wizard, dragons? What mess am I getting myself into...?

"I was told you can use magic," the priestess said, surprised. "The lights you summoned last night…"

"We are all taught a little of it and we can channel the power of our dragons… but a wizard is something completely different – they use elements to –"

She raised her hand, smiling.

"Forgive me, the intricacies of Western magic are beyond my understanding."

Tokojiro noticed she brushed over the mention of the dragon as if the boy said he was a cart driver.

A dragon. Where is it now...?

"The boy I've seen – he used magic…" the foreigner said.

"Oh, there are some wizards in Kiyō!" The High Priestess nodded. "Satō's father is one, for example. Because of our trade with the Bataavians and Qin we are not as wary of Westerners and their knowledge as the rest of the Empire."

He saw a frown pass the boy's face at the mention of "the Empire".

He has no idea what this place is like. For his sake, I hope he never learns.

"And yet I am not allowed to leave the walls of this precinct?"

"It is illegal for any foreigners to be in Yamato without a permit and a state-appointed guardian. It wasn't so bad a few years ago," the priestess explained, "but now you'd probably just be killed straightaway. The streets are full of armed men who would cut you on sight. Even castaways are not exempt."

The boy nodded slowly, more to himself, as if remembering something.

"What is to become of me?"

"We are working on a solution, but it may take time. In the worst case scenario you'll have to wait until Minazuki..."

"That's two months from now," Tokojiro added an explanation to his translation.

"…when the Dejima magistrates make their annual report to the city masters," the priestess continued. "We could smuggle you into their entourage then."

"Can't you at least get the message out?"

"As soon as the Overwizard arrives back from Edo, we will let him know of your plight, of course."

The boy looked at Tokojiro quizzically.

"Edo is the capital city," the interpreter said, "far to the north of here."

"And what's an Overwizard?"

He really knows nothing!

"The Bataave commander at Dejima."

"Is there anything else you would like to ask?" Lady Kazuko interrupted their exchange.

"I just wanted to congratulate Sir Tokojiro. His Seaxe is very good."

The interpreter bowed, surprised at the praise.

"Thank you. I studied with Black Raven Somerled."

No reaction to the name.

Of course, why did I expect otherwise?

"Now, if you are willing to answer," the priestess interjected, "I would ask you my own questions."

"Naturally."

"Tell me, what happened to you before arriving in Yamato – on a beam of light, if Nagomi is to be believed."

The boy hesitated.

He does not want to reveal too much, thought Tokojiro. *Black Raven was just the same when we asked him how he got to Kiyō.*

"I… was on a ship sailing along the shores of Qin with my father," the boy finally said. "There was a disaster at sea.

I invoked a… spell, which for some reason brought me here."

"Your father was a Dracalish sailor?"

"He is a free man of Gwynedd, as am I," the boy announced proudly. "An officer and a diplomat."

"I'm sorry, I don't understand," Tokojiro interrupted.

"Gwynedd lies to the west of Dracaland. There is no border between the two, and one monarch sits on both thrones, but we rule ourselves as a separate nation."

"I… I see."

The interpreter turned to Lady Kazuko trying to translate the complicated sentence as best as he could, but she silenced him, not interested in the foreign politics.

"Your father," she asked instead, "do you know his whereabouts?"

"We were separated in the disaster. I… don't know where he is now, but I believe he's alive."

The priestess gave the boy a long, inquisitive look.

"The items you have with you," she continued, "I was told about them. Can you tell me how they have come into your possession?"

"The dragon figurine was a gift from my father, he found it on one of his travels."

"And the black box?"

The foreigner paused again.

"My grandfather sailed these seas, and he once came to this very city," he divulged at last.

"Your grandfather was a Bataavian, then?"

"No, a man of Gwynedd as well. He was on board a Dracalish ship called *Phaeton*."

Lady Kazuko's eyes widened. Tokojiro remained professionally calm, even though he also recognised the ship's name.

240

"I remember. I was Nagomi's age then. It was a famous incident. The commander of our fleet committed suicide because he was unable to stop the warship leaving the harbour."

"Suicide…?"

"Such is the law of this land. There can only be one punishment for failure. It was after the *Phaeton* incident and the great fire of Dejima that the law against foreigners was strengthened, but the sailors from that ship never landed in the city, as far as I know – so how did your grandfather come to have a Kutsuki lady's jewellery box?"

"Is that what it is? What's a Kutsuki?"

"The markings on the box, that's the crest of the Kutsuki clan of Fukuchiyama Castle, far to the north, beyond the Imperial Capital."

"I don't know anything about the clan or the castle," the boy said, shaking his head, "but the box was brought to the ship by a woman who fled from the city. It seems she and my grandfather had… been friends for some time."

"How curious," the priestess said, "I don't think I ever heard that part of the story. You wouldn't know who the woman was, or why she was fleeing from Kiyō?"

"All I know is that her name was Ōmon. Her picture is in the box, and I can only guess that golden buckle also belonged to her. I think she died not long after meeting my grandfather. In his diary he mentions a man clad in a crimson robe, who was chasing after her, but I don't know anything else."

"A man in a crimson robe?"

"*A flowing crimson robe, his hair was long, dark, flowing in the wind and his eyes gleamed like nuggets of pure gold,*" the boy recited, obviously having learned the diary off by heart.

"I see."

241

The priestess's brow furrowed in deep thought. They were both silent now. A single grey starling chirped outside as the sun slowly climbed up the morning sky. Tokojiro looked from the priestess to the boy, waiting to continue the translation. He hoped it would not last long; his throat was parched and his head throbbed after the night at the inn. Lady Kazuko stood up.

"I must now proceed to my duties. Your conversation has given me much to think about," she said.

The boy stood as well. The High Priestess rang a small porcelain bell.

"The girl who brought you here will take you back to your room. She is sworn to secrecy, but not everyone is, so be careful. I want to assure you we are doing what we can to help. The streets outside may be dangerous, but you are in the care of the shrine now. You are safe here."

"I am grateful for your help," the boy said, bowing.

"We could do no less."

You could have sent him to the magistrate, thought Tokojiro, *and saved us all a beheading.*

By the evening Bran began to grow hungry. The sunlight was fading outside, and the twilight choir of birds hiding in the rose and magnolia bushes started in earnest. Little shy wrens and chatty redstarts, noisy finches, blackbirds and thrushes with their artisan melodies, all erupted into song, a concert punctuated by the regular staccato of a lone cuckoo somewhere in the distance.

The entire part of the building seemed cut off from any visitors. There were faint noises and voices all around the compound and in the garden, but never near his room. Through the window he saw some women pass from one pavilion to another and once he thought he caught a glimpse

242

of the red-haired girl. As the night drew in the garden fell quiet, and only a few women remained - priestesses or shrine attendants, he guessed. The atmosphere was calm and focused, monastic, the people moving purposefully and in peace.

The place was having a strange effect on him. He felt acutely alone, melancholic. He realised he had been feeling like this not just since waking up in the Itō's household, but for much longer… since leaving Brigstow at least. Perhaps, he thought, he had been alone all his life, but only now with his mind so clear in this meditative atmosphere had he began to notice it.

He wished there was somebody he could tell about all his adventures, but there was nobody waiting for his stories back at Llambed. Of the people whom he could have counted among his friends, Eithne was lost beyond the Hawthorn Wall at Mon, Hywel had joined the dragoons and was probably already seeing his share of the world, and Madoc had never been interested in what lay outside Gwynedd. Would any of them even remember him when he returned – *if* he returned? Bran had no knack for making his friendships last.

He sighed, looking out through the window. The moon peered between the branches of the gingko tree as in a beautiful painting. So much wonder, lost in his own head… If he died now it would perish, like the memories of those poor souls gone down with the *Ladon*. Perhaps he should start writing a memoir, like his grandfather? He opened his satchel and took out the Keswick pencil and what remained of the notepad, but his hand hovered with no purpose over the oiled-paper sheet. He didn't know what to write. He didn't even know what date it was.

His stomach rumbled and he remembered he hadn't eaten anything since breakfast. He was resigned to going to sleep hungry when a female voice called him from outside the room. He slid the door away cautiously and saw the elderly woman who questioned him earlier, her long, greying hair let loose down the flowing light green robe. She was holding a tray with several bowls of food and a lit oil lamp. It was already getting dark outside. The woman observed him intently with wise gleaming eyes set deeply within a wrinkled face.

The interpreter had called her "Lady Kazuko", he remembered - the High Priestess. She had been very inquisitive in their morning conversation. Bran was uncertain how much of his story he should have revealed to her. In practice, MFS *Ladon* was, at the moment of the disaster, a navy ship at war, and its expedition to Jiankang was a military matter. Bran knew enough of army protocol to be wary of mentioning too many details. Why did she care so much about the contents of his satchel? What use was it to her or to anyone? Eventually, though, he'd had little choice but to answer her questions. The woman most probably held the key to his release. Certainly she had good connections – after all, she had managed to procure a Seaxe interpreter at short notice. He was surprised they even had one in a city so cut off from the outside world. It seemed prudent to stay on her good side.

He took the tray from her and bowed as best he could.

"Thank you, Lady Kazuko," he said in Prydain.

The woman smiled silently, turned away and disappeared into the darkness of the corridor without a sound.

Bran was nonplussed.

What was all that about?

244

The exquisite smell of food reached his nostrils and he remembered how famished he was. An entire mackerel grilled to perfect crispiness and an aromatic broth with thick noodles accompanied the usual bowl of rice and cup of *cha*, the hot bitter drink. He put the tray on the straw mat and waited for the meal to cool down – he could still only eat it with his fingers, the way to use the wooden sticks remaining a mystery. The mackerel was large and fat, oil dribbled down his chin and stained the purple kimono as he sank his teeth into the soft moist flesh.

I must seem like a barbarians to them, he realised. *It's a good thing nobody's here to see my clumsiness.*

Bran was writing down some of the new Yamato words he had just learned from Nagomi. "*Phoode*" - brush, he started, "*soomee*" - ink, and so on, adding words he had learned earlier until he reached the end of the page. The red-haired girl had provided him with writing utensils the locals used and explained in mime how to create the thick ink from black stone and water, but the thin brush was too unwieldy for Bran and he reverted to a pencil.

The next sheet was invitingly blank, but so was Bran's mind. He glanced out the window and tried to draw a sketch of the scene outside, branches of a tall gingko tree strikingly black against the blue, cloudless sky and the rooftops of the shrine compound, grey and black in the sun.

He looked down at his piece of paper and sighed. The sketch was just a poor jumble of shoddily drawn lines. To top it off, the paper itself was full of smudges where his hand clumsily smeared over soft graphite. The Academy had taught him to draw maps from dragonback – a necessity for a future soldier – but that was the limit of his artistic abilities. Bran reached for his satchel's front pocket and took out a small sharpening knife. He had to be careful – now that he had no idea how long it would take him to get out of this place, every sliver of pencil was precious. The knife's blade was dull and beginning to rust– he had forgotten to take proper care of it since his arrival in Yamato. It snapped and cut him on the index finger.

Clenching his fist to stop the blood trickling from the small wound, he leaned against the wall and closed his eyes, listening to the soft wafts of the wind whistling gently through the gutters and roof tiles, the rushing of the flat, fan-shaped leaves of the tree outside and the incessant tweeting of a family of swallows building an early nest in the eaves of one of the buildings.

Did she really mean they'd keep me here for two months? There must be another way…

He hadn't told anyone about where the dragon was yet. He could tell Emrys was getting near. What if it would find its way to Kiyō? Bran could only imagine the chaos the city would be thrown into by the appearance of the jade green beast. He wondered where the dragons of Yamato were kept – he had not seen any yet, although they seemed omnipresent in the carved ornaments and painted ceilings throughout the shrine. Perhaps they were all kept on the other island the interpreter had mentioned. How big was this country, anyway? Tokojiro called it an "Empire" – was it just a case of mistranslation, or could there really have been enough ocean to hide a land the size of Qin or Rome? Not for the first time Bran wished he had paid more attention to geography…

The ring on his finger lit up like a flare. He was overwhelmed by a flood of images and emotions. He could barely gather his bearings, but he was on a beach somewhere – in the waves – on a rocky reef – in the trees – back on the

246

sand. Panic and anger swept through him, danger and pain. A group of people - short stocky men with spears, nets, bows and arrows – approached him, creeping. He tried to get away, but a net entangled his arms, his legs and his... wings?

Bran opened his eyes, the images perished. He immediately realised what he had just seen – Emrys had been captured. Its abductors looked like the Yamato, but he couldn't be sure, as everything had happened too quickly. The boy did not know if what he had just experienced happened now or was an echo of some earlier events. He tried to focus again, but there was no more response.

The dragon rider fell back against the wall, his heart racing. He could not wait any longer until whenever his hosts deemed him ready to sneak to the Bataavians. He had to do something, but what? Leaving alone was out of the question. He had tried this once already, and it had only brought trouble. Besides, now he had even less idea in which part of the city he was and how to get from here to Dejima. No, to save Emrys he needed to get help from the few Yamato people he already knew.

CHAPTER XVII

Yamato, Spring, 7ᵗʰ year of Kaei era

Keinosuke arrived late. He sat down by the table beside Shōin, unpacked his bag and prepared for the lesson, while the others waited.

Satō glanced at him with irritation, but said nothing. *He dares to come? What's he playing at?*

"We're talking about Elemental Affiliation today," she explained, and continued from where Keinosuke's arrival interrupted her, "can you guess what element is your teacher's preferred one?"

"*Sui* – water," moaned Shōin, rubbing his arm in remembrance of the freezing punishment then laughing.

Satō laughed too. Keinosuke was silent and distant, obviously thinking about something other than the lesson. The wizardess bit her lips, but decided to ignore the boy's behaviour.

"You will choose your element, eventually, or rather, it will choose you. You will find some of the transformations are easier to perform, some invocations don't require as much effort, some enchantments come more naturally. Through practise and understanding of the nature of your Power, you will learn more of this special communion with elements."

"Do all wizards suffer from this limitation?" Keinosuke asked, suddenly breaking his broody silence.

"We don't regard this as a limitation, it's just a way the Power manifests itself..."

"It *is* a limitation if you confine yourself to just one aspect over others."

"It's only as much of a limitation as becoming a samurai confines you to not being a farmer or a merchant," Satō argued.

She preferred him when he was simply sitting quietly and listening to the lecture. The boy was barely capable as a wizard, in fact, Shōin, for all his giddiness and goofing off, had much greater innate talent and showed much more progress, but was boastful and arrogant, and interested only in self-aggrandisement.

"Nonetheless, are there wizards able to wield all elements with the same ease?"

Satō rolled her eyes.

"Yes, they are called Prismatics and they only appear once every few generations. They reach great fame and power – then they die young," she added grimly.

"Why is that?" Keinosuke pressed her, undeterred.

"Their life energy is spent too fast. They accomplish wondrous feats of magic, but the conflicting elements within eventually tear them apart."

The lesson continued in peace and quiet. The boys wrote down a long list of historic wizards and their biographical notes then tried to freeze a cup of water. Shōin managed to cover the surface of the liquid with a thin layer of frost remarkably quickly. At the same time, Keinosuke's cup barely cooled down. Frustrated, the boy decided to heat it up instead. He clutched the thin-walled clay cup in his hand. Suddenly it broke apart. A potsherd scratched his palm and he started bleeding.

Satō quickly wrapped the wound in a piece of cloth. Keinosuke was beaming.

"Did you see it? I only wanted to heat it up, but it exploded! Does that mean I am a fire wizard?"

"You squeezed it too hard and it snapped, that's all."

Stupid boy.

The training mugs were quite expensive, having been imbued with four elemental runes at the bottom to make the exercise easier. The shards of the cup she picked up weren't even warm.

"*You lie!*" the boy shouted.

Satō looked at him sternly. Even Shōin turned serious.

"You shouldn't say that to the *sensei*," the merchant's son said.

"Or what?" Keinosuke stood up, clutching his bleeding hand. "I know your lies and secrets, *sensei*, and you can't do anything about it!"

Here we go.

"Be quiet, boy."

"I won't! You can't make me! I'm a samurai and you're just a girl!"

"You're not a samurai yet. You're just a spoiled brat."

"I could cut your head off for this!"

I'd like to see you try.

"Shōin, the lesson is over," she said, standing up, "please leave us."

The boy swiftly picked up his belongings and made for the door. He turned around before leaving.

"Same time next week, *sensei*?" he asked.

"Yes, of course," Satō said, not looking in his direction, as she was concentrating on Keinosuke's arrogant burning eyes.

Shōin stepped outside and slid the door behind him.

"You have something to say, apart from insults, Keinosuke?" she asked when they were alone.

"I lost a coat two nights ago. I would like to have it back, *sensei*."

"I don't know anything about it."

"It was black and white with the crest of my clan. I lost it near the Sōfukuji Temple. I thought you might have seen it, it wasn't far from the Itō house."

"Little boys should not wander around the town at night."

"Daughters of disfavoured samurai should not become acquainted with criminals."

How does he even know so much about politics? What has his father been telling him?

"Mind your words, boy. I don't know anything about your coat or any criminals hiding in the night. What is it exactly that you want from me?"

Keinosuke smiled mischievously.

"I would like to read about dragons. If you were bring me a book I could forget all about the coat, or how I came to lose it."

This was too much for Satō to bear. She would not let herself be blackmailed by anyone, especially this boy. She drew her sword and invoked the Power of flame. This wasn't her affiliated element, but she felt ice or water would not be dramatic enough to make a lasting impression. She wrote a Bataavian fire rune in the air. A barrier of flames rose around the boy, who had lost all his smugness.

"I am the heir of the Takashima *Dōjō*, I wield the power of *Rangaku*, I command the elements!" she cried in her best theatrical voice - she adored the theatre and often sneaked herself into the performances. "I will not be threatened by little boys!"

Keinosuke turned pale and instinctively reached for the dagger at his belt. Satō flicked her sword, and a tongue of flame licked the tip of the dagger's hilt. Keinosuke yowled as his hand got burned.

"You're heir of nothing! You're a girl! You'll never be allowed to inherit anything!"

Satō's eyes narrowed. The wall of flame tightened around the boy, singeing his hair.

"You mad sow, that hurts!"

"It will hurt more if you don't apologise."

"What? I'll never... *Ow!*"

"Apologise to your teacher!"

"I'm sorry, I'm sorry!" cried the boy with tears in his eyes.

Satō's forehead trickled with sweat. This show of power was exhausting her.

"If you ever talk about this to anyone, these fires will devour your flesh. Even your old man can't save you from the Curse of the Flames."

There was no such spell, but she hoped the boy would never dared to check. She dispersed the fiery circles with a wave of her hand.

"Do not ever come here again, boy. Your lessons are over."

Keinosuke picked up his books, his burned hand still trembling, tears of rage and fear trickling down his cheeks. As he reached the door he turned his head and seethed.

"You'll regret this, Takashima Satō. One day I will gain power far greater than you or your father."

When he had left, the girl sat down on the floor, breathing heavily. She reached for the remaining cup of ice-cold water and drank it in one gulp. She recalled all the inauspicious prophecies, omens and forebodings of the past months, and her father's strange words. She was naïve to think she could handle this situation. With one word whispered to a willing ear, Keinosuke could easily bring doom upon the Takashima household, already in a precarious situation.

Oh, why did the Gaikokujin have to wander outside in the dark! How thoughtless of that Ine to leave the door of her house unlocked!

Shūhan already had enough trouble on his shoulders. They were running out of money and the *Taikun*'s officials were coming to the end of their patience with his increasing connection to the Bataavians. There was already a faint rumour circulating about the conspiracy her father was a member of, not enough to act upon, but enough to grow suspicious. He was already in the court's great disfavour – Satō dared not think what would have been the next step taken against the family if the rumour had grown any further.

She could almost see the thick dark clouds envelop her and her home.

The door to Satō's room slid open noiselessly. Shūhan's bare feet stepped quietly onto the straw mat. He looked at his daughter in the light of a small paper lantern. Satō had rolled off her futon onto the floor, arms and legs spread apart, her blanket kicked off in the corner.

Shūhan picked the blanket up and covered the girl. She stirred, but did not wake. He started to softly sing a lullaby.

"Nen, nen kororiyo, okororiyo…"

He couldn't remember the rest of the words, so he put his hand on her head and gently ran his fingers through the girl's short hair.

It could be as beautiful as your mother's, he thought, *if only you'd let it grow…*

The old wizard slid the door close and headed back to his room. He cast a guilty glance at a pot of cold *chazuke* – rice with tea broth and pickled plums. Satō worked hard to prepare his meals and he kept forgetting to eat them, too busy with his experiments and research.

A family shrine stood in the corner of the room. Shūhan opened the little black lacquer doors and lit a couple of incenses. The light of the lantern flickered playfully on the brass and golden ornaments, but the tiny figurine of the *Butsu* god seemed stern, serious. He began praying to the Spirits of his ancestors, silently, careful not to wake anyone.

By night the house seemed even more empty. Only his daughter and a few old servants remained in the great residence. The Takashimas had once been a rich and powerful family. Shūhan's father had been a master of defences of the Kiyō harbour, dismissed after the *Phaeton* incident – getting into trouble with the government was becoming a family tradition... Now Satō was the last of the line - an heir to everything and nothing in particular; an empty house and a school without students.

"It's a good thing you gave me no sons, dear." He smiled bitterly as he prayed before the Spirit tablet representing his wife. "What kind of legacy would I give to a son?"

He was aware that several neighbouring families still hoped their sons would inherit the prestigious school through marriage to the master's daughter, but that was different. Without the tainted Takashima name, the school could start again. Ever since Satō had turned twelve and was of engagement age, various relatives, friends and matchmakers had started to appear at the house with talk of marriage, suitors and courtship, but she would hear none of it. His daughter was satisfied with her life as it was. She was getting used to walking around the streets of Kiyō in male clothes, with her head held high, hair combed straight and simple. She had often told him -she could not bear the thought of having to follow some fool of a husband, with small steps enforced by her kimono tied just that little bit too tight as noble ladies did. Shūhan was willing to indulge her for a few more years. She would have to conform to what was expected of a Yamato woman eventually, but he was too soft-hearted to command her. Without his wife, he had no idea how to raise a daughter properly.

He would not yet consider adoption either, another common and obvious solution to the problem of inheritance.

"What is wrong with my son, Takashima-*sama*?" a proud parent would enquire when another supplicant for the legacy was refused. "Is he not the best of your pupils? You're not getting any younger. It would be a shame if the school was to perish when you're no longer with us."

"If he defeats my daughter, he will be worthy," had been Shūhan's only response, and it was enough. None of his students matched Satō's skill, raw talent, power and dedication.

"She has a rare gift, our girl," the old wizard said, still kneeling before the family altar.

The Yamato people often lacked the innate talent needed to perform western magic with ease, but Satō showed a remarkable natural aptitude.

"She will be far greater than me one day."

If she's ever given a chance, he thought.

"I did everything a mortal could to protect her," he told the Spirit of his wife, "now it's up to you. Please, keep an eye on our daughter."

Shūhan bowed then closed the altar. One last time, he made sure all the traps and magic barriers he had set up throughout the house were in good order then went to sleep.

Satō entered the lecture hall and slipped past the small crowd of *Rangaku* scholars. In her usual black-vermillion *Rangakusha* attire, with the Matsubara sword stuck proudly in the sash, she could easily pass as one of them. They were all too focused on Grand Master Tanaka Hisashige's speech to pay attention to her, anyway. Only one man cast her a curious glance. *A* Taikun *spy*, she thought, *here to note who comes to the lecture*.

Master Tanaka was a renowned expert on mistfire and enhanced hydraulics. He had come to Kiyō all the way from Saga to give the lecture, and Satō was happy her father had managed to obtain an entrance permit. The scientist read from a Bataavian book on engines and presented his famous masterpiece, the Myriad Year Clock.

The mechanism was a miraculous feat of engineering and magic, combining western technology and thaumaturgy with eastern geomancy and astrology. The mistfire-powered dials showed not only the precise time and date, days of the week, months and years, phases of the moon, times of sunrise and sunset, signs of the zodiac - both the yearly of the Qin and monthly of the Western Magi - but also the predicted elemental alignments for the day, geomantic measurements and a brief divination chart for the start of each week. Master Tanaka claimed he was planning on having the prophecies match in accuracy those produced by the shrine Scryers themselves.

"It is made of one thousand mechanical parts, bound by two hundred Words of Power. Eight elementals are trapped inside, and the mistfire engine inside is of my own design. It's taken me three years to reach its current form, and I am now working on a second, even more precise, prototype."

Eight elementals! Shūhan's precious airguns contained only one Wind Spirit each. This was fantastically impressive machinery and Master Tanaka's efforts were loudly fêted by the gathered *Rangakusha*. Satō sneaked forwards to touch the clock. She could feel the trapped elementals buzzing inside a case of brass and teak wood, the power of *thaumaturgie* binding the iron springs and copper tubes together – Grand Master Tanaka was one of only a few scholars in Yamato powerful enough and sufficiently familiar with this magic to use it. She could hear the tiny engine puffing away quietly in the middle of the clockwork, beyond the panels of glass and copper.

"Ah, you must be Shūhan's heir," the old scholar said, having noticed her among the other scholars.

"Yes Sir."

"Too bad your father couldn't make it. I really wanted to see him. Ah, but I *do* have something, will you give it to him from me?"

"Of course!"

The old mechanician reached deep into the wooden chest and took out a small bundle no bigger than a grown man's hand. He unwrapped it carefully and showed the artefact to Satō.

It was a fingerless glove of thick brown leather, with a couple of gears, cranks and clockworks attached to it, a large dial on the outside and an oblong bulge on the inside. Satō could feel the binding enchantment buzzing throughout the mechanism.

"What… What is it?"

"Something I worked on with your father. This should help combining swordsmanship with *Rangaku*. I'm not a glover, so it may be a bit unwieldy…"

"But what does it do?"

"Oh, I'm sorry. It does all sorts of things. This dial shows the life energy quotient, and into these gears below you compose a spell pattern… Your father will know what to do with it."

"He will be very grateful."

"Oh, and look out for this spring," he added, pointing to the oblong bulge, "it pops out a needle conduit."

Satō was appalled.

"Blood magic?"

"Your father's request; I copied the design from an old Vasconian book."

"I see. Thank you, Tanaka-*sama*."

Satō bowed and pulled back into the crowd of scholars, each of whom wanted to have a chance at conversation with the celebrated mechanician.

"Fafnir the Green of Osning Forest was the Broodfather of the Forest races: the Viridians, the Celadons, the Verts and the Emeralds. These are robust practical races, beneficial for civilian labour, known for their reliability and stamina."

A detailed ink drawing of a large green *dorako* in flight, hauling a huge load of stone on a platform tied under its belly, filled out a third of the page. The dragon's wings moved slowly, and a man sitting on the stones waved to the reader merrily. Underneath, the black runes on a yellowed parchment spelled mysterious words with no apparent meaning. Even though Shūhan, unlike his daughter, had a cursory knowledge of Seaxe, the particular jargon in which the *Dracology, Student's Handbook* had been written was hermetic and complicated.

Some fifteen years ago, Shūhan had bought a copy of an incomplete Seaxe wordbook from a Bataavian merchant for a hefty sum. The dictionary, written by someone called Medhurst, had lain unused on the upper shelf of the library until another smuggler had brought the enigmatic *Dracology Handbook*. It had taken the old wizard a while to recognise the language of the book and remember where he had hidden Medhurst's piece. The dictionary itself was difficult to work with; its author seemed not to be aware the Yamato wrote in a vertical fashion, used only one of the three writing systems and was completely unfamiliar with the consonant markers or long vowels. Still, without the dictionary, the Handbook would have remained just an undecipherable set of runed pages bound in thick leather.

Always a regular person, Shūhan devoted every third day's afternoon to his attempts at decoding the book. He knew Satō was also sometimes sneaking into the library to take a peek at the pages, but he didn't mind as long as she put it back safely every time. It did spoil the surprise a little, as he planned the book as a gift for the girl's eighteenth birthday next year, but he wanted to provide her with as complete a translation as he could manage.

It was the day of Grand Master Tanaka's visit to Kiyō, and the wizard was all alone in the residence, apart from servants and guards. All his students and friends, including his daughter, had gone to see the great engineer's famous

260

Myriad Year Clock. Days like this were when the house arrest felt most inconvenient. Shūhan really wanted to see the wondrous machine for himself. On the other hand, he had an entire afternoon to work on the translation in peace and quiet.

He was stuck on a long, many-vowelled word that he could not find anywhere in the dictionary, when he heard a cracking and shattering noise coming from downstairs, as if somebody had broken through one of the thin paper walls. At first he thought one of his old servants was being particularly clumsy, but the sound repeated, accompanied by brief, but bloodcurdling, shrieks of pain. Shūhan stood up, alert, and reached for his sword. The house was under attack.

Too soon. She's not ready yet.

The enemy, whoever it was, managed to scale the staircase in two great leaps. With a third leap, the assailant appeared in the doorway, sliding the delicate panel away with a force that made it break out from the grooves and fall to the floor with a loud crack.

"The barbarian," seethed the man in the crimson robe, "where is he?"

She almost skipped along the way, like a child at play. The sun was shining brightly, warming her face in spite of the crispy, cold mid-spring air. Just a few white clouds were hanging over the horizon. Black kites and sea hawks screeched resolutely over the harbour as fishermen were returning with the first haul of the afternoon. The day couldn't get any more perfect. Everything would work out, she told herself, she was sure of it.

She stopped by the Fukusaya bakery to buy a piece of moist castella cake then she remembered she was supposed to get some rubbing alcohol for the laboratory. She headed for the Itō house – the family of physicians held ample supplies of the medicinal preparation.

Satō turned in front of the Sōfukuji Temple onto a narrower lane leading up the hill to the Itō residence. The entrance door was wide open, but there was nobody in the vestibule. This was unusual. Satō immediately remembered her worries. Warily she went inside the house. A servant was lying in the entryway, his skull cracked on the wooden floor, bleeding. Satō knelt by his side.

"Save... Ine-*sama*..." the old man moaned.

Satō ran up to the first floor. All the thin sliding panel walls were shattered, all the rooms exposed. There was debris everywhere. Ine was lying against the wall, bruised but conscious.

Satō helped her to sit up. The woman looked at the girl with blurry eyes.

"What's happened here?"

"There was a man here – a strange man. He was looking for the boy – the *Gaikokujin*."

"Bran-*sama*?"

"Yes, who else!" Ine coughed. "He tore through the walls and when he had found nothing, he – he leapt through the window."

He will go to my house next, Satō thought.

"Will you be all right here? I must see if my house is safe."

"Yes, I'll be fine. You'd better run to your father!"

The guards at the gates of the Takashima residence house had already been gruesomely disposed of by the time she arrived. They were not slain by a sword or spear, rather their throats seemed to have been torn apart by a wild animal. One of them – Satō recognised young Kaiten – was sprawled

262

across the threshold, slain in a brave, but futile, attempt to defend the residence.

Foolish boy, Satō thought briefly. *I told you - keep people in, not out.*

The gate had been crashed open. Satō dashed across the courtyard to the main hall and up the stairs straight for her father's study. She could hear the sounds of a fierce battle inside. Her father fought against the invader with all his power.

She entered the room, stepping over a discarded lightning trap, its deadly energies spent. The study was ravaged by flame, ice, wind and lightning thrown from Shūhan's sword and other focus artefacts scattered all over the floor, as the energies within the room soared to a point of oversaturation. All the hair on Satō's body stood on end, electrified, and the air smelled of ozone and burnt plums.

This magical onslaught was not enough to stop the enemy, who slowly inched towards the *Rangakusha* holding a long bronze knife. Another blade of the same kind was lying at Shūhan's feet, its tip bloodied. A great two-handed sword was slung over the stranger's back. A loose flowing robe of crimson fluttered in the hurricane of energies.

Satō shuddered, recognising a demonic presence in the room. Having trained partially in the arts of the *onmyōji* magic she was sensitive to evil Spirits, and could tell that whoever stood before her was no mere human. The smell of blood and death filled her nostrils. She drew her sword and released the most powerful enchantments she knew, adding to the already magically permeated atmosphere. A cascade of energy enveloped the assailant, vapour in the air crystallising into chains and shards of ice. Icy spikes and icicles threatened to pierce and crush the crimson-clad man.

THE SHADOW OF BLACK WINGS

The mysterious enemy simply shrugged off the chains of frost, dispelled the icicles and turned towards the girl with deliberate slowness. There was a strange hypnotising beauty in his long gaunt face, pale like the moon. The almond-shaped, predacious eyes gleamed pure gold and when he opened his mouth in a scowl, sharp blackened fangs glistened behind bloodless lips. Transfixed, Satō observed how in one smooth, dance-like move, the man threw his bronze dagger towards her. She moved, but not fast enough. The long bronze blade dug deep into her left shoulder up to the hilt.

At that moment, Shūhan yelled and leaped at the enemy, pinning him to the floor.

"Satō, run! Hide yourself!" he screamed as the creature held him in a lethal embrace.

Their bodies became enveloped in the crackling black and purple energy of fierce raw magic, overcoming each other's defences.

Satō felt her strength seeping out of the wound. She tried to launch another barrage of spells, but the enchantments fizzled out and all the ice melted. The creature's willpower was too strong.

"On your mother's name, girl," Shūhan cried again, "*save yourself.*"

Satō swore through gritted teeth. She could not disobey this command, and she could do nothing else to help Shūhan. The mysterious blade seemed to be sapping all her magic away. The black and purple vortices swelled, filling the room, threatening to envelop the wizardess. She was well aware of the dangers of finding herself within uncontrolled currents of raw magic.

"Be brave, Father," she said, her voice shaking, "I'm going to get help."

She ran away, tears rolling down her cheeks, her father's dying screams ringing in her ears, the bronze dagger tearing through her skin and muscle with every step. At last she pulled it out and threw it away, screaming with pain. Leaving a trail of blood on the dirt of the street, she ran north towards the Suwa Shrine, the only place she knew was safe in this time of darkness. The last thing she saw were people running towards her to assist, their hands stretched out helpfully as she fell down.

"Suwa Shrine... Help – my father..." she managed to whisper before the world around her was enveloped in a thick, black impenetrable shadow.

Jōtarō passed under a stone torii gate, over a bridge spanning the moat and onto the artificial island in the middle of a large pond. He moved slowly, bent, supporting himself on a sturdy bamboo stick, holding a long bundle of black silk under his arm.

Struggling through the overgrown beech grove, he located a low earthen wall and, hidden under a massive tangle of wisteria, a large round boulder. With strength defying his fragile form he ripped away the thick dense mass of purple-blooming vine, grabbed the massive rock and rolled it away, revealing a dark round entrance. He picked up a bronze lantern from a niche in the wall, cleaned it up, filled with fuel and lit it with a Qin firestick.

He descended down the corridor leading deep into the earthen mound. As he walked the light flickered, reflecting on lime-plastered slabs of fine granite, dancing on immeasurably old frescoes, paintings of zodiacal beasts, phoenixes, turtles, tigers and dragons. Jōtarō passed under fading images of courtiers and court ladies whose names and titles had long been forgotten, of princes and emperors never mentioned in the chronicles. He moved on, paying no attention to any of these wonders. He had seen them so many times…

The passage narrowed slightly and ended with a large bronze door. Jōtarō grabbed the round handle, turned it and - this time with considerable effort - pushed the great bronze slab in. It moved with a dreadful creak, disrupting the age-long silence of the vast cavern beyond. A plume of dust whirled from the floor as fresh air whooshed inside.

The walls of the perfectly round chamber were painted with pleasant scenes of courtly life - hunting, playing, lovemaking. Once it had been filled with treasure, bronze mirrors, spearheads, swords, clay figurines of Gods and ancestors, pots of coins and rice. All that had been long gone, save a few broken potsherds and unrecognisable bits of metal scattered in the thick layer of dust, unworthy of the attention of generations of grave robbers.

In the very centre of the chamber, on a square pedestal, stood a large richly carved chair made of cryptomeria wood. Sitting on it was a statue of a tall samurai clad in a purple cloak thrown over rich, extravagant, garishly coloured clothes. A shallow saké cup rested in the samurai's hand.

The statue wore an unmarked black helmet and a moustached face mask with fierce demonic eye slits. The helmet and the mask were the only pieces of clothing on the sculpture that seemed truly ancient. They were cracked and stained in places, the pigments faded.

Jōtarō hung the lantern on a hook on the wall, climbed the two steps of the pedestal and started dusting the sculpture, removing cobwebs and stains of moisture that seeped through cracks in the ceiling. He was in no hurry. Nearly an hour passed before he was satisfied with the outcome. The statue shined like new in the flickering light of the lantern.

The old man then drew a sharp dagger from a sheath hidden in the folds of his robe. Without flinching, he cut a long deep wound into his forearm. Blood dripped into the saké cup in the statue's hand. When it was full, Jōtarō put the cup to the open lips of the demonic mask.

As the liquid dripped into the opening he spoke in a trembling, but loud, voice.

"Bennosuke-*sama*! I call upon you with the name your father chose for you on the day you were born. It is time!"

This had no effect, so Jōtarō spoke again, louder.

"Shinmen-*sama*! I call upon you with the name you chose for yourself on the day you killed your first man. It is time!"

Still nothing happened, so the old man straightened himself and cried at the top of his lungs.

"Niten-*sama*! I call upon you with the name the Great *Butsu-sama* himself chose for you on the day you started your new life. *It is time! The Shard has returned!*"

There was a cracking sound. The statue stirred, its arms moved. A grunt came from beneath the demonic mask. Eyes flickered opened in the slits. The statue's hand reached for the helmet and cast it away.

The face that appeared from beneath the mask was that of a man in his early thirties. The top of his head was shaven bald, with fringes on the sides and a thick, straight shaggy ponytail sticking out at the back. His lower face sported a thin whisker and the pointed beard of Vasconian fashion.

The man grimaced and stretched his jaw, trying out muscles he had not used for a very long time. He flexed the fingers of his right hand then the left and wiped the blood stain from his lips. The skin on his hands, and on his face, was yellowy pale and paper-thin. His almond-shaped eyes, slightly bulging from under bushy eyebrows, glistened with cunning, intelligence and cruelty. They were the colour of pure gold.

When the man spoke, his voice was hoarse and broken.

"Is this true, Jōtarō? Has the Shard really returned?"

"Yes, *tono*, just as had been foretold."

On hearing these words, the samurai slowly stood up to full height and stepped forwards from the pedestal.

"How long has it been?"

"Almost fifty years."

"And what of the Seven?"

"They have already made their first move, *tono*. I am ashamed. I was unable to stop the Crimson One."

"No, you wouldn't have been. I never gave you enough power. Very well, give me my swords."

Jōtarō untied the silk bundle and unwrapped two swords of nearly equal length, sheathed in plain, featureless black scabbards. His master stuck them both into his sash then pulled out one of the blades and examined it carefully.

"You have taken good care of them, Jōtarō. There is not a spot or blemish."

The old man only bowed, but said nothing.

"Is everything ready for my return?"

"Just as you have ordered, *tono*."

"Excellent. This makes me very glad. What reward do you wish for your efforts?"

Jōtarō raised his head, and his sad wrinkled eyes met those of his master.

"My *tono* knows my desire."

"You have not changed your mind then?"

"Never."

"Very well, you have served me faithfully, and the time has come. You deserve nothing less. Assist me outside, please."

Jōtarō raised the lantern and lit their way out of the mound. Once outside, his master stopped, gently touched the light pink flowers covering the tomb's entrance and looked at the sun. He breathed in the fresh crisp air of the morning and grinned. His eyes turned plain brown.

"On ceaseless breeze," he improvised, "sweetly lingers the scent of wisteria flowers."

"*Tono*," Jōtarō reminded patiently.

"Oh, forgive me. It's been so long…"

The samurai approached him and put a hand on the old man's shoulder.

"I release you from my service. You are free to join your ancestors."

A shudder came through Jōtarō and he felt his body start to painlessly scatter into ash. He raised his eyes up, tears streaming down his ancient, cracking face.

"Thank you, *tono*," he managed to speak one last time.

"Farewell, friend," the samurai said solemnly.

THE END

APPENDICES

GLOSSARY OF TERMS

(Bat.) — Bataavian

(Yam.) — Yamato

(Pryd.) — Prydain

(Seax.) — Seaxe

aardse nor *(Bat.)* spell word, "Earth Tomb"

amazake *(Yam.)* a traditional sweet drink from fermented rice

ardian *(Seax.)* the Commander of a Regiment in the Royal Marines

banneret *(Seax.)* the Commander of a Banner in the Royal Marines

bento *(Yam.)* a boxed lunch, usually made of rice, fish and pickled vegetables

bevries *(Bat.)* spell word, "Freeze"

biwa *(Yam.)* fruit of loquat tree

blodeuyn *(Pryd.)* spell word, "Flowers"

bugyo *(Yam.)* chief magistrate of an autonomous city

bwcler *(Pryd.)* magical shield covering a fighter's arm, a buckler

cha *(Yam.)* green tea

chwalu *(Pryd.)* spell word, "Unravel"

Corianiaid *(Pryd.)* a race of red-haired dwarves from Rheged

cwrw *(Pryd.)* beer

dab *(Pryd.)* creature, thing or a person

daimyo *(Yam.)* feudal lord of a province

daisen *(Yam.)* chief wizard

dap *(Pryd.)* the same size and shape as something

dengaku *(Yam.)* a meal of grilled tofu or vegetables topped with sauce

denka, —denka *(Yam.)* honorific, referring to the member of the royal family

derwydd *(Pryd.)* druid

dōjō *(Yam.)* school of martial arts or fencing

dono, —dono *(Yam.)* honorific, referring to a noble man of a higher level

doraco *(Yam.)* Western dragon

doshin *(Yam.)* chief of Police

dōtanuki *(Yam.)* a type of katana, longer and heavier than usual

draca hiw *(Seax.)* spell word, "Dragon Form"

draigg *(Pryd.)* a dragon

duw *(Pryd.)* a swearword

dwt *(Pryd.)* a young child

egungun (Yoruba) a holy spirit, also a shaman dancer representing Egungun

enenra *(Yam.)* a spirit born of smoke

faeder *(Seax.)* father

fudai *(Yam.)* an "inner circle" clan; one of the vassals of the Tokugawa Taikun before the battle of Sekigahara

futon *(Yam.)* a roll-out mattress filled with rice husks

gaikokujin *(Yam.)* a foreigner, non-Yamato person

genoeg *(Bat.)* spell word, "Enough" (to mark the end of a continuous spell)

gornestau *(Pryd.)* magical duel

graddio *(Pryd.)* school graduation ceremony

gwrthyrru *(Pryd.)* spell word, "Repel"

hakama *(Yam.)* split trousers

hamon *(Yam.)* visual effect created on the blade through hardening process

haori *(Yam.)* a type of outer jacket

hatamoto *(Yam.)* the Taikun's retainer, samurai in direct service to the Taikun

hime, —**hime** *(Yam.)* honorific, referring to women of high position

igo *(Yam.)* a board game for two players, using identical black and white tokens

ijslaag *(Bat.)* spell word, "Ice Layer"

inro *(Yam.)* a wooden container for holding small objects, hanging from a sash

inugami *(Yam.)* a dog spirit

jawch *(Pryd.)* a swearword

jutte *(Yam.)* police truncheon

kabuki *(Yam.)* a form of classical dance theater

kagura *(Yam.)* a type of theatrical dance with religious themes

kakka *(Yam.)* honorific, referring to lords of the province or heads of the clans

kambe *(Yam.)* a shrine servant taken from an adjacent village

kami *(Yam.)* God or Spirit in Yamato mythology

kanpai *(Yam.)* Cheers!

kappa *(Yam.)* a water sprite, reptilian humanoid

katana *(Yam.)* the main Yamato sword, over 60cm in length

kaya *(Yam.)* a bright yellow wood used for making igo boards

kekkai *(Yam.)* a magical shield, similar to tarian

kimono *(Yam.)* official layered robe of the noble class

kirin *(Yam.)* a chimerical creature of Qin, body of a deer and the head of a dragon with a large single horn

kodachi *(Yam.)* a short Yamato sword, less than 60cm in length

koenig *(Seax.)* the monarch of the Varyaga Khaganate

kosode *(Yam.)* basic, loose fitting robe for both men and women

kun, **—kun** *(Yam.)* honorific, referring to young persons of the same social status

kunoichi *(Yam.)* a female shinobi assassin

kuso *(Yam.)* a swearword

lloegr *(Pryd.)* Dracaland east of the Dyke

llwch *(Pryd.)* spell word, "Dust"

long (Qin) Qin dragon

mam *(Pryd.)* mother

mamgu *(Pryd.)* grandmother

Matsubara *(Yam.)* the family of katana swordsmiths

metsuke *(Yam.)* inspector representative of the Taikun

mikado *(Yam.)* the divine Emperor of Yamato

mikan *(Yam.)* fruit of tangerine tree

mithraeum (Latin) temple of Mithras

mitorashita *(Yam.)* worshippers of Mithras

mochi *(Yam.)* a sweet made of rice gluten

mogelijkheid *(Bat.)* magical potential

monpe *(Yam.)* workman's trousers

naginata *(Yam.)* a polearm formed of a katana blade set in a bamboo shaft

nodachi *(Yam.)* a large, two-handed sword, over 120cm in length

noren *(Yam.)* a curtain hanging over the shop entrance, with the logo of the establishment

oba (Yoruba) chieftain

obi *(Yam.)* a silk sash wrapped around the waist

obidame *(Yam.)* a buckle for tying the obi sash

oden *(Yam.)* a type of stew

omikuji *(Yam.)* fortunes written on a strip of paper

onmyōji *(Yam.)* a practitioner of traditional Yamato magic

onmyōdō *(Yam.)* traditional Yamato magic

oppertovenaar *(Bat.)* overwizard of Dejima

pilipala *(Pryd.)* spell word, "butterfly"

proost *(Bat.)* Cheers!

rangaku *(Yam.)* "Western Sciences", study of Western magic and technology

rangakusha *(Yam.)* a practitioner of Western magic

reeve *(Seax.)* the Staff Sergeant in the Royal Marines

rhew *(Pryd.)* spell word, "frost"

ri *(Yam.)* measure of distance, approx. 4 km

rōnin *(Yam.)* a masterless samurai

ryū *(Yam.)* a Yamato dragon

Saesneg *(Pryd.)* (slur) Seaxe

sakaki *(Yam.)* a flowering evergreen tree, used to produce **sacred** paraphernalia

sama, —sama *(Yam.)* honorific, referring to peers of the same social status

sencha *(Yam.)* popular kind of tea

sensei, —sensei *(Yam.)* honorific, referring to teachers and doctors

shamisen *(Yam.)* a three-stringed musical instrument

shinobi *(Yam.)* assassin

shōchū *(Yam.)* strong liquor (25-35% proof)

shōgi *(Yam.)* strategic board game similar to chess

shukubo *(Yam.)* accommodation for temple pilgrims

sokukamibutsu *(Yam.)* a self-mummified monk

stadtholder *(Bat.)* the ruler of Bataavia

swyfen *(Seax.)* a swearword

tabako *(Yam.)* tobacco

tadcu *(Pryd.)* grandfather

tafarn *(Pryd.)* tavern, inn

tafl *(Pryd.)* strategic board game, played on a checkered board

taid *(Pryd.)* grandfather

taikun *(Yam.)* military ruler of Yamato

taipan (Qin) leader of a trading company

Taishō *(Yam.)* field marshal, commander-in-chief of all the forces in the field

tarian *(Pryd.)* magical shield surrounding entire body

tengu *(Yam.)* a forest goblin

tenpura *(Yam.)* small fish and vegetables fried in batter

teppo *(Yam.)* a "thunder gun" — hand-held lightning thrower

terauke *(Yam.)* a passport produced by an affiliate temple

tono, —dono *(Yam.)* honorific, referring to a noble man of a higher level

torii *(Yam.)* wooden or stone gate to the shrine

tozama *(Yam.)* an "outer circle" clan that was forced to become the vassal of the Tokugawa Taikun after the battle of Sekigahara

tsuba *(Yam.)* a handguard of the katana

twinkelbal *(Bat.)* sparkleball; a stone used for thaumaturgy practice

twp *(Pryd.)* insult, "stupid, simple"

tylwyth teg *(Pryd.)* Faer Folk, a race of tall, silver- or golden-haired humanoids

waelisc *(Seax.)* (slur) Prydain

wakashu *(Yam.)* an "unbroken" youth, a virgin

wakizashi *(Yam.)* a short sword used as a side arm, 30-60cm in length

xiexie (*Qin*) "thank you"

y ddraig goch *(Pryd.)* Red Dragon

yamabushi *(Yam.)* an ascetic mountain hermit

yōkai *(Yam.)* evil spirit, demon

yukata *(Yam.)* casual summer clothing, simple light robe

GWYNEDD

CANTRE'R GWAELOD

IFOR AP MEURIG o Cantre'r Gwaelod

b. 2541 a.u.c. Midshipman on *Phaeton* under Captain Broughton Reynolds. Married to Branwen ferch Rhodri.

DYLAN AB IFOR o Cantre'r Gwaelod

b. 2566 a.u.c. Ardian of the Second Dragoons Regiment of the Royal Marines. Married to Rhian ferch Rhys.

Mount: Highland Silver, Afreolus (*Unruly*)

BRAN AP DYLAN o Cantre'r Gwaelod

b. 2590 a.u.c. A graduate of Dracology at the Llambed Academy of Mystic Arts.

Mount: Rhos Jade, Emrys (*Ambrosius*)

LLAMBED ACADEMY

YWAIN MAB URIEN

b. ca. 1200 a.u.c. (assumed) Headmaster of the Llambed Academy. A Corrie.

INGRID MAGNUSDOTTIR

Dean of Dracology

Mount: Highland Grey, Grima (*Shadow of the Night*)

NICOLAUS CAMPION

Head of Astrology

WULFHERE of WARWICK

b. 2589 a.u.c. A student of Dracology, descendant of Richard Warwick the Kingmaker.

Mount: Highland Azure, Eolhsand (*Amber*)

EITHNE MacALPIN

b. 2591 a.u.c. A student of Geomancy from Alba.

HYWEL AP CADELL o Llyn

b. 2590 a.u.c. A student of Dracology.

Mount: Eryni Ruby, Taran Goch (*Red Thunder*)

MADOC AB OWAIN o Llyn

b. 2590 a.u.c. A student of Dracology.

Mount: Eryni Ruby, Barfog (*Bearded*)

THE SHADOW OF BLACK WINGS

MFS *LADON*

EDERN mab Gwyn

b. 2526 a.u.c. Banneret of the Second Dragoons Regiment of the Royal Marines. A Tylwyth Teg.

Mount: Highland Silver, Nodwydd (*Needle*)

GWENLLIAN ferch Harri

b. 2577 a.u.c. Reeve of the Second Dragoons Regiment of the Royal Marines.

Mount: Highland Silver, Tywyll (*Dark*)

SAMUEL ben Hagin

b. 2546 a.u.c. The ship's doctor.

AKINTOYE

Former *Oba* (ruler) of the city of Éko, reinstalled by the Dracalish Navy.

BOU MAI

A Tanka fish merchant in Fan Yu.

ISAMBARD BRUNEL

b. 2559 a.u.c. Arch-wizard of the Clistane Academy, designer of *Ladon*.

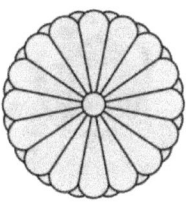

<u>YAMATO</u>

DEJIMA

HENDRIK CURZIUS

b. 2566 a.u.c. *Oppertovenaar* (Overwizard) of the Bataavian outpost of Dejima.

SAKUMA

SAKUMA ZŌZAN

b. 2564 a.u.c. A scholar of *Rangaku*.

SAKUMA KEINOSUKE

b. 2594 a.u.c. A student at the Takashima School of Wizardry.

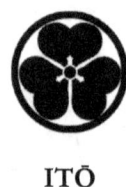

ITŌ

ITŌ TAKI, neé Kusumoto

b. 2556 a.u.c. Wife of Itō Keisuke, a Western-style physician, owner of the Sōfukuji Infirmary.

ITŌ INE

b. 2580 a.u.c. A nurse and physician at the Sōfukuji Infirmary.

ITŌ NAGOMI

b. 2591 a.u.c. An apprentice at the Suwa shrine.

TANAKA

TANAKA HISASHIGE

b. 2552 a.u.c. A scholar of *Rangaku* magic, mechanician and thaumaturgist.

TANAKA DAIKICHI

b. 2598 a.u.c. Heir and apprentice of Hisashige Tanaka.

TAKASHIMA

TAKASHIMA SHŪHAN

b. 2544 a.u.c. A *Rangaku* scholar, head of the Takashima School of Wizardry.

TAKASHIMA SATŌ

b. 2589 a.u.c. Heir of Takashima School of Wizardry.

YOSHIDA SHŌIN

b. 2594 a.u.c. A student at the Takashima School of Wizardry.

SUWA SHRINE

HOSOKI KAZUKO

b. 2567 a.u.c. High Priestess of Suwa Shrine.

NAMIKOSHI TOKOJIRO

b. 2581 a.u.c. An interpreter of Dracalish language.

SATSUMA

SHIMAZU NARIAKIRA

b.2562 a.u.c. Daimyō of the province of Satsuma, lord of Kagoshima Castle.

SHIMAZU ATSU

b. 2589 a.u.c. Adopted daughter of Shimazu Nariakira, princess of Satsuma.

Thank you for reading *The Shadow of Black Wings*.
If you enjoyed it, why not leave a comment on Amazon or
Goodreads?

The Year of the Dragon cycle contains the following volumes:

The Shadow of Black Wings

The Warrior's Soul

The Islands in the Mist

The Rising Tide

The Year of the Dragon: Books 1-4 Delux Edition

THE WARRIOR'S SOUL PREVIEW

CHAPTER I

"So you're saying the neighbours saw nothing?"

"Nothing, *doshin* Koyata. The silk merchant from across the street heard some screams and noises, but that's all."

"What about the girl? We still can't reach her?"

"She's hiding in Suwa – outside our jurisdiction."

Koyata stood before the entrance to the Takashima Mansion's main building, squinting at the afternoon sun. This day was too long. The plain grey overcoat marked with the red pentacle badge of the Kiyō police lay heavily on his shoulders. His clues were as scarce as his resources – the precinct could only spare two men to help him. The bodies of the guards had disappeared before anyone could inspect them. The members of the household were all either dead or missing and, worst of all, nobody could investigate the scene of the crime.

"I will try again," declared Koyata, whose high rank of a *doshin* meant he was responsible for supervising all crime-fighting activities in the district.

"Be careful, Koyata-*sama*," Ishida, the shorter and fatter of his two subordinates warned him earnestly.

Dismissing their fears, he entered the building and climbed the narrow steps to the first floor. He stopped in front of the remnants of the broken sliding panel separating the ruined study from the corridor. He carefully reached into the room with the *jutte* truncheon. Nothing happened. Encouraged, he stepped forwards, crossing the threshold.

Lightning struck him in the chest, and he flew a few feet into the air before landing painfully on the other side of the corridor.

"Koyata-*sama*!"

The two policemen hurried to his assistance.

"I'm all right. *Kuso*! When is Sakuma-*dono* going to help us with this barrier?"

"He said he won't leave his son's bed as long as the kid is unconscious," explained Ishida.

"Such a tragic accident…" added the other.

"If it *was* an accident," Koyata said under his nose.

"You don't think – "

"I think it looks like somebody's targeting the *Rangaku* scholars, and I think that's why Sakuma-*dono* doesn't want to leave his house."

The only item found at the scene of the crime was an antique bronze dagger, covered with dried-up blood, discovered on the road a few yards away from the gate of the residence. Koyata recognised the pattern from his days in the forgery trade – he would not have progressed so high up in the hierarchy if he hadn't a keen eye for such detail. The dagger was at least two hundred years old, of the type used in the Yōkai War. The bronze blades were manufactured with a singular purpose – to vanquish magical creatures, or users of magic.

He rotated the bronze dagger in his fingers. He could feel the barely noticeable buzz coming from the blade, a confirmation of the latent magical ability he did his best to conceal from his colleagues and superiors. He had always admired real wizards, in secret. Takashima-*sama*, Sakuma-*dono*… Those names meant much to him. It worried him greatly that somebody would wish to hunt them down.

"Well, if you ask me, I won't be sorry if they all go to hell," said the taller policeman. "Just look at all this barbarian junk on the floor," he added, pointing to the books and magical artefacts scattered all over the study. "I bet he just killed himself with one of these contraptions."

"There would at least be a body," Koyata replied, dismissing the idea outright.

"Exploded, melted, eaten by a demon," the policeman said with a shrug.

The *doshin* looked sharply at his subordinate and clapped his thigh.

"Hirata, you're brilliant!"

"I am?"

"We'll just say the wizard did it to himself! That will save us all the work!"

And keep the superiors off my back, he thought. Already the magistrate officials had contacted him regarding the mysterious attack.

"We are certain you will find evidence incriminating the Bataavians." The city bureaucrat's fat jowls shook as he spoke.

"I'm not so sure, *tono*. You know as well as I do that the Bataavians regarded Takashima-*sama* with great esteem. What possible motive – "

"I don't think you understand, *doshin*. You *will* find the necessary evidence."

"I… I see."

An accident – due to mishandling Bataavian technology. *You'll have your evidence, but good luck incriminating anyone with it. What do you say to that, you fat brush-pusher?*

"It's a good idea," Ishida agreed. "It's just as believable as an abduction by rival mages, or a *shinobi* attack, or any other mad theory spun by the folks back at the precinct."

"Are they really talking about a *shinobi* attack?" the *doshin* asked, laughing.

"Old Jūzō does. He sees ninjas and demons everywhere."

"He's been watching too many *kabuki* plays. The *shinobi* are extinct. Let's go back and write this one off; there's nothing more for us to do here."

Koyata grinned. His mood improved. He would still try to solve the mystery of the Takashima Mansion, of course – but now he could do it in his own time, by his own rules.

He shook off the doziness and yawned discreetly. He retreated behind the frame of a ground floor sliding panel and observed the courtyard outside through a hole in the paper. The hours of waiting paid off – somebody *did* appear at the Takashima residence.

An unmarked palanquin stopped at the gates. The night was pitch-black, illuminated only by a single paper lantern carried by one of the priests accompanying the vehicle. A youth wearing a wide-brimmed, face-concealing hat stepped out of the palanquin and limped towards the main hall, supported by the priest with the lantern. This must have been Shūhan's heir, Satō, Koyata realised. He had heard rumours the wizard's daughter preferred to wear male clothes – and a sword. In any other city this would have been reason enough to arrest and disgrace her. In Kiyō this was merely an eccentricity.

Koyata sneaked after the heir and two priests. As she climbed the stairs, the girl dispelled all the protective spells with a wave of her hand. She entered her father's study without a hindrance.

The residence, like all aristocratic houses built in times of the assassins, was full of hidden corridors and hideouts, and the *doshin* had all day to discover most of them. With the magic barriers gone he could now reach a small concealed alcove from which he had a good view of the entire study.

The girl gingerly touched the floor. The air crackled with remnants of a powerful spell. She gasped with pain, touching her shoulder.

"We did warn you, Takashima-*sama*," the priest with the lantern said in a worried voice, "the wound has barely sealed. If you will not rest now, it may never be healed completely."

"It doesn't matter. I have to take care of my legacy. Help me clear these up."

The girl and the priests gathered all of wizard's belongings into a great pile in the library. Koyata watched it in horror. Was she planning to burn it all? So much knowledge, so much research… If she did, the *doshin* would have to come out of his hiding place and stop the girl, he decided, even if revealing his continued interest in the case brought the wrath of his superiors upon his head.

The girl reached for a large black book at the bottom of the pile and picked it up tenderly. The cover and the edges of the pages were burned. Several pieces of paper fell out from between the pages, scribbled with composed writing.

"It's difficult to carry such a bulky tome," remarked one of the priests.

"I know." The girl sighed and threw the book back onto the pile. "I don't need it anymore."

I need to find out what that book is.

She lifted one of the floorboards and picked up a roll of golden coins. A fortune in gold! Koyata gulped. He had only ever seen so much money in the treasure houses of the gambling dens he had raided.

"There is nothing else I want to take," the girl said. "All these things…" she pointed to the pile of magic contraptions, books and documents, "I can neither carry nor leave to the robbers or magistrate."

Right, that's it. Koyata grasped the handgrip of his truncheon, ready to pounce, but the girl turned to the accompanying priests and said something which made him stop and let out a quiet sigh of relief.

"Throw it all into the dry well by the cemetery. Bury it deep. My father and I will come and retrieve it once this is all over."

She arrived at the servants' quarters dressed in the simple common uniform of a shrine attendant; a grey cloth *monpe*, pantaloons that ended at half-knee, and a brown jute tunic. It was itchy and chafing compared to silk, but Satō found it remarkably easy to walk, even run in the narrow trousers.

It was Lady Kazuko's idea for her to hide in the servants' quarters. Even though the shrine was probably the safest place in the city, its walls still could not provide a complete guarantee of safety.

"This will be the last place anybody would look for a samurai's daughter, and it will help you to pick up some of the language and behaviour of the lower classes in case you need to disguise yourself."

"Why would I need to disguise myself as a serf?"

"Do you not intend to look for your father?"

"Of course I do!" the girl blurted out.

Finding Shūhan was the only thing on her mind right now. No body had been found at the mansion, and she had recognised the faint pattern of a transportation hex still lingering on the floor of the study. The thought of her father being still alive, somewhere, was the only thing keeping her from breaking down.

"Well then, you can hardly travel as Takashima Satō, as long as there's an unknown enemy waiting for you outside the shrine's gates."

"I suppose not," she agreed reluctantly, "but a *servant*? They are so uncouth and – and *smelly*!"

"Just try to see how they live," said the High Priestess, "they may surprise you yet."

The poor commoners were employed by the shrine to assist with the simplest menial tasks – carrying luggage for the guests, chopping firewood, transporting heavy goods. Satō entered the quarters with hesitation, holding her breath, expecting to find it in a state little better than the village of *eta*, the untouchables. But, though very poor and simple, the rooms were as clean as any and, to her surprise, everyone inside seemed rather cheerful.

Despite her being dressed like one of them, the servants immediately fell to their knees.

"I, uh... why are you kneeling? I'm just a commoner like you..."

One of the girls raised her face, smiling broadly.

"*Tono*, if you want to hide among us lowly serv'nts then by all means you can, but you ain't foolin' nobody 'ere just by wearing the garb of a common'r."

Satō winced on hearing the peasant's crude accent.

"Please stand up, all of you. I need to learn how to be more like one of you, and quickly."

The servants stood up slowly. The girl who spoke first approached the wizardess boldly.

"Please come, *tono*."

She led Satō to sit beside her on the bedding. Satō looked at the quilt reluctantly, expecting bedbugs and fleas to scurry off it the moment she sat down, but it too was clean and freshly washed.

"First off, you need to grime yerself. Ye'r not tanned 'nuff, yer skin's too pure. Any fool can see you come from a good 'ouse."

"What do you propose?"

"Lessee… Why don't you rub some walnut juice on yer skin? Not too much or ye'd look like an *oni*. There ain't that much sun now, so it needn't be much. An' maybe some lamp oil if yer don't mind t'smell."

"What else?" encouraged Satō, wondering how many other fugitive nobles before her had been through the same ordeal. The girl seemed experienced.

"Yer need to slouch, like this. See how every'un is bent, that's from carryin' all them heavy bags and such. Yer walk straight, proud. That's a samurai walk. Walk low, don't look at the high-up folk."

"I see."

"An' yer looking mighty grim, if you don't mind me sayin' so. You should always smile."

"How so?"

"If we don' smile, a samurai could think we don' like summat about'em, and that be trouble, so we smile. An' what's not to smile about? Our life's a good'un."

"*Eeh*! You call this a good life?" Satō cried out.

She looked around at the squalid dormitory full of people whose combined wealth was maybe less than a tenth of a golden coin, if that.

"Sure, *tono*, an' why not? As long as we do our duty well, we ain't got nuttin' to care about. T'shrine gives us food and a place to sleep. That's more than we'd'ave in our home village. We ain't be needin' no more than that and we're all in the same boat, so we don't fight or bicker with each other. Ye'll see if yer spend a day 'ere, this life's as good as it gets."

Satō pondered the girl's words for a while.

"What is your name?"

"They call me Ikō, *tono*," the girl answered, still with the same beaming innocent smile.

"And how did you come to live in the shrine?"

"I'm a *kambe*; a payment, like," she proceeded to explain. "When t'news of great famine came from up north, all villages in Saga ran to the priests like 'ens to a cock. Ours was a poor place and t'only thing we could promise to t'great shrines were t'first girl babies born after 'arvest. The famine never came after all, but a deal was a deal. On t'day after the 'arvest feast, me mom bore three daughters in one birth. When we were five, we each got sent to one of t'great shrines – 'ere, Karatsu and Kirishima."

"Have you ever seen your sisters?" asked Satō. The three shrines were quite a distance apart from each other, even for a wealthy traveller.

"Only once, we all came back to t'village for our brother's wedding five years back. But I know them's all taken care of well, just like me, and that makes me 'appy."

"And your parents?"

"Me mom's died a few years ago, but she lived a long and good life, bless her. Me dad perish'd with t'pox when I was but tiny. 'scuse me, *tono*, but I mustn't tarry no more, there's work to be done, always. Ye'll be arright 'ere, *neh*?"

The girl stood up, leaving Satō on the jute quilt alone with her thoughts. The wizardess found her gloominess had disappeared. If the girl managed to stay so merry despite the hardships of her life, what right did Satō have to stay depressed? She was healthy, well fed, a roll of golden coins she'd taken from her father's safe box – a real fortune by any account – tightly wrapped on her stomach. She had friends and allies. Her father was very likely alive, and even if not – such was the lot of a samurai. She would continue his legacy and rebuild the dōjō. Yes, she decided, there would be no more misery. Like Ikō, she would meet her fate with a smile.

There was some commotion outside and the few servants remaining in the room scrambled to the small window to see what was happening. Satō stepped up and they politely let her closer to the opening. She could see almost the entire main courtyard from here, as the servant quarters were built on a low prominence to the west of the main gate.

The High Priestess, accompanied by several other priests and attendants, was arguing loudly with a troop of samurai. The warriors carried themselves very pompously, their rich kimonos gaudily festooned with golden dragons and silver leaves, boasting wealth and prestige. A sign of mallow was embroidered on their collars, and their leader, wearing a wide-brimmed lacquered hat, frantically waved a narrow wooden paddle, the symbol of high status.

"It's *bugyō*, the *Taikun*'s magistrate!" Satō whispered, recognising the markings of high office. The magistrate was the highest ranking official in Kiyō, equal to the provincial *daimyo*s.

The servants at the window, and Satō with them, gasped audibly as one of the magistrate's retainers pulled out his sword by an inch. Lady Kazuko halted her protestations for a moment, before renewing them with even more vigour. At last the magistrate gestured his men to calm down, barked a few more words indignantly and turned away.

The High Priestess watched the officials march away down the stairs then turned her face towards the servants' quarters. Satō could not see her face clearly at that distance, but she could imagine the look of anxious concern in Lady Kazuko's eyes.

Even the Suwa Shrine was no longer a safe place.

Lady Kazuko had barely managed to confront the magistrate at the gate when Nagomi approached her with news that the Westerner suddenly grew very agitated.

"He keeps saying, "Kazuko-hime, Kazuko-hime"," reported the girl.

The priestess pursed her lips. What other unpleasant surprises would this day bring?
It took her priests an hour to find Tokojiro in some tavern by the harbour. By the time she finally called for the Westerner, he had managed to calm himself down.

"It's about my dragon. I didn't think there would be any need to mention this," the boy said apologetically. "We… I was separated from it in the disaster and I had little hope of seeing it ever again. However, I believe it has now been captured – somewhere in this land."

"How do you know this?"

"I have a… link, a mental connection with my dragon. I can tell it arrived on a beach somewhere – to the south of here, if I have my bearings right – and was captured by armed men."

The priestess closed her eyes and prayed for guidance. How could she have missed that? Of course a dragon rider would have a *dragon*. She was silent for a long while.

"This is all too much for me, especially considering the other events... I need to consult the Spirits."

"What other events?"

He does not know, the High Priestess reminded herself.

"Satō's house was attacked – by a man in a crimson robe," she said.

"Crimson robe… you mean – "

"With long black hair and eyes like nuggets of gold, apparently."

She let the news sink in as she observed the boy.

"I must leave this place." He stood up. "I am putting you all in danger."

The boy thinks, the priestess thought with satisfaction.

"Sit down, please," she said. "The shrine is still the safest place for you to be right now, if not for very long. The others are also under its protection. We can think of something together."

"But I need to find my dragon. It can't be kept in a cage for too long. It may even die if it's not taken care of properly. Besides, it… it's my friend."

A friend?

Lady Kazuko glanced at the interpreter. Tokojiro nodded and shrugged.

"Does your… *friend* pose any danger to others while in captivity?" she asked.

"I don't know." The boy shook his head. "It depends on how long it is kept imprisoned, and in what conditions… If it turns – "

There was a word that Tokojiro did not understand and had to have explained by the boy.

"Goes wild, breaks the link with me, its rider. A feral dragon will burn villages, slaughter livestock - kill people… Even a small one, like mine, can be terribly dangerous."

"I have heard enough," said the High Priestess, her hand raised. "We will help you, I promise," she told the boy, "we will find a way, we need just a little more time. Have faith. Make sure you stay out of sight – at all times. I predict further trouble coming our way."

And I don't need the Spirits to tell me that.

At the back of the shrine gardens, in the part most overgrown and unkempt, stood an old teahouse. Funded by one of the *Taikun*s of old, the small square building with walls of unpainted wood and bamboo was the quintessence of simplicity and aesthetics. These days, the High Priestess alone used it for her contemplations. Only she and a few gardeners even knew of its existence. The roof of dark straw badly needed repairing and the tea stove begged for replacement, but it was still the best place to meditate in the entire shrine.

A flock of blue-winged magpies darted, screeching, from among the pink azaleas growing wildly over the earthen walls of the pavilion as Lady Kazuko sat on the narrow veranda overlooking a small lotus pond with a cup of fragrant, frothy *cha* in her hand. She liked the cup. It was covered in a sky-blue glaze, spotted and cracked in a deliberate, yet seemingly random, pattern. She had bought it in Heian, a long time ago. The best potteries in the country were selling their wares on the approach to the great Kiyomizu Temple. An old frail woman had walked among the rich merchants trying to sell just this one bowl. She was blind, and this was the last vessel she had created before her eyes died.

"You have a gift of seeing," the old woman said, touching Lady Kazuko's hands.

"I do," the priestess agreed. There was no point in asking how the woman knew.

"I could tell you this cup is mystic and will aid you in your divinations, but all I can say is that it will hold the *cha* without spilling, and that the glaze will not peel or lose its shine for many years."

"That is as much as I expect from a teacup."

Despite the old woman's words, Lady Kazuko did enjoy making her divinations while drinking from the cup.

Perhaps the gentle blue of the glaze helped to clear her mind, or perhaps the amount of *cha* it held was just right.

She reached for the small round bamboo box and shook it vigorously. A single stick fell out. She picked it up and smiled. Forty-four - life is a game of *shogi*. All success depends on cunning and strategy.

The sticks were just a toy, of course, a souvenir from the Qin district, but in the shrine, where the air itself was permeated with spiritual energy, even children's toys could tell the truth. The sticks simply confirmed what she had already learned from all the other divinations - the yarrow, the compass, the bones, the Four Pillars, the Six Planets, even the *omikuji* ribbons… She had spent the better part of the day trying to pierce the veils of fate and, of course, she had visited the Waters. The Spirits were most obliging, providing her with many detailed visions, but little guidance as to which of the futures was the most probable one. It was often a problem with the Waters of Scrying. Only very rarely were they as straightforward as when they had presented Nagomi with her first prophecy. And clear answers were what she needed most on this day of decisions.

She could still have given away the foreigner to the authorities. She could say he had been brought to the shrine against her will, that she knew nothing about it. None would dare question the word of a High Priestess, not over that of a drunken unemployed interpreter and two children. This would be the clever, rational solution. The shrine would be safe, her duty to the *Taikun* fulfilled; but she did not need the bamboo sticks or twigs of yarrow to see that the boy's arrival was no accident. One did not give away the gifts from the Gods.

She had had ample time to observe the foreigner, ever since she had requested his presence at the shrine. The circumstances of his arrival, as reported by Nagomi, piqued her curiosity. Then the blue ring on his finger caught her attention - a shard of sapphire stone, like the ones Nagomi saw in her vision. The boy said at first it was just a gift from his grandfather, but then admitted that it, too, had come from Yamato. A coincidence? The High Priestess knew there was no such thing when it came to divination. The other parts of the puzzle started falling into place. The crimson robed enemy assaulting Satō's and Nagomi's houses, and now the boy's *dorako…*

The mightiest will fall, remembered Lady Kazuko. She was bound to serve the Edo court with wisdom and advice. In exchange, the shrine was given protection from the domain lords and city magistrates. But the prophecy was older than the castle of Edo, and it concerned more than just the *Taikun.* The priestess had to consider the fate of all Yamato before making a decision. It was a heavy burden, but she was prepared to carry it.

Where did the foreigner come into all this? Would this boy bring the darkness upon Yamato, or deliverance? Was he just a harbinger of doom?

The situation required a decisive unorthodox solution.

"Cunning and strategy," reminded the bamboo sticks.

The High Priestess lifted her head and looked towards the top of the mountain, where the forest was the darkest and most dense. Sudden understanding dawned on her. For a moment she had gained a prophetic vision of the threads of Fate, all converging on Suwa, the Shrine in the middle of the tangled, glistening spider's web. Nagomi's apprenticeship and prophecies, Satō's escape, the boy's arrival - even Tokojiro's old, forgotten debt of gratitude, all played a part in the greater divine scheme.

The Suwa Shrine was not just a place where all these things had happened, she realised. The shrine itself was the solution.

I need to write a few letters.

CHAPTER II

The shrine bell struck nine times. The door to Bran's room slid away. The red-haired girl's slim, almond-eyed face was lit by a small flickering flame in her hand. He got up and straightened the creases on his new *kimono*, a deep, dark purple silk gown embroidered with the crest of a triangular mountain reflected in the water. The High Priestess had given it to him as a gift, and taught him how to wear it properly.

He pursed his lips and inhaled deeply in unsure anticipation.

"Kazuko-*hime*," the girl said, their limited mutually known vocabulary making it impossible to explain further what she wanted. "*Dōzo*," she added, giving him a rolled up piece of paper.

It was a letter from the High Priestess, written in the elegant, if oddly spiky and angular, handwriting that he guessed belonged to the interpreter, Tokojiro.

Please follow the girl.
Do not fear. Keep your mind clear.
I will help you find what you are looking for.
Trust us, we all want to help you.

This was all very cryptic and vague, and did not inspire trust in him at all. Why couldn't the priestess just send the interpreter to explain what was going on?

A whole day had passed since he had reported about the dragon and nobody had come to see him except the blind girl bringing him food and some strange moustached man who carefully studied his sword and then left without a word. What did they want from him now?

He looked at the girl, but she only stood, smiling shyly, in silence.

"*Dōzo*," she repeated, gesturing him to follow her outside.

They walked down the long winding corridors and then, after putting on uncomfortable wooden sandals, out of the building into the night. The moon was waning, but still bright. The garden was completely silent. They passed through a small gateway leading out of the main compound, walked across the bridge over a stream – here there was, at last, a sound, the trickling of a waterfall and the croaking of frogs – then the path started ascending steeply into a deep forest growing beyond the northern limits of the shrine.

The wood here was different from the cultivated orchard of the inner shrine. It was ancient, thick, not even a sliver of moonlight filtering through the dense canopy. There was something sinister in the darkness, giant gnarled trees brooded over the narrow path and invaded it with their black roots, covered with moss, vine and cobwebs.

"Where are you taking me?"

Bran was losing his patience. He had trusted the girl and the priestess so far, but his trust was running thin. Where was the translator? Why were they taking him deeper into the forest? Cold sweat trickled down his spine – what if they were going to sacrifice him to their Gods? He was, after all, in a temple, and he knew nothing of the religions of the locals…

"Kazuko-*hime*," the girl repeated, and from the helpless look in her worried eyes Bran guessed she knew as little of the purpose of their nightly escapade as he did.

At last they reached the end of the trail, the heart of the forest. By the light coming from the stone lantern standing between two enormous cedar trees, Bran saw a cross-beam gate of cinnabar wood and, beyond it, a little shrine, no bigger than a shed, made of round white stones under a thatched roof. The bargeboards of the roof crossed and formed a fork at the top of the gables. The structure was leaning a bit to the side, the stones covered with thick pillow moss, and the thatch was black with age.

The red-haired girl drew a sharp breath seeing the building. The inquisitive boy – Satō, the wizard's son, Bran remembered - and Lady Kazuko were also there, waiting for him. The boy's arm was bandaged. The High Priestess reached out her hand expectantly.

"What do you want from me? Where's Tokojiro?"

"Tokojiro-*sama dame*."

The priestess shook her head and crossed her arms.

"Forbidden?" Bran tried to guess, "Is the translator forbidden to come here?"

There was no answer. He looked at the red-haired girl. She tried to smile encouragingly, but the concern was still in her eyes.

Lady Kazuko said something and he sensed urgency in her voice. He took her by the hand at last and, lowering their heads under a thick straw rope hung across the entrance, the two entered the tiny shrine. There was barely enough room for them to stand here, slightly bending their backs. It was pitch black, cold and damp. He could hear water dripping somewhere far below. The air smelled faintly of sulphur.

When his eyes got used to the darkness, only faintly brightened by the stone lantern outside, he noticed a flight of steps carved into the rock, leading downwards, damp, slick and coated with lichen. Somehow he managed not to slip and tumble down, slowly following Lady Kazuko. Soon they reached a vast underground chamber filled with smoke and mist.

There was a wide lake at the bottom, its waters sparkling and shimmering with their own pale light as if the moon was trapped underneath the surface. The blue light dispersed on the whirling mist, carving fantastic shapes from the shadows. The smell of rotten eggs and ammonia was now almost unbearable. The rocks around the pool were coated in fine yellow powder.

Bran glanced at the priestess nervously.

"What now?"

She made a gesture he did not understand at first, but when she repeated it he realised she wanted him to disrobe and enter the water. This was not another hiding place. There was to be some kind of ritual performed on him, but the priestess was frail and unarmed, he couldn't imagine her wanting to harm him. There was something in the old woman's eyes that made him believe her good will. If only they could somehow communicate… There was only one way to learn exactly what it was she wanted to do with him on that mysterious night - obey the command and see the ritual through to the end.

Bran cast the dark robe to the floor and undid the loincloth. He was naked, but not cold. The warm mist surrounded and caressed his body, as if it had a mind of its own. He stepped forwards and touched the surface of the water with his toes. It was bubbling and hot, almost as hot as the water in the *Oyū* bath. He looked at the priestess and she nodded. He took another step. The stone bottom of the pool descended steeply and before long he was submerged up to the chest.

The experience was not altogether unpleasant. His muscles relaxed, his joints lost their stiffness. He could sense underwater flows and currents warming his thighs and calves, streams of heat emerging from cracks in the bottom of the lake. He stepped deeper and the water covered his shoulders. He inhaled deeply.

The mist around him became denser and thicker, now milky-white. The thicker it became the deeper breaths he had to take and the more of it he took into his lungs. He was starting to feel nauseous, and turned around to come out of the pool before it was too late. The priestess observed him intently, but made no move.

Suddenly the mist whirled around him again and some shapes appeared in the fumes, wisps of thicker yellowish smoke. For a second he thought he saw a human face looking at him curiously. Then another appeared, and now he was certain - there were eyes gazing at him from the steam, faces of all shapes and sizes, small, large, narrow and round, gentle female ones with sad eyes and fierce male ones frowning under bushy eyebrows - dozens of them, swirling around in silence, crowding and pushing each other to get nearer.

Some of the faces then grew necks, shoulders and arms. The hands of smoke started touching him, stroking and poking his flesh. He yowled as wandering fingers pinched him on the back, on the shoulder. He was surrounded by a crowd of hands, a forest of palms, now scratching and punching each other to get closer, and some of the scratches and punches would reach him by mistake. "Stop it!" he wanted to say, but the mist had enveloped his head and mouth, making it difficult to breathe or speak.

He was terrified. He could not get back to the shore. The ghosts were pushing and pulling him around in a whirlpool of limbs, fighting for the prize of a young body. He noticed the female faces had now gone from the immediate vicinity, as stronger, more virile Spirits of men took their places in the front. Some of the ghosts procured weapons of smoke and fog, swords of mist, spears of steam, and started fighting each other in a manner of warriors on a battlefield. Misplaced blows fell on Bran's arms and head. He raised his hands, defending himself from the strikes, and closed his eyes…

As suddenly as it had started, the chaos stopped. Bran opened his eyes. The ghosts were still there, a troop of grizzled warriors armed to their lucid teeth, but they were no longer fighting. The throng parted, making way for somebody coming in from the darkness - a Spirit of a huge man in full armour, wearing a masked helmet with a fan-shaped ornament. In his chest stuck an arrow, still trembling as if it had been shot mere seconds ago. The Spirit raised a great, narrow-bladed halberd and pointed it in Bran's direction. Other ghosts bowed in respect and pulled back.

The warrior Spirit roared and lunged towards the dragon rider. Bran's mouth and eyes were forced open by an unseen power. The Spirit transformed into several wisps of white smoke that entered Bran's body. The boy felt an exquisite pain, as if molten lead was poured down his mouth, nostrils and ears. He wanted to scream, but he couldn't.

After what seemed like an eternity, the High Priestess climbed up the stone stairs and out of the shrine carrying the

Westerner's limp unconscious body on her back. Immediately, Nagomi jumped to her aid and, with Satō's help, took the burden off the woman's shoulders.

"Did it work?" she asked.

She didn't exactly know what was supposed to work, or how.

"We won't know until dawn," replied Lady Kazuko, catching her breath.

"Why, what happens at dawn?"

"Patience, child, you'll see for yourself. Until then, we must wait and pray. Let's take him back to the shrine then beg the *kami* for a happy outcome."

Nagomi helped carry the boy's body down the hill, through the dark forest and quiet garden. It seemed lighter than what she remembered from the beach.

"Take him to my quarters," the priestess commanded.

They laid the unconscious boy on the straw mat floor in the Crane Room and sat beside him. Lady Kazuko closed her eyes and started chanting a monotonous droning invocation to the *kami* of Suwa. Nagomi joined her quietly, still casting worried glances at the Westerner.

"What is going on, Kazuko-*hime*?" she asked at last, when the chant finished, "what happened in that cave?"

"I'll tell you in a moment, but let me start with what happened yesterday. This will help you understand why I had to do what I did."

"You mean the magistrate agents," said Satō.

"Yes. They came to search the shrine for a harboured fugitive. Luckily, the *bugyō* made a mistake – he came without a proper warrant, so I could refuse his request and buy us a little time. However, when he's back with the *Taikun's* seal I will have no choice but to let him in."

"The magistrate should be investigating my father's disappearance, not chasing after harmless Westerners," Satō said, clutching her fists.

"How did they know Bran-*sama* is here? Who betrayed us?" asked a worried Nagomi.

"I'm afraid they were not looking for the boy. They were looking for you, Satō. Your family has been outlawed. *You* are now a wanted fugitive."

"*What?*" Satō cried out.

The boy stirred on his bed and moaned.

"I'm sorry," she said, remembering her manners, "but… I don't understand…"

"I'm not exactly sure what is going on here, either," the High Priestess admitted. "Perhaps the magistrate decided to use this opportunity to finally get rid of the Takashima family… They claim that your father perished through his unlawful experiments and you, as his heir, are equally dangerous."

"At least the boy is still safe," Satō said, biting her lip.

"But you're not. I told them you have already left the shrine in search of your father. This is what you will do today, at any rate, before they return."

"Today…?" The wizardess looked outside. It was still dark, the sky in the east slowly turning grey. "But, I don't even know where to go – what to look for…"

"And you will take Bran-*sama* with you," continued Lady Kazuko, "he will help you and you will help him."

"How can he help me – he's just a lost boy," Satō scoffed, "and he'll be slain the moment he steps out of the shrine."

"He may be lost, but there is a reason why he became lost here, of all places. This is not the first time his kin has met with the man in the crimson robe. He told me his grandfather met a similar being once before."

"So he came here because of the crimson robed man?" Nagomi guessed, trying to make sense of the fast-changing events.

"That I don't know, but there is more. If it was only a matter of hiding from the man in the crimson robe, or the authorities, I believe I could manage this without going through today's ordeal. But the boy must leave the shrine and the city. There is something he must go looking for."

"What's out there that's so precious to him?"

"The boy's *dorako*."

"The beast? It's *here*?"

Satō could not contain herself again, rising from her knees, almost standing up with excitement.

"That's what the boy said. He can somehow sense the creature coming. He says it landed somewhere south of the city."

"*Monsters from without*," whispered Nagomi. Lady Kazuko gave her a sharp warning look.

"*Eeh*?"

Satō turned to her friend.

"Nothing," the apprentice replied quickly and shook her head.

"South… Father told me to go south if anything happened to him," said Satō, now remembering her own urgency. "Kumamoto, Kagoshima… If our family still has any friends left, that's where they would be."

"You have been brought together by Fate," declared Lady Kazuko prophetically. "I have meditated on this for long hours and I am now certain beyond any doubt. The boy, the dragon, your father, the Crimson Robe, the strange items in the boy's box… You must venture south together, to find out the solution to this puzzle."

"But how?" Satō still doubted. "Are we to wrap his face in bandages and pretend he's a leper? Are we to mime our way throughout Yamato?"

Before the High Priestess could respond, the first ray of dawn pierced through the latticed paper window. The Westerner stirred again, violently this time, agony twisting his face.

"It has begun," said Lady Kazuko. "Now you will have your answer. Observe!"

He dreamt of a battle, a siege of a great stone castle overlooking a raging sea, with walls smooth and curved, rising high towards the clouds. Horsemen charged against the sallying defenders with long swords and great bows and arrows. Footmen in black armour scaled the walls, rectangular banners flying on their backs. Bronze cannons roared, spewing cannonballs over the battlements.

A Bataavian man-o'-war of ancient design sailed up to the castle. A terrifying broadside from its guns shook the walls to their foundations. Still the defenders stood strong, jeering and mocking the hapless assailants for asking the barbarians' help.

The final charge, one last push against the keep was his last chance to prove himself as an apt commander before the *Taikun* relieved him of his duty. All men were ordered forwards, all guns screamed in unison. The assault was exhilarating in its totality, a formidable rush of battle fever. They climbed past the first rampart, the second, reached the third…

A stray arrow buried itself in his chest. He fell off his horse. His men rushed to him, but it was too late. A retainer

leaned over to listen to his final words - the death poem of a
dying samurai.

> *"Among the bullets,*
> *At the start of the year,*
> *The name of*
> *Scattered flowers remains*
> *The only certainty."*

Satō was the first to notice the transformation.

"Look at his face!" she whispered, astonished. "What –
"

Lady Kazuko silenced her with a raised hand then
leaned over the boy.

"Now is the crucial moment. Everything hangs in the
balance."

The Westerner's face started melting and changing. His
features rounded, his eyes narrowed, his nose became
shorter and wider, his skin pale. There was a faint creaking of
bones and strained ligaments. The boy squirmed in pain, but
did not wake up. Nagomi turned her eyes away, unable to
look at his suffering. At last the metamorphosis was
complete, and on the bedding lay not a Western boy but a
Yamato one, not unlike any of the boys she knew from the
streets of her city.

"It's not over yet," the High Priestess remarked quickly.
"We must pray that the Spirit who is in Bran-*sama*'s body
does not overwhelm him and take over. The boy is strong
and the power of his will is great but anything may yet
happen at this point."

She chanted another invocation. Her hand resting on
the boy's forehead glowed up with white light and the
Westerner started grunting in his sleep.

"He's waking up," Lady Kazuko noted. "Satō, dear, would you call for Tokojiro-*sama*? He should be waiting in the common room."

"Yes, High Priestess."

The wizardess stood up, cast a confused glance at the boy's transformed face and disappeared outside.

"I'm sure you have noticed the significance of the events we spoke about today," the High Priestess said.

"The Prophecy," Nagomi answered, not looking at Lady Kazuko.

She was focused on the unconscious boy, trying to understand what had just happened. The transformation was like nothing she had ever heard about. She had no idea the High Priestess was in possession of such power.

"Things are happening much faster than I expected," continued Lady Kazuko. "Bran-*sama* and Satō must leave the shrine and the city - that much is clear. I will have Tokojiro-*sama* accompany and assist them, but what shall we do about you?"

"Me…?" she asked, looking back at the Priestess.

"You were there when the boy fell from Heavens and I believe your visions from last year portended his coming. It is obvious you too are greatly involved in this matter. But their quest is a dangerous one and I cannot put this burden upon you against your will."

"Oh, I understand." Nagomi lowered her head Her heart sank. When the High Priestess had spoken of Satō and the boy venturing upon a journey south, she naturally imagined herself accompanying them. Had she been expecting too much?

"Of course, if my duties to the shrine…"

The High Priestess scoffed.

"There are many ways to serve the *kami*, child. No, I don't mean you are to stay here when your friend embarks on a perilous mission, but it is something you must choose to do of your own accord."

"Oh, Kazuko-*hime*!" Nagomi said, lifting her eyes in renewed hope. "Need you ask? Of course I will go. Wherever Satō goes I will follow. If I am allowed, of course," she added hastily.

"You have my permission, child, and I'm glad you've agreed. The quest could prove impossible for just Satō and the boy. With you, it will be merely difficult. They will need your protection."

"*My* protection? But… they are the warriors, the wizards. They have swords and magic. I can only heal …"

"You can do much more than this. There are perils that cannot be subdued by steel or spell."

What does she mean?

"I will do what I can – if there is anything I can do."

"You can be yourself, for a start," the priestess said with a smile. "Satō will need your cheerfulness, and Bran-*sama*…" She turned her head towards the door.

"I can hear Tokojiro-*sama* coming. Could you leave us alone for a moment?

CHAPTER III

He winced, opening his eyes. His face felt sore, tense, and there was something wrong with his vision, although he couldn't pinpoint what. He was lying in the Crane Room, the High Priestess and the interpreter, Tokojiro, sitting by his side staring at him intently.

"Why are you looking at me like that?" he asked the interpreter.

Tokojiro glanced at the High Priestess. Without a word she produced a small, round, mirror of polished bronze. He looked into it warily and then dropped it.

"*By Owain's Sword*! What… What trick is this…?"

The face in the mirror was not his - flat wide nose, narrow eyes, pale-yellow skin, high angular cheekbones. It was the face of a Yamato man. He knew now what was wrong with his vision. He was used to seeing the tip of his hooked Roman nose in the middle of his face. It was gone. He touched his skin. It felt alien, flabby, soft.

"What is this…?" he said, still in shock.

"You have asked me for help."

Tokojiro translated Lady Kazuko's words.

"If you want to seek your *dorako* throughout Yamato, you will need more than just a good disguise. Your current appearance is that of one of the Ancestors in the Cave of Scrying. I trust the ritual was not too painful for you."

"Seek my…"

This wasn't what he had in mind at all. When he had asked for help, he hoped the priestess would use her contacts to expedite his transfer to Dejima or at least let the Bataavians know of the danger posed by Emrys. He never considered actually *travelling* across the unknown alien land in search of the dragon. Certainly not looking like this…

"Can I – can I change back?"

Lady Kazuko smiled encouragingly. "Why don't you try?"

"How? I don't know…"

"Remember how you normally look. Focus your will. The change will come."

It wasn't easy to remember his own face. Bran did not yet shave, so he had little reason to be looking in mirrors. Even though he tried his best, nothing happened at first, but then several muscles in his jaw crackled and moved. He cried out with pain and surprise.

"It hurts," he moaned.

The transformation continued against his will, muscles and joints slithering underneath his skin like living creatures.

"It will get better in time," Lady Kazuko said, leaning over him and touching his face, "so I've read."

Her hand was warm and soothing, but her words were not.

"You've *read*? Then this was something you had never done before?"

"The ritual of the Caves had not been performed since the Civil Wars," the High Priestess admitted with slight embarrassment. "The Spirits in those days had turned… belligerent. It was getting difficult to conduct the ritual peacefully."

Spirits? he thought, trying to understand. *Ancestors? What kind of magic is this? What happened to me in that cave?*

"But you knew it would work for me?" he asked.

"I had prayed it would, but there was always a risk."

"Why didn't you warn me?"

"You told me the *dorako* was your friend. Would you not have faced the risk for a friend's sake?"

Bran thought carefully about the answer. Yes, the priestess was right. What good was notifying the Bataavians? Emrys was *his* dragon, *his* responsibility. He had to find it on his own.

"I would," he admitted at last.

The priestess's face wrinkled in a gentle smile.

"Remember about how you feel right now. Remember this conviction. It will help you go through the hardships of the journey."

Hardships?

"Your face has returned to normal."

The priestess presented him with the mirror again. It reflected his round, jade-green eyes in a Prydain, lightly olive-toned face.

"Try not to do that too often. If you forget to transform back and are seen in public, your life is forfeit," she warned him, and clapped her hands twice.

The door slid open and the two familiar youths came in.

"Now, I believe some introductions are in order." The High Priestess gestured to the two. "You will, after all, travel together."

"We will?"

Bran blinked. How much of this had the woman prepared beforehand? Was it really fine to trust her?

The boy approached first, looking at him slightly suspiciously. He bowed deeply and spoke in a bright tinkling voice. The interpreter tried his best to translate the formal noble manner of the boy's speech.

"I am Takashima Satō. My father is Takashima Shūhan, son of Takashima Shirobei. I am the heir to the Takashima-Ryū School of Western Magic. Pleased to make your acquaintance."

Bran nodded. School of Western Magic… Lady Kazuko had mentioned there were wizards in Yamato and Satō's father was one of them, but a whole *school?* Was Satō a wizard as well?

He looked at the red-haired girl.

"Itō Nagomi…" she said, shyly, "daughter of Itō Keisuke. I'm the apprentice here in Suwa, training to become a priestess. I was with Satō when we found you on the beach…"

Bran bowed back.

"I am Bran ap Dylan o Cantre'r Gwaelod." His name sounded strange to his own ears. "Graduate of Llambed College of Mystic Arts, dragon rider."

"You will all need new identities," declared Lady Kazuko, "and disguises – except Bran-*sama*, of course, he's already as disguised as is possible for a man…"

"Wait," Bran said, raising his hand, "this is all happening very fast, I need time to…"

"I'm afraid there is no time. You must leave today."

"*Today*! But…"

"We don't know when the magistrate will return with a search warrant, how long your *dorako* can stay in captivity. This all means our time is short – very short."

"*The magistrate*? I don't understand any of this."

With Lady Kazuko's permission, Tokojiro quickly explained to Bran the arrival of the magistrate officials at the shrine. The news shook him. Focusing on his own problems he had forgotten of the risk his presence was posing to the others. He glanced at Satō's arm injured arm; the boy was hurt because of him. And the High Priestess – what could happen to her if she was discovered disobeying the laws of the city? He still did not fully understand the situation, but he could clearly sense the overwhelming sense of danger.

"Now you see why we must hasten," the High Priestess said.

"Still – " he replied slowly, hesitating, "is it really safe for me to go outside? I may look like one of you, but I can't yet speak your language, don't know your customs…"

"You have sworn the vows of silence," declared Lady Kazuko, and Bran again wondered how much of this she had planned ahead. "Tokojiro-*sama* has agreed to come with you – as translator and guardian."

"Guardian?"

Bran looked at the young interpreter doubtfully. He noticed Satō doing the same.

"I have the reputation of being as skilled with the sword as with the tongue," Tokojiro said, bowing slightly and smiling. He then repeated it – Bran guessed - in Yamato, for the benefit of incredulous-looking Satō.

"Let us pray your reputation never needs to be tested," said the High Priestess. "If you should encounter on your journey anything you're not capable of dealing with, send word. As long as I'm alive, Suwa will assist you to the best of its abilities. Now, let's not dwell too long on this. Bran-*sama*, a bath is ready for you."

Bran agreed, still a little dazed. He was conscious of the smell of sulphur and sweat that his body emanated and for some reason he was growing increasingly ashamed of it. Nagomi and Satō bowed and left the room hurriedly. Bran stood up, his head spinning slightly, and headed for the door.

"You will need to tie your hair in the samurai manner," Tokojiro said after consulting with Lady Kazuko. "I will help you with that, and with the proper way to walk. Playing dumb will only get you so far if you don't learn a few basics."

What's wrong with the way I walk now?

"*Hai* – yes."

"I'm sorry everything's so sudden," the High Priestess said, pursing her lips. "I know it must be difficult for you."

"It's fine," he replied, though he wasn't certain it was. "I understand it is for the best."

"I'm glad somebody thinks so," she said.

He made sure all the elements of the dark kimono were properly adjusted, the mountain crest on his shoulders – he was now a member of an *Aoki clan*, he reminded himself, like the man whose kimono he was wearing – in plain view. He then felt to see if the newly tied knot of hair at the top of his head was in place, buckled the leather satchel tightly and thrust his Prydain sword into the silk sash. The metal scabbard was painted black and the shrine blacksmith – the moustached man from earlier – had prepared a rough replacement hilt, a long wooden handle wrapped in black cord, that made the cavalry blade look almost like the swords he had seen other Yamato men wear. The proudly sculpted dragon-shaped handgrip, far too elaborate for the simple local style, was hidden in the satchel.

He was trying to wrap his mind around what was happening to him. His face and body changed. He traced the still unfamiliar features with his fingers. The intricacies of the magic involved evaded him – maybe he would understand it better if he knew thaumaturgy. The transformation was perfect, seamless; after the initial odd sensation had passed the new face felt as if it had always been there.

His thoughts… There was something going on there too, something the priestess had not told him about. When he had been given a bowl of breakfast rice, after his bath, his fingers reached for and deftly grasped the quaint bamboo chopsticks. His hand brought morsels of food to his mouth without hesitation, without mistake.

The many-layered robe felt much more familiar than before. The bowing seemed more natural than handshaking. *Something* was happening to him, and he wasn't sure he liked it. The High Priestess didn't know all the details of the ritual. What if the Spirit within was slowly taking him over?

He looked out through the door at the pouring rain. There was no more time to linger. According to Lady Kazuko's plan, Satō, Nagomi and Bran were to leave the shrine one after another at intervals and meet inside an inn at the bottom of the long stairs. Bran was to go last, accompanied by Tokojiro. The interpreter waited impatiently outside under the grey-tiled eaves. It was their moment to leave.

The dragon rider gingerly touched the cold red scabbard of Satō's sword, lying on the straw mat floor. As the Yamato boy was disguising himself as a commoner, he could not bear a weapon – it was decided that Bran would carry it for him. Bran had already noticed that most noblemen in Kiyō walked around with two swords at their belts, so it made sense for him to do so as well. Curious, he pulled out the blade for a few inches. It was of damascene steel of great quality, razor sharp, with a rich hardening pattern and a blacksmith's signature carved near the circular guard.

His Prydain weapon, a sturdy heavy blade of ancient design, was more a mark of his graduation from the Academy than a martial tool. A proud sign of an age-old legacy going back ten centuries to the times when wild dragons roamed the land and brave warriors stood in their way, and later, when dragon riders flew to battle alongside regular horse cavalry against humans cast in steel and mail. A little more than a decorative piece of iron, although the edge was still sharp enough to cut through muscle and bone. Yes, it could maim and, in skilled hands, kill. The runes carved along the fuller shimmered with gentle magic at the touch. They enabled the sword to break through magical shields and armour. Bran was taught how to use it to hack and slash with great force, like a carving axe or, in a bind, thrust.

A sword was never the primary weapon of the dragon rider – Soul Lance against the scale, magic against the shield, dragon against everything else. This was what the Academy had taught him. Other than the symbol of prestige, the sword would only be used in self-defence, when all else failed. Some young riders even went as far as to forgo the sword and replace it with a lightning pistol or pneumatic rifle. They would certainly prove more useful in this age of mistfire and thaumaturgy.

Looking at Satō's sword Bran recognised a weapon designed with just one purpose in mind – to kill a man with a single, fast, precise strike. It was sharp enough to cut through a falling piece of paper. It was well balanced, swift and strong, flexible enough not to snap and hard enough not to bend. The steel was of fantastic quality, the craftsmanship involved incredible – but there were no ornaments on the hilt other than a butterfly crest on the handguard, no superfluous carvings on the scabbard. This was the product of a culture that still esteemed swords as the main armament of a warrior, and knew their value. The boy was certain the blade could easily slash off a man's arm, leg, or even, with enough skill and strength, a head. But there was no magic about it. A simple *bwcler* would hold the deadly edge back. This was the most interesting bit of information, and Bran made sure to remember it well.

He thought again of the two men duelling in the streets of Kiyō and wondered whether Satō had also been trained to so ruthlessly destroy a human life. He must have been. The Yamato boy was of a soldier's age and bore the sword effortlessly. Admiring the blade, Bran was glad to have its owner on his side.

I owned a blade like this once, he thought. *It's a Matsubara if ever I saw one.*

"No, I didn't," he corrected himself immediately, startled. "I have no idea what a Matsubara sword is."

He waited for a moment to see if the strange memory would return but there was nothing but silence inside his head now. He sheathed Satō's sword, stuck it in the sash beside the Prydain blade and went outside.

END OF PREVIEW